BATTLESAURUS

Clash of Empires

BRIAN FALKNER

SAURUS

Clash of Empires

Farrar Straus Giroux
New York

Farrar Straus Giroux Books for Young Readers
175 Fifth Avenue, New York 10010

Copyright © 2016 by Brian Falkner
All rights reserved
Printed in the United States of America
Designed by Andrew Arnold
First edition, 2016
1   3   5   7   9   10   8   6   4   2

fiercereads.com

Library of Congress Cataloging-in-Publication Data

Names: Falkner, Brian, author.
Title: Battlesaurus : clash of empires / Brian Falkner.
Description: First edition. | New York : Farrar Straus Giroux, 2016. |
  Series: Battlesaurus ; 2
Identifiers: LCCN 2015047553 | ISBN 9780374300777 (hardback)
Subjects: | CYAC: War—Fiction. | Dinosaurs—Fiction. | Science fiction. |
  Europe—History—1789–1815—Fiction. | BISAC: JUVENILE FICTION /
  Animals / Dinosaurs & Prehistoric Creatures. | JUVENILE FICTION /
  Historical / Military & Wars. | JUVENILE FICTION / Action &
  Adventure / General. | JUVENILE FICTION / Historical / Europe.
Classification: LCC PZ7.F1947 Bap 2016 | DDC [Fic]—dc23
LC record available at https://lccn.loc.gov/2015047553

Our books may be purchased in bulk for promotional, educational, or business use.
Please contact your local bookseller or the Macmillan Corporate and
Premium Sales Department at (800) 221-7945 ext. 5442 or by e-mail at
MacmillanSpecialMarkets@macmillan.com.

For Sandra and Mick Thornton, who added a little madness.
And for Mike Rehu, who added a little magic.

PROLOGUE

September 24, 1815

CHÂTEAU DE BREST, FRANCE

The young French soldier shivers, and not from the cold, although here at the parapet of the castle the wind is icy and pitiless.

From behind him and below come deep grunting sounds and the rattle of chains. That area of the castle courtyard is covered with hastily erected screens of sailcloth to keep out prying, spying eyes. He cannot see what is there. But he knows what is there.

A bellow rumbles around the stone walls of the courtyard, loud enough to shake the tarpaulins and tremble his sword in its scabbard. The devil's creatures walk the cobblestones below him but even they are not the reason for his terror. The soldier does not fear the creatures as much as he fears the devil, and the devil surely stalks the castle this night.

The castle is old. Some of the stones of its walls were cut by Roman slaves, fifteen centuries before. It stands at the mouth of the Penfield River in Brest, at the westernmost tip of France, isolated on a rocky outcrop, protected on three sides by the sea and on all sides by high walls, towers, and ramparts. The stonework is dark and imposing, rising on a sharp angle from the rock-strewn shore.

At night the castle has a presence of its own, as if it has absorbed the souls of those who have died defending and attacking its thick walls.

The young soldier stands to attention at the battlements, his musket beside him, stock on the ground, barrel nestled in the crook of his right arm. He faces the sea, which smolders with embers of moonlight.

He is grateful for the moon. Without it he would have nothing but the flickering amber of the storm lamps that line the wall.

The silvery light falls also on the ships, moored at the wharves in the river mouth below the castle. Their masts sway in the strong breeze. The creaking and groaning of wood and rope is relentless.

More ships lie at anchor in the middle of the river. Many ships. *Enough for an invasion*, the soldier thinks, but he does not express this thought out loud, not even to Corporal Joubert. Words can be overheard, and to talk to anyone of an invasion fleet, or of the monsters caged below him, would surely lead to the separation of his head from his body.

Where is Joubert? He disappeared many minutes ago and has not yet returned.

Desertion of duty, even for a moment, is an offense punishable by the most torturous death. Joubert knows this, but as a veteran of the Peninsular War, and of the recent victory in the Southern Netherlands, near Waterloo, Joubert thinks himself to be untouchable. He is wrong.

The young soldier stands guard alone, shivering.

On the far side of the river are the taverns and bawdy houses of the town, and as the wind shifts occasionally, it brings the shouts, laughter, and music of the sailors making the most of their shore leave.

Now there are footsteps on the walkway behind and the soldier immediately turns and presents arms.

"Halt," he says. "Who goes there?"

"Put away your bayonet before you stick yourself with it," comes a hushed voice and suppressed laughter. Then out of the shadows of the staircase swaggers Joubert. He is not alone. He has his musket in one hand, and the other hand is entwined in the smock of a girl. She is perhaps seventeen, slender but womanly. As they approach, the soldier can see that she is both attractive and afraid.

"I caught a stray," Joubert says. His words are a little slurred and the soldier thinks he has shared rum with some of the sailors.

"Parisian pig," the girl says.

Her beauty is marred by a crooked nose, broken and long-healed. Perhaps this girl is not unused to a fight.

"She must leave," the young soldier says. "We must attend to our duty."

"Why should the ship rats have all the fun tonight?" Joubert asks. "There is no danger to guard against. Europe is ours and Napoléon has the British cowering like pups on their lonely rock."

"If . . . he . . . was to see this, your death would be an unpleasant one," the soldier says.

"You are too serious," Joubert says. "He is tending to far more important matters, or is asleep in his warm bed. Come, we will have our fun tonight also."

He wrenches at the girl's smock as he says this and there is a ripping sound. The girl spits at him and slaps his face. He laughs drunkenly.

"I will even stand guard and give you the first kiss," Joubert says.

"I will not," the young soldier says, and turns back to the battlement, standing again to attention.

"As you wish," Joubert says, and there is another tearing sound.

"You should pray that the devil does not see you," the soldier says.

Joubert begins to laugh but stops abruptly as a new voice intrudes.

"Who is this devil you speak of?"

The soldier spins, raising his musket. "Halt," he says. "Who goes there?"

"Colonel Valois," is the reply.

Joubert lets go of the girl, who falls to the ground and then picks herself up, trying to piece her clothing back together. He snatches his musket, which he had leaned against the battlements.

Valois is the commandant of the castle. He emerges slowly from the darkened staircase as another figure comes into view behind him.

Valois says, "And General Thibault."

The young soldier freezes, unable to move or speak.

The devil stands before him on the castle wall.

This was a handsome man once. He wears the uniform of a general in the imperial guard, yet without the bicorne hat that befits his rank. Three parallel scars extend from the top of his head diagonally down his face, taking with them his right eye and ear. On his scalp they plow furrows where no hair grows. His sideburns are thick and he has an earring of gold in the ear that remains. He has one complete arm: his right. The left is a withered, scarred stump, ending just below his elbow. His skin is black, not all over like an African, but in patches around the scars, perhaps from infection, or disease. His only hand is encased in a black leather glove.

The girl is rigid, paralyzed at the sight. She sways, then General Thibault takes two steps toward her, surely more swiftly than any human could move. He grabs her. He tucks the remains of his left arm under her legs and lifts her effortlessly, murmuring soothing words into her ear.

"This is how you guard my precious creatures?" Thibault asks. His tone is light, but his voice is a rasp, the scars across his throat evidence of why.

Neither Joubert nor the young soldier speaks.

"By making whores of the young women of the town?" Thibault asks.

Still there is silence.

"This is the daughter of the baker," Thibault says. "I know him and I know his family. His baguettes and brioches are the best in Brittany. You would sully the daughter of my friend?"

"Your names," Valois demands.

Now Joubert finds his voice. "Joubert," he says, and with a nod at the soldier, "and Lefevre. But I am at fault. Lefevre had no part in this."

The young soldier, Lefevre, leans his musket against the castle wall. He withdraws his sword, kneels, and offers it hilt-first to the general.

Thibault sighs. "Put away your sword," he says.

Lefevre bows his head before rising, sheathing his sword, and retrieving his firearm.

"But this is the last time you will neglect your duties," Thibault says.

"Yes, sir," Joubert manages in a shaky voice. "Never again, sir."

"I know your names, Joubert, Lefevre," Thibault says. "I know you."

Lefevre can barely breathe.

Thibault stares at them with his one good eye. It burns into the young soldier. Thibault says, "This eye sees you when I am standing before you." He turns his face, bringing his eye patch into the light of the storm lamps. "And this eye sees you when I am not."

A cold shudder shakes the young soldier so violently that he almost drops his musket.

The girl wakes, staring at the soldiers as if she cannot bring herself to look at that which holds her.

"Rest, girl. These men will not bedevil you again," Thibault says.

She turns her head toward his face and freezes, rigid like a statue.

Thibault turns to the sea, taking a deep breath of the salty sea air and gazing over the forest of masts in the river and at the wharves below.

"Come, Valois," he says, turning back toward the staircase, the girl struggling in his arms.

Valois turns abruptly after glaring fiercely at the two guards.

Another bellow comes from the courtyard below and Thibault stops. He turns in that direction, smiling, as if he approves of the sound. He leans out over the inner wall and casually opens his arms. There is no sound from the girl as she hits the topmost sailcloth with a flat, smacking sound and slides off the edge.

There is another sound, a moist thud as she hits the cobblestones of the courtyard, far below, followed by the rattling of heavy chains and the scraping of immense feet.

Then come the screams, but they are brief.

"She would not have seen anything, General," Valois protests as they descend into the shadow of the stairs.

"You can be sure?" Thibault asks.

"No, General, I cannot," Valois says with sadness. "What about the guards? Are they to escape punishment?"

"You would rather I took their heads?" Thibault asks.

"Their offense was great, yet they seem to have escaped lightly," Valois says. "You have frightened them, no more."

"Scared men I can use," Thibault says. "Dead men are no good to me."

Book One

September 25–October 4, 1815

SAUR-KILLERS

The officer at the Royal Artillery Barracks in Woolwich, southeast of London, wears the uniform of an artillery major of the Third Netherlands Infantry Division. But he is neither a soldier nor Dutch.

His papers identify him as Major Johannes Hendrik Lux. But that is a lie.

Willem Verheyen is the name he has used since he can remember, although even that is not his true name.

Playing the part of a soldier and an officer came awkwardly at first to Willem. But now he wears the role as comfortably as another would wear a cloak. "Major Lux" is merely an illusion and Willem is a masterful magician.

The sky is overcast, a typical dull London morning. In the dismal shadows of the high-walled courtyard at the rear of the Royal Artillery Barracks the cold air bites like saur-bugs and every breath hangs in crystalized white.

Willem stands in the center of the courtyard, observing as a group of six artillery lieutenants approach a line of tethered herbisaurs.

Today is the final day of their training. It is Willem's last day also.

In a week he will be behind enemy lines.

He puts those thoughts out of his mind and watches. The

nervous, wide-bellied, duck-billed herbisaurs rear up on their hind legs as the soldiers draw near. Not to attack, for that is not in their nature, but to flee. They cannot: the leather collars, chains, and heavy metal stakes keep them in place. They emit warbling calls of alarm and thrash their necks from side to side, but the stakes are strong and deep in the ground.

These saurs are imported especially from Asia. They are large, nearly twice the height of a man. They were the largest known saurs in the world before Waterloo, although still not nearly as big or anywhere near as ferocious as Napoléon's battlesaurs.

If the circumstances were different Willem might smile at the awkward-looking creatures with their wide, childlike eyes. But he does not smile. He knows what is coming.

"Ignite," Willem calls.

The soldiers strike flints, creating a constellation of tiny stars.

The British soldiers call these "sparkle sticks." A mixture of gunpowder, magnesium, and glue along a stiff wire. They burn like the souls of sinners in the misty morning gloom.

"Begin," Willem calls.

The stars begin to move as the soldiers weave an intricate pattern with the sticks. Bright lines fade slowly on the gentle mist of the soldiers' breath.

The saurs pull away in fear, then settle slowly as their attention is captured by the dancing lights.

"Approach," Willem calls.

With one exception the soldiers are young men, most not much older than Willem. Willem watches their faces as they move even closer to the large saurs. He pays particular attention to a tall Scotsman, Hew McConnell. McConnell has a feeble mustache and a thin strip of beard down his chin.

McConnell is the son of a nobleman. The others call him Sir

Hew behind his back, although he does not hold that title. They do it because of the way McConnell wears his birthright like a badge of honor. McConnell has the potential to be a good soldier, Willem thinks, but he has a weak character, which he covers with bluster and bravado. He will pass this training, but Willem worries that he will be found wanting on the battlefield.

For different reasons Willem keeps a close eye on the exception, the oldest and largest of the lieutenants, Joe Hoyes. He is Irish and a grizzled veteran of many campaigns, a former sergeant promoted (against his will) in the aftermath of Waterloo. A battlefield commission, like many, to help fill a shortage of lieutenants after so many were killed in that hellish encounter. Big Joe, as they call him, sports a bushy mustache and a cleft chin. His face bears a jagged scar. He has a healthy disrespect for everything military, but has impressed Willem with his great steadiness and determination.

"Hold," Willem calls as McConnell reaches too soon for his scabbard.

The saurs are ready, but Willem wants the men to see how long they can be held this way.

"The longer the dance, the deeper the trance," he says. Then, finally, "Draw."

Now the soldiers pull swords from their scabbards, holding them ready in front of them. Still the sparkle sticks etch their patterns on the cold air.

"Strike," Willem calls.

A flash of steel as the swords jab upward at the soft tissue on the underside of the herbisaurs' jaws.

Blood gushes.

A short, sharp thrust up into the brain, as Willem has taught them, then a quick extraction before the head can fall and trap the blade.

The herbisaurs remain standing for a moment after they are dead. They look at their killers with startled, confused expressions, if that is possible for a saur.

Almost in unison they collapse, to the front or to the side, falling in awkward piles of flesh and pools of blood.

He should feel bad, Willem thinks. But these lieutenants will face much worse in battle and this is the only way they can truly learn. Besides, he has done this often enough now that he has ceased to feel anything; his heart is as steel at the sight of the slaughter. At least that is what he tells himself.

"Withdraw," Willem calls.

Stepping back, the soldiers drop their exhausted sparkle sticks and wipe blood from their swords with oilcloths.

One of the lieutenants, a prematurely balding eighteen-year-old named Weiner, is smiling, but Willem thinks it is not happiness at the kill. Weiner's expression is a permanent smile that might be mistaken for insecurity, or even a lack of intelligence. But Willem has found it to be a reflection of a constant good humor.

Already the butchers' carts are moving in to dismember and remove the carcasses.

"Good work, gentlemen," Willem says. "Stand down."

"They seem . . . efficient," a voice says behind Willem. He turns to see the young blind army officer, Lieutenant Hunter Frost. He had not heard Frost arrive. Next to him stands an equally young subaltern, clearly acting as his guide.

"You saw this?" Willem asks, although he knows this cannot be true. Frost wears two eye patches.

"I smell the smoke and hear the sound of the scabbards," Frost says. "I hear the rupture of skin and the quieting of the beasts' breathing. I smell the blood. It paints a picture for me almost as clear as your eyes do for you."

Willem nods. Frost has not let the loss of his sight affect his spirit or his career. Such is his character. He has earned special dispensation from the War Office to remain a serving officer. He no longer serves in the artillery, nor even in the infantry. A soldier without eyes cannot sight a cannon, aim a pistol, or fight with a sword. Instead he now reports to Lieutenant Colonel Grant, of the Intelligence Service. Willem has heard that his incisive mind and sharp wits have already proved invaluable in analyzing information gained from spies and intercepted enemy dispatches.

"Thank you for coming, my friend. It is good to see you," Willem says. "How is Whitehall?"

"A battlefield of a different sort," Frost says with a smile. "I would not bore you with the details."

"And you got my letter?" Willem asks.

"I did," Frost says. "But do not let me interrupt your training session." He turns to the subaltern and dismisses him with a quiet word.

Willem turns back to the line of soldiers.

McConnell is bragging about his fighting skills. He was born with a sword in his hand, it would seem. He demonstrates with cuts and thrusts and appears, to Willem's eye, genuinely talented, although the other lieutenants conceal their disdain behind fixed expressions.

"Gentlemen," Willem says, recapturing their attention. "Take a break. Go and select a trojansaur. Join me on the parade ground in an hour."

McConnell sheathes his sword and all six lieutenants stand to attention and salute before making their way from the courtyard.

"You have become quite the dashing young major," Frost says when they are out of earshot.

"An illusion," Willem says. "Smoke and mirrors, nothing more."

"So what do you really think of your new saur-killers?" Frost asks.

"Do you inquire as a friend or as an officer of the Intelligence Service?" Willem asks.

"Does it matter?"

Willem shrugs. "I think they are well equipped for an attack by an army of herbisaurs."

"And battlesaurs?" Frost wonders.

"There is only one way to find out," Willem says. There is more that he could say, but he doesn't. Not even to Frost.

"Hew McConnell?" Frost asks. "Is he ready?"

Willem is amazed at how little escapes Frost's notice, even without eyes.

"He is the one who worries me most," Willem says. "He is a braggart, and I think of very little substance."

"He may surprise you," Frost says. "My father knows his father. We spent time together as children."

"I apologize," Willem says quickly. "I did not realize he was your friend. I meant no offense."

"None was taken, and I do not count him as a friend. Far from it," Frost says. "We were ill-suited to each other's temperaments. But I know this: Hew has lived all his life in the shadow of a great man, his father. Even as a child he was constantly trying to prove himself worthy. Perhaps he will. He comes from good stock."

"I hope you are right," Willem says. "Come, let us warm up for a moment in the officers' mess."

He takes his friend by the arm and leads him toward the main entrance of the barracks.

"I have heard many stories about you," Frost says. "You have achieved a certain infamy on the other side of the English Channel."

"What kind of infamy?" Willem asks.

"They call you the Wizard of Gaillemarde," Frost says. "Napoléon's soldiers fear you. They say you are no conjurer but a sorcerer, capable of true magic."

"Let them think that," Willem says. "Perhaps it will work to our advantage."

"Napoléon of course spreads word that it is not true," Frost says. "That you are just a boy with a box of conjuring tricks. But his soldiers believe that you can turn yourself into a dinosaur, that you can control the weather, that you can disappear from one place and reappear in another."

"If that were so, this war would already be won," Willem laughs. "I would turn myself into a battlesaur and appear in Napoléon's quarters during a thunderstorm."

He mimes picking meat from between his teeth.

"If only this were true," Frost says.

"But we will have to make do with my 'simple conjuring tricks' when we reach the forest," Willem says.

"When do you leave?" Frost asks.

"Today is the last day of training," Willem replies cautiously.

Frost stops in his tracks. "Do you not trust me?" he asks.

"Of course," Willem says, encouraging Frost forward with a gentle tug on his sleeve. "Again I owe you an apology. You are perhaps the one person in this country whom I do fully trust. We sail in seven days."

"How many men?" Frost asks.

"Just six," Willem says.

"Six?"

"Six trained saur-killers." Willem smiles to cover his own anxiety. "Along with the two hundred infantry who will overwhelm the abbey and allow us to slay the battlesaurs in the cavern below."

"You will emerge through the cave?" Frost asks.

Willem nods. "Right in the heart of the abbey while the French are occupied with the threat from without."

Frost nods. "The journey to the Sonian will not be easy."

"We go by night," Willem says. "The Royal Navy will create a diversion near Zeebrugge while we slip quietly down the Oosterschelde."

"Surely there are lookouts," Frost says. "Even at night they will see you and raise the alarm."

"You no doubt remember Sofie and Lars, who helped us escape from Antwerp?" Willem asks.

"I did not meet Sofie," Frost says. "But Lars would be hard to forget."

Willem smiles. Lars is a giant of a man.

"I have sent word to her and received a reply," Willem says. "The lookouts along the Oosterschelde will be looking the other way, or sleeping. Those who can be bribed, will be bribed. The others will be dealt with. Sofie has many friends in that part of the Netherlands."

"And after you land?" Frost asks.

"Lars will meet us in Krabbendijke," Willem says. "And guide us past any French encampments."

Frost frowns.

"You seem concerned," Willem says. "Is there something I should know?"

"I did not say anything," Frost says.

"And yet you are holding something back," Willem says. "Is it about Héloïse? What have you learned?"

Héloïse, the wild girl, who lived for many years in the Sonian Forest outside Willem's village after her mother was taken by a firebird. She was one of the few survivors of the massacre at

Gaillemarde. She had helped Willem, Frost, and Jack Sullivan escape from Europe, traveling with them through the sewers of Antwerp and sailing out of the harbor under the nose of Napoléon himself.

Within a week of her arrival in England, Héloïse had bitten a British officer and was taken to the St. Luke's Hospital for Lunatics despite the loud protestations of Willem and Frost. She escaped twice in the first week, was recaptured both times, then disappeared altogether.

"Is Jack here?" Frost asks. "I should like to see him."

Now it is Willem who stops walking, which stops Frost as well. He looks at Frost for a moment, trying to read his expression.

"The officers' mess can wait," he says. "Jack builds and maintains the trojansaurs."

"Really?" Frost says.

"But you already knew that," Willem says. "As I think you already knew the details of our mission. Come, let us go find him."

Frost manages to look suitably offended as Willem takes him by the arm and leads him toward the workshops.

CAPTIVITY

The abbey is old. Older than Cosette can comprehend. She cannot look at the crumbling walls without thinking of those who built this place so very long ago. It is older than the church in Waterloo or the ancient saur-wall at Brussels. She thinks the world must have been young when men carved out this clearing in the dense Sonian Forest and quarried stone to build the high walls and even higher bell tower.

Who were they? Why did they come here to build a place of worship in such isolation? And why did they build the abbey over the entrance to a vast underground cave? Was it as an escape route if the abbey came under attack?

Napoléon's men have enlarged the opening to the cave, walled it off, and fitted it with great wooden doors. She keeps well away from that part of the abbey. She knows what lies beneath.

A few weeks earlier Cosette and Madame Verheyen—Willem's mother—had been confined to their cell with no reason given. They cowered and held each other as the floor and even the thick stone walls trembled. The light from the high stone window had dimmed as something vast passed by. Then another. And another. She could not see them, but in her mind's eye she had clearly pictured the malevolent eyes, cold steam breath, and huge, jagged teeth of the terrible thing that had lunged at her that night in the village.

Now she hurries through the courtyard with breakfast: a bowl of rice gruel to share with Marie Verheyen in the church that is the base of the bell tower. They spend most of their day there. Their cell is too small, merely a square room with two sackcloth beds and a pail for toileting. After a few weeks of imprisonment Marie negotiated with Baston to allow them to use the church. The French soldiers do not use it, except on Sundays for mass.

A soldier is tending one of the vegetable patches that take up most of the courtyard. Private Deloque, a brute of a man with a brute of a beard who seldom speaks except for grunts and lewd remarks when she passes. He is turning earth with a hoe, mixing in manure. It smells like dinosaur dung.

He steps out of the garden as she approaches, blocking her path. She steps to the side but he moves in the same direction and when she steps back, he steps back also. He grins, a gap-toothed smile, and grunts unintelligibly.

"Excuse me, sir, I would pass," Cosette says.

Deloque grunts again.

Cosette makes to step to the left, but changes direction quickly to the right, stepping nimbly around Deloque. He thrusts out the hoe as she passes, however, catching her foot, and she falls, sprawling into the vegetable patch.

"What is going on here?" A voice comes from over her right shoulder. Cosette sits up, covered in mud, manure, and gruel, to see Belette, a lumpy-looking sergeant, emerging from a doorway.

"Merely an accident, monsieur," Cosette says. "I tripped."

Belette steps swiftly forward and extends a hand to help her up.

"Thank you, monsieur," Cosette says with a small smile.

Belette has always been pleasant to her, finding her extra rations or treats such as a piece of soft cloth for her bath.

"Private Deloque, back to work," Belette says.

Deloque glowers but steps back into the garden and resumes his hoeing. Belette picks up the empty gruel bowl.

"Your breakfast?" he asks.

Cosette nods.

"Here," Belette says, holding out a cloth. It is knotted at the top and filled with something. It smells like bread. "Something fresh for breakfast for you and your mother," he says. "And some butter as well."

Marie Verheyen is not her mother, but it was a necessary subterfuge that they have maintained. The soldiers' belief that she is Willem's sister is what has kept her alive.

"That is very kind, monsieur," Cosette says cautiously.

"I have no doubt that your stay is arduous enough," Belette says. "I am happy to do what I can to ease the passing of the days."

"I am indebted to you, monsieur," Cosette says. She takes the cloth-wrapped bundle.

Belette falls in step alongside Cosette as she continues to the church. "Allow me to escort you," he says. "With both General Thibault and Captain Baston away, I fear the discipline of some of the men is not what it should be."

"It was merely an accident, monsieur," Cosette says.

"But of course," Belette says.

The entrance to the church is a large pointed archway. Belette leaves her there with a smile and a small bow.

Inside, the seats are wooden and new, replaced by the French, although the altar is made of stone and as old as the church itself.

Marie is waiting there. She looks up, her nose twitching as Cosette enters. "What happened?" she asks.

"An accident in the garden," Cosette says. "Courtesy of Private Deloque." She grimaces. "I smell like the back end of one of their fiendish saurs."

Marie uses a foul word to describe Deloque.

"But now we have fresh bread and butter," Cosette says. "Courtesy of Sergeant Lumpy."

Marie laughs. "Belette is an odd-looking man."

"He has a kind heart," Cosette says.

She sets the cloth down on the pew next to Marie and wipes her hands as best as she can on her dress.

"Now your dress smells as bad as you do," Marie says.

"I will go to the rock pool to bathe after breakfast," Cosette says. "I will wash the dress then also."

"I will go after you return," Marie says, and Cosette nods.

Only one of them is allowed to leave the abbey at a time.

Cosette sits and they break the bread together. Marie sniffs at it.

"It is not fresh," she says. "In fact, I would barely call it bread."

"But still better than the rest of the slop they call food," Cosette says.

"Sadly true," Marie says.

"Deloque grows more impertinent by the day," Cosette says. "Belette says we must take extra care now that Thibault and Baston are away."

"Belette is right," Marie says. "These are foul, brutal men. We have been lucky so far. The soldiers fear Thibault and respect Baston but with them both gone I fear for our safety. Horloge is a milksop."

Captain Horloge is in charge in Baston's absence. He is a small man, no older than eighteen and still struggling to grow more than a short fuzz on his upper lip.

Marie breaks off a crust and dabs it at the butter, then chews it slowly. "When we first came here, what did I tell you?"

"To survive," Cosette says.

"Whatever it takes," Marie says. "Your honor and your virtue are precious, but not as valuable as your life. This ordeal will end. Do whatever you have to do to survive."

"How is Monsieur Verheyen?" Cosette asks, uncomfortable with this line of conversation. Back in the village of Gaillemarde, her sister, Angélique, had done what was necessary to survive and had ended up as a meal for a monster.

Marie does not answer, but stares at Cosette until the girl nods.

"I will do whatever it takes," Cosette says. "How is your husband?"

Maarten Verheyen had been thought long dead, until they had discovered him incarcerated here in the abbey.

"I fear for him," Marie says. "He grows weak. He has been a prisoner here too long, without proper food or fresh air. We all have."

THE TROJANSAURS

Jack is up a ladder working on Harry's face when the lieutenants arrive. Some have blood spatter on their uniforms. Most look a little shocked, although one or two seem exhilarated. He knows this look. They have just killed herbisaurs. For most of them this was their first kill of any kind. Not for the tall Irishman, Big Joe Hoyes, though, Jack knows. He has seen much worse on the battlefield.

Jack ignores them and concentrates on his work.

The trojansaurs are lined up outside the carpentry workshop, in the open air. Jack would like to see them inside, out of the elements, but they are too large to fit through the workshop doors.

There are six trojansaurs altogether, named after the legendary wooden saur of Troy. The upper body of a dinosaur mounted on a gun carriage. A practice dummy. When the trail of the gun carriage is resting on the ground and the dinosaur head raised into the air, each is twice the height of a man. That is where Jack is now. He set the ladder carefully and checked it three times for stability before daring to climb it. He focuses on the face so he won't look down. He does not like to look down.

The faces are nightmarish, bony-ridged brows over eyes foiled with silver. They reflect even the dull light of the overcast London sky. The nostrils are deep-set and keyhole-shaped. The "skin" is painted with intricate scales. The jaws are open, and white-painted wooden teeth gleam with menace. Each head has taken Jack more than a week to carve and paint in painstaking detail, using skills he learned from his father.

He has styled them after the six men on his gun crew, lost at Waterloo: Harry, Sam, Douglas, Dylan, Ben, Lewis. In his carvings he has tried to capture something of each person: Dylan's narrow-set eyes, Ben's single thick eyebrow, Harry's wide smile.

He misses the lads. They always treated him well. They were like brothers. Here he has no brothers and few he could count as friends. Like other survivors of the battle at Waterloo, he is not regarded as a hero. Far from it.

He marks cuts with a stick of chalk, then holds the chalk with his mouth and takes a chisel and mallet from his belt.

The lieutenants wander along the line of trojansaurs as Jack chips carefully away at the corner of Harry's smile.

The Scotsman, McConnell, stops next to Jack's ladder.

"I'll take this," he says.

"Harry's not quite ready, sir," Jack mumbles through the piece of chalk in his mouth.

"*Harry's* not quite ready, sir." McConnell mimics Jack, and laughs. "They have names."

"Yes, sir," Jack says. "After me friends. Who died at Waterloo, sir."

"Yes, Waterloo," McConnell says. He takes hold of the ladder with both hands. "This ladder doesn't look stable to me. Is it safe?"

"Yes, sir, I hope so, sir," Jack says, not daring to look down at him.

"Let me check," McConnell says. He shakes the ladder, grinning around at the others as he does so. Jack's chisel slips and adds a cruel gash to the corner of the wooden lip. He grabs for the huge, carved wooden teeth of the trojansaur. The chisel clatters off the cobblestones below him, landing at McConnell's feet. Jack had not even realized that he had dropped it.

"Are you afraid, Sullivan?" McConnell laughs. "Like you were afraid at Waterloo?"

Jack says nothing. It is true. He was terrified at Waterloo.

McConnell rattles the ladder again. Jack clings on desperately. "Well, Sullivan?"

"Sir, yes, sir. I'm a bit afraid of heights," Jack manages.

"Will you run away?" McConnell asks. "As you ran at Waterloo, leaving your friends behind?"

"I didn't run, sir," Jack says.

"I think you did, Sullivan," McConnell says, shaking the ladder again. "And that's why you lived and they all died."

Jack loses one foot from the ladder rungs and frantically scrabbles to find it. He cries out in fear and indignation. "That ain't what happened, sir!"

"Oh, I'm wrong, am I?" McConnell asks.

Somewhere nearby a horse squeals and a man shouts. The sounds echo coldly off the stone walls of the courtyard. McConnell glances around, then back up to Jack, raising an eyebrow.

"Yes, sir, I didn't run, sir," Jack says.

"Are you arguing with an officer, Sullivan?" McConnell asks. "That is insubordination."

"No, sir, I was agreeing with the officer, sir," Jack says. "About you being wrong, sir."

Jack is getting terribly confused now, and sweating despite the cold. He is aware that he is on dangerous ground. Insubordination can be punishable by death.

"You're a liar and a coward, Private Sullivan," McConnell says.

Jack is silent. There is nothing he can think of to say that won't make matters worse.

"I'd be leaving the boy alone, if I was you." It is the gravelly voice of Big Joe, the Irishman.

"You stay out of this," McConnell says, "or I'll have you up for insubordination as well."

"Now you can't do that, an' all," Big Joe says with a broad grin. "I'm a lieutenant, just as you."

McConnell sniffs in disdain. "For how many weeks, is it? Three or four?"

"Eight. And I earned my commission," Big Joe says. The grin is gone. "And it were hard earned. It were not bought for me by my da."

McConnell clenches his fists and starts to step forward, then stops himself and turns to the other lieutenants. "This is what happens when they allow commoners to become officers."

The others maintain stony faces. Big Joe may be a commoner, but there is clearly more respect in the group for him than for McConnell.

"If you want to insult me, you'll have to be doing better than that now," Big Joe says.

"Oh, I can do much better," McConnell says. "But I wouldn't waste my breath on muck like you, or this sniveling, lying coward up the ladder here."

A dangerous silence settles into the mist of the courtyard.

"You can take that back," Big Joe says with a sigh. "I don't care what you say of me, but you'll treat the boy with respect. He was there. He saw the beasts."

"And he ran," McConnell sneers.

"Of course he ran," Big Joe says. "And you'd a done the same."

"I would not. I am no coward," McConnell says.

"You've no idea what you would have done, because you weren't there," Big Joe says.

"I know what Jack did," McConnell says. "He ran."

"Did he now?" Big Joe steps forward. Even the mist seems to draw back from him. He closes in, face-to-face with McConnell.

"He saw the battlesaurs and he ran," McConnell says, not backing down. "He's a coward."

"I ran!" Big Joe roars, the scar across his face suddenly red. "I was there and I ran. Everybody ran. If you'd been there, you mewling kitten, you'd have run too."

From his perch at the top of the ladder, Jack sees that McConnell's hand has dropped to the hilt of his sword.

"Jack did not run." A soft voice filters through the silky mist.

Jack knows this voice. Lieutenant Frost is standing with Willem at the entrance to the courtyard. "Lieutenant Frost, sir!" he cries out.

"Jack remained at his cannon when all others ran," Frost says. He speaks calmly. "He helped me fire the shot that brought down one of the great saurs. He fended off another with nothing more than a ramrod. And then he saved my life. Jack, you are no coward."

"No, sir. I didn't think I was a coward, sir," Jack says with great relief. "I'm a good lad."

"Yes, you are, Jack," Frost says. Then he steps forward, led by Willem. He finds McConnell's ear, and although Jack is not supposed to hear, he does.

"And any man who calls him otherwise will regret it immensely."

There is such quiet ferocity in his voice that anyone would forget that it is a blind man who makes the threat. McConnell backs away, then turns abruptly and storms off. Hoyes moves to the base of the ladder and steadies it.

"You did not run," he says as Jack descends. "I did not know that. Would that I had half your courage."

He steps back as Jack reaches the base of the ladder. Jack looks around once his feet are on solid ground and realizes that Big Joe is saluting him. That is unheard of, for an officer to salute a private without the private saluting first.

Jack quickly returns the salute, and realizes as he does so that the other lieutenants—Gilbert, Smythe, Weiner, and Patrick— have lined up behind Hoyes, and are saluting him also.

"I weren't brave," he says, embarrassed. "I just did what I had to because I didn't know what else to do."

"And that is as good a description of bravery as I have heard," Frost says.

Jack forgets himself completely and races over to Frost, wrapping him in a bear hug.

"That'll do, Jack," Frost murmurs after a moment.

"Yes, sir, sorry, sir," Jack says, standing to attention but wiping his eyes. "It's been a while, sir, and I've missed you, sir."

"It's good to see you, Jack," Frost says.

"And don't you worry about Lieutenant McConnell," Big Joe says. "He's as popular around here as a cup of cold sick on a frosty morning. We'll make sure he doesn't bother you again."

DEPARTURE

The riggers and topmen are high in the masts unfurling the sails, just the light-air canvas until they clear the river mouth. The bosun barks orders and the dockhands make ready to cast off the mooring lines. The sun has not long risen and the docks are still stirring, like some great animal slow to wake.

Major Thibault stands on the fo'c'sle near to the sheep pen. Hurrying sailors flow around him as around a rock in a seaway. They do not acknowledge him. Many make the sign of the cross after they pass him.

This does not concern him.

The ship is the *Duc d'Angoulême*, a first-rate vessel of a hundred and ten guns spread over three decks. She is a mighty and majestic wolf of the sea, with a powerful bark and bite. Beneath Thibault's feet, engraved into the wooden planking of the deck, are the words *Honor, Motherland, Valor, Discipline*. The same words are found on the deck of every ship in the French Navy. Many of which are anchored here in the harbor, which is a flurry of sails as the fleet prepares to depart.

Thibault glances up at the Château de Brest, the great castle overlooking the harbor, high, strong, and still, now that his battlesaurs have been moved.

He is joined by Captain Montenot, the head saurmaster. Montenot is a man who has seen many battles and bears the scars of most of them. He was present at the great victory at Waterloo, and at Berlin and again in Rome. He is a joyless man with skin tanned to leather by years of campaigning. They do not speak, but quietly watch the activity on the dock.

A horse gallops into view around a corner of the riverbank. The rider is hurrying, raising dust from the horse's hooves. More than one person has to leap out of the way. The rider, in the uniform of a captain, pulls to a halt at the gangplank and dismounts, tossing the reins to a shore hand. The horse is led away, breathing heavily, sweat steaming from its sides in the cold morning air. The captain glances up, catching Thibault's eye, then bounds up the narrow plank and strides forward to the fo'c'sle.

"Baston, my friend, it is good to see you," Thibault says, kissing him on both cheeks. "I feared you would not make it before our departure."

"It was a close thing, General," Baston says, after greeting Montenot as well. "I was delayed at Calais."

"By Napoléon?"

"He was sleeping when I arrived. His aides did not dare wake him," Baston says.

"He is not the man he was before Elba," Thibault says. "But you did not hear those words from me."

"I heard nothing," Montenot says.

"Nor I." Baston smiles. "But if I had, I would surely have agreed."

"What news do you bring from the Sonian?" Montenot asks.

"The juvenile battlesaurs near maturity," Baston says. "Their training is complete. And a new batch of eggs has hatched."

"This is good news," Thibault says.

"The tricorne riders grow restless with their training," Baston says. "They wonder when they too will be brought to the battle."

"Soon enough," Thibault says. "What of the boy, Willem?"

"There has been no sign," Baston says.

"You must find him," Thibault says. "He poses great danger to us."

"We have been searching for him for months," Baston says. "He hides in a deep hole, and by the time he emerges it will be too late for him to cause us harm."

"And if you are wrong?" Thibault asks. He paces back and forth along the railing, thinking. "We never found who helped him in Antwerp."

"No. We spent months searching and interrogating but found nothing," Baston says. "But no one knew anything, or if they did, they wouldn't talk. Perhaps if we started executing suspects . . ."

Thibault shakes his head. "There are only two forces in the world, the sword and the spirit. In the long run the sword will always be conquered by the spirit."

"Monsieur?"

"These are the words of our great leader. Napoléon believes you conquer with the sword, but to rule you need the spirit of the people," Thibault says. "He wants to be seen as a father, not a tyrant. He has expressly forbidden executions of those not directly engaged in deeds against us."

"Then we are no closer to finding the boy's collaborators," Baston says.

Thibault stops pacing abruptly. "We have Willem's mother and sister. They must know something," he says.

"I have interrogated them myself," Baston says. "The sister knows nothing. The mother, perhaps, but she would die the most excruciating death before she would reveal it. I could torture the sister perhaps, to force the mother to talk."

"There will be no need," Thibault says. "Use the other boy."

"François?"

"Get him to make contact. Perhaps he can earn their trust."

"I will see it done," Baston says.

There is a muted growl from somewhere beyond the stern of the ship, a low rumble that shakes dew from the canvas sails. The nearby sheep mill around nervously in their pen. One panics and jumps, leaping on the backs of other sheep, which only creates further anxiety in the small flock.

"The battlesaurs are well secured for the voyage?" Baston asks with a quick glance up at the stern of the ship.

"Well enough," Montenot says. "Although you would not think it from the faces of the sailors."

Baston nods his understanding. "Which did you bring?"

"Mathilde, Valérie, and Odette," Montenot says. "The rest remain with the army in Calais."

Three mighty saurs in three barges towed by three ships. Spreading the risk, should one of the ships founder.

"Just three greatjaws, all females," Baston comments.

Thibault nods. "Plus some demonsaurs. Napoléon prefers the males. He thinks the size makes them more potent weapons. I prefer the ferocity of the females."

"He will learn," Baston says.

They all laugh, a private joke.

"We cast off," Thibault says, with a glance at the captain. "I will see you in a few weeks."

"We shall drink champagne together in London," Baston says.

"In the throne room at St. James's Palace!" Montenot declares.

Baston does not look back as he disappears down the gangplank.

The high-pitched sound of the bosun's whistle echoes off the buildings on the dock as the heavy ropes that tether the ship are heaved from their bollards and hauled back on board. Wind tugs at the sails in uneven gusts, easing the ship away from the dockside. The deck takes on a slight lean as the ship begins to move toward the darkened mouth of the river. Thibault turns to the rear, adjusting his footing, watching two heavy towropes on the dock begin to unwind. The ropes uncoil like striking snakes as the ship picks up speed. There is a shouted order from the quarterdeck and the ship slows. The thick ropes slide from the dock into the water, then reemerge as they tighten further.

"Brace yourself, Montenot," Thibault says, placing his own hands on the railing of the gunwales.

Montenot is slow to move and is almost knocked off his feet by the shudder as the ropes lift high out of the water and snap tight. For a moment it seems that the ship has stopped, then the barge behind begins to move. The ropes slacken and tighten again as the ship takes the ungainly but stable barge under tow.

The "barge" is little more than a huge wooden box, wallowing in the wake of the ship. There are narrow slits in the sides to allow air for what is chained inside.

The captain approaches. He is plump and short, with a little too much powder on his hair and rouge on his cheeks. He is strongly perfumed. He bows elegantly. "We are cast off," he says in a voice that is strangely rough and deep, and does not seem to suit his elegant countenance. "Might I now be permitted to know my orders?"

"The need for secrecy was impressed upon you, was it not, Captain?" Thibault asks.

"It was. But we are now clear of land and the time for such games has passed," Captain Lavigne says.

Thibault regards him for a moment.

"You will lead the fleet through the Raz de Sein," he says.

Lavigne nods. "Of course, to avoid the British blockade. I am no fool. And then?"

"That I shall inform you once we are clear of the passage," Thibault says.

There is a bellow from the barge behind them. The men instinctively glance to the stern.

"As you wish, General," Lavigne says. "I should warn you that there is foul weather moving in and we must be through the Raz de Sein before it arrives. It is a narrow and difficult passage in the best of conditions, let alone while towing a deadweight."

"Thank you for your concern, Captain," Thibault says.

Montenot sighs as the captain disappears. "A pompous little dandy," he says quietly.

"We are guests aboard his ship," Thibault says. "He may be as pompous and as dandified as he chooses, as long as he gets us to our destination expeditiously."

NAPOLÉON

"He is not to be trusted," Marshal Michel Ney says.

"Thibault has been a faithful and loyal general," Napoléon says. "And successful."

They stand together on the battlements of the fort at Calais. In the harbor beyond, under the protection of the great guns of the fortress, lies the invasion fleet, sails glowing in the embers of the predawn.

Beyond the safety of the harbor are the ships of the British Royal Navy, blockading the port, determined to prevent any crossing of French troops to England on the other side of the Channel.

"I fear he serves his own agenda," Ney says.

"And what reason do you have to think this?" Napoléon asks. "What evidence to refute what I see with my own eyes?"

"None but my instincts," Ney replies. "But they have seldom let me down."

"A less magnanimous leader than myself might detect a note of jealousy in such words," Napoléon says.

"Such a leader would be cruel and wrong," Ney says. "What possible cause is there for envy?"

"Thibault commands the first invasion fleet," Napoléon says. "His troops will be the first to set foot in Great Britain. Would that not be cause for resentment?"

"A small force only," Ney says. "A diversionary tactic."

"Yet an important one, one that will open the door to England," Napoléon says.

"Even so," Ney says, "it is I, not he, who will be leading the main force. Who will march first in the streets of London and demand the surrender of their king."

"Actually, it is I who will accept the sword of capitulation from the English," Napoléon says. "Although it will be from their prime minister, I would imagine, not their old, sad, mad king."

"Of course." Ney bows his head. "You are correct on both counts. But still I count it a greater privilege to be riding alongside you than to be in charge of a lesser piece in this magnificent chess game of yours. And that notwithstanding, I urge you to exercise great caution when dealing with Thibault. You have my loyalty until the day I die. I fear Thibault has a lesser commitment."

"I will heed your words," Napoléon says. "Now come, we must breakfast."

THE RACES

The six wooden trojansaurs have been lined up at the far end of the parade ground in Woolwich. The horse teams are now uncoupling and drawing away. Behind them the gun crews assemble, ready for the exercise.

To the south of the parade ground are the training fields. A series of sharp reports sounds from a battery of cannon and the acrid smell of cannon smoke is carried on a sharp and bitter wind that cuts through the jacket of Willem's uniform. The combination of cold and smoke makes his skin burn and his eyes water.

"This weather is sharp and foul," Frost says. "Use your magical powers and bring us some sunshine."

Willem laughs.

To the north is the façade of the main barracks building, a huge brick edifice, dotted with long lines of windows, three stories high and stretching to the end of the long parade ground. All the buildings in Willem's tiny village home of Gaillemarde combined would fit inside this one with room to spare.

The main entrance consists of three archways flanked by massive white stone pillars. Above them statues of a lion and a unicorn form the British royal crest, with the motto in French: *Dieu et mon droit* ("God and my right").

It seems odd to Willem, the language of the enemy on the British crest.

"You have yet to answer my question about Héloïse," he says as they wait for the horse teams to leave. "Do you bring me good news?"

"The answer to your question is complex," Frost says. "That is why I came to see you in person."

"You have either found her or not," Willem says, a little more brusquely than he intends.

"I have," Frost says.

"She is alive? She is in good health?" Willem asks. "I need her for the mission. She is the only one who knows the way through the caves."

"She is alive, and well in body," Frost says reluctantly. "The doctors do not say the same for her mind."

"She never belonged in that place," Willem says.

"I agree," Frost says. "But the doctors have their own view. And now . . ."

"Where is she?" Willem asks with sudden concern.

"Héloïse's identity and whereabouts have been kept most secret," Frost says. "As have yours."

Willem nods his understanding. The French have many spies in England.

"But Héloïse was recognized," Frost says. "Another patient at St. Luke's was the widow of a British officer. This lady was at her husband's side at Waterloo, and by his deathbed in the field hospital in your village."

Willem is not surprised to hear that the officer's widow had lost her mind. What he witnessed in the makeshift hospital in the aftermath of Waterloo was enough to drive anyone to madness.

"For security, the High Command decided to move Héloïse to another . . . location," Frost says.

Willem wants to ask more but refrains as the six lieutenants approach within earshot and form a line in the center of the parade ground, directly in front of where Willem, Frost, and Jack are standing. They look expectantly at Willem.

"Load," Willem orders.

The soldiers draw their flintlock pistols. They feel for powder cartridges in their leather pouches, insert them, and ram them home.

"Ready," Willem calls.

At the start line, the gun crews lift the trails of the carriages, lowering the heads of the wooden saurs. Some soldiers take hold of the wheels.

"Attack!" Willem calls.

The soldiers strain and the trojansaurs begin to move, slowly at first, but increasing in speed. The soldiers gasp and grunt, calling encouragement to one another. At the other end of the parade ground the lieutenants wait, raising their pistols as the trojansaurs approach. Faster and faster the carriages rush down the parade ground.

As they draw closer, the soldiers holding the trails of the carriages lift them higher, lowering the heads as if they are stooping to attack.

The pistols sound, a ragged series of *crack*s, and from each muzzle spurts a cloud of pepper, enveloping the oncoming wooden heads.

This is the real point of the exercise. The "race" is merely to add speed and urgency. The officers must learn to stand their ground in front of a charging battlesaur, holding their nerve until the beast is within range of their pepper cartridge.

The lieutenants leap to the side, crouching down out of the path of the carriages and reloading as the trojansaurs rumble slowly to a stop.

"Lieutenant McConnell, I declare you the winner," Willem says, not without some reluctance. McConnell's trojansaur, Harry, was a foot in front as the wooden beasts crossed the line.

McConnell struts and preens as if it was he who had pushed the carriage, not his men. Willem observes a few sour expressions and rolled eyes among his gun crew and thinks McConnell would have been wiser to thank them than to steal their glory.

"Is that it?" Frost asks.

"Two more races to go," Willem says. "Best of three, then a final if there is no clear winner."

The gun crews drag the trojansaurs back to the start line. The lieutenants follow, to give instruction and encouragement.

"Where is this other location?" Willem asks. "You sound uneasy."

"It is very old and has a dark history," Frost says.

"Then we must go to her," Willem says. "Today."

"Willem, I understand your desire to see her," Frost says, "but the doctors say she is unwell."

"She is not mad," Willem says. "She is just odd. As would you be if you had lived for so many years alone in a forest cave."

"The doctors say differently," Frost says.

"You owe her your life!" Willem says, aware of the heat in his voice. "We all do. Have you forgotten our narrow escape from Antwerp?"

"We owe her a great debt," Frost says. "But that does not heal her illness."

"It is more than that," Willem says. "The mission cannot succeed without Héloïse. Only she knows the secret forest paths and the ways through the underground tunnels."

"We do not even know for sure that your mother and Cosette are at the abbey in the Sonian Forest," Frost says.

"It was you who told me they were," Willem says, angry now, despite himself. "Do you doubt your own spies?"

"I believe the information was good," Frost says. "But they could have been moved."

"And wouldn't your spies know if that was so?" Willem asks.

"Most probably," Frost admits.

"What do you know that you are not telling me?" Willem demands.

"It is not my place to talk about your mission," Frost says.

"I ask you not as an officer, but as my friend," Willem says quietly.

They fall silent as the lieutenants line up once again in front of them.

This time Lieutenant Patrick, a round-faced man, wins it by a nose. It earns him a sour look from McConnell. Patrick congratulates his crew, shaking each of them by the hand.

"Race three," Willem calls, and the gun crews haul the trojansaurs back to the starting line.

He turns to stare at Frost, who seems aware of it.

"Willem, there is talk that your mission will be canceled," Frost says.

Willem draws in a sharp breath.

"That cannot be! I have an agreement with the Duke of Wellington himself," Willem says. "I trust the honor of a British officer, a nobleman, in upholding his promises."

"Promises he may find it hard to keep," Frost says. "This is the news I dreaded telling you. Word has come that Napoléon encamps his army in Calais. An invasion of England is imminent."

"An agreement is an agreement," Willem says.

"Until it is not," Frost says. "He will need every man to resist the invasion."

"He is coming tomorrow for the rocket demonstration," Willem says. "I will ask him about it then."

"And if he says no?" Frost asks.

"Then I will go on my own," Willem says bitterly.

"Not on your own," Frost says, and smiles.

Willem breathes in deeply and exhales his aggravation in a soft white mist. He finds that he has clenched his fists, and slowly relaxes them. His anger is misdirected. And Frost is wrong. The duke will not go back on their agreement. Willem is sure of it.

The third trojansaur race begins, but halfway down the course one of McConnell's men trips and falls. The man behind him stumbles over him and falls also. Their carriage slews to the side and the trojansaur comes to a brief stop before the men pick themselves up. They resume the race, but well behind.

Five out of the six pistols sound. Five of six trojansaurs cross the finish line. Lieutenant Patrick's team again is in front. Willem is about to declare them the overall winners when McConnell lowers his pistol and draws his sword. Before Willem can say anything McConnell rushes at Harry, yelling an incoherent war cry.

He reaches high and slashes up at the wooden face using both hands in a powerful strike. Paint and wood chips fly.

"Lieutenant McConnell!" Willem calls. The tall Scotsman does not seem to hear. He raises the sword again, but it is wrested out of his hands and he flies backward onto the cobblestones as the trojansaur rumbles slowly past him to a halt.

Jack towers over the lieutenant. Willem is too shocked to speak. He has never seen Jack angry before.

McConnell scrambles back to his feet, his face red with rage and embarrassment. He shouts, "You have struck an officer! You will hang for this, Private."

Jack tenses, then he lowers the sword, looking around at

Willem with a horrified expression as he realizes the extent of his crime.

McConnell snatches the sword out of Jack's hand, raises it, and cuffs him across the side of the head with the hilt. Jack staggers and blood flows from a cut above his ear.

"Withdraw, Lieutenant," Frost says, taking a few quick steps toward them. Even without eyes he seems to know what is happening.

"This man has struck a British officer and the son of a peer," McConnell says, drawing himself up. "Call for the provost marshal, I will see the private court-martialed."

"I saw nothing," Frost says.

"Need I point out that you have no eyes?" McConnell says.

"Major Lux," Frost says, using Willem's pseudonym, "you are the ranking officer here. What did you see?"

Willem steps forward to join him.

"Lieutenant McConnell, I saw you disobey clear training procedures and directly attack an enemy battlesaurus," Willem says. "An action that, in battle, would lead to your death and that of your men."

"It was only a wooden—" McConnell begins.

"Are you interrupting me, Lieutenant?" Willem asks, acting every inch the officer that he is not.

"No, sir," McConnell says, standing to attention.

"Even in training, what you did was dangerous," Willem says. "Running in front of a fast-moving gun carriage. What I saw was a brave private risking his own safety to push you out of the way." He looks around at the other trainees. "Did anyone here see differently?"

There is silence. Weiner struggles to conceal a grin.

McConnell stares around at them, fuming.

"The matter is settled," Willem says. "Thank you, gentlemen. Your training is complete. Lieutenant Patrick's crew is the winner. I will have my final reports with the commander of your regiment by the end of the day."

The lieutenants salute as one. Willem returns the salute and the lieutenants and their gun crews depart.

"Jack," Frost says.

"Yes, sir," Jack says.

"You are being addressed by a senior officer," Frost says. "You will stand to attention."

"Sir, yes, sir," Jack says, immediately snapping to attention, his back ramrod straight, his arms making crisp lines down his sides.

"What did you think you were doing?"

"I don't know, sir. I'm very sorry, sir," Jack says. "It won't happen again. It's just that he was hurting Harry, sir. It all came over me in a rush, sir."

"Jack, that's not Harry. Harry is dead. That is a wooden dinosaur," Frost says.

"Yes, sir. But—" Jack says.

"But what?" Frost asks.

"But he was hurting him, sir," Jack says.

There is a tutting sound and Willem turns to see a lieutenant colonel standing quietly behind them. Sir William Congreve is the comptroller of the Royal Laboratory at the nearby Woolwich Arsenal. A scientist and inventor. The creator of the artillery rocket. He is a tall man, small-mouthed and thin-lipped, hatless and balding. His hair is graying yet his luxurious sideburns are unaccountably fully black.

"Your man was very lucky today," he says.

"You saw the incident differently, Sir William?" Willem asks.

"Let us agree that I arrived after the incident," Congreve says.

"I would not wish to deprive the barracks of its most talented wood-carver."

Jack looks both relieved and embarrassed.

"I am grateful, Sir William," Frost says. "He's a good lad."

"You really think to use pepper against dinosaurs?" Congreve asks.

"We do, sir," Willem says. "We have already tested it against a meat-eater."

"Against a firebird, I have heard," Congreve says. "Not a battle-saurus."

"I believe it would have the same effect on the eyes of the greater saurs as it does on the lesser ones," Willem says.

Congreve examines Willem slowly and from his expression seems to find him wanting in many respects. Willem is suddenly conscious that he wears a rank he has neither purchased nor earned, although Congreve would not know this.

Congreve says, "From accounts, these beasts are savage enough already. I fear the pepper will just enrage them further, and endanger more of our troops."

"I do not dispute that, sir," Willem says. "But a French battle-saurus under the control of its rider is a danger only to our soldiers. A maddened, blinded dinosaur is equally dangerous to friend or foe."

"Perhaps," Congreve says. From his expression it is clear that he does not agree.

"Willem's methods are our best hope of defeating these creatures," Frost says.

"I hardly think so, Lieutenant," Congreve says, looking down his nose at the young lieutenant. "Pepper guns and sparkle sticks against battlesaurs? It is my rockets that will bring down the giants, not your toys."

"I don't—" Willem begins, but Frost cuts him off.

"Of course, Sir William," Frost says. "And at battle's end they will be shouting your name as they bury the carcasses of the beasts. But there are only so many rocketeers, and the dinosaurs could attack from any direction. Do you not agree that our artillerymen should be given every chance to defend themselves?"

"Yes, yes, of course," Congreve says, glancing around as if he has somewhere better to be. "But Napoléon will think twice about risking his dinosaurs on the battlefield once we have killed a few of them with my rockets. You will see, at the demonstration tomorrow."

He turns abruptly and strides away.

"What was he doing here?" Jack asks.

"I have no idea," Willem says. "He has shown no interest in our work until now."

"Sir William does nothing without good reason," Frost says.

"Do you think he is right?" Willem asks, his shoulders slumped. *Pepper guns and sparkle sticks.* What he has been teaching the soldiers seems suddenly trivial.

"He is wrong. For a genius, he is a fool," Frost says. "And when the battle is over it will be your name, not his, that echoes across the field."

Willem stares at him and after a moment Frost smiles. "I do not have to hear your words to know what you are thinking," he says. "Yes, our debt to you is great. We will go to Héloïse, but I caution you to steel yourself for the sights you will see."

"We must leave at once," Willem says.

Frost shakes his head. "I have important matters to attend to this afternoon that I cannot avoid or delay. We will go tomorrow, but early so we are back before the demonstration." He puts a hand on Willem's arm. "Earl Wenzel-Halls of Leicester will also attend tomorrow's events."

"He is returned from the Near East?" Willem asks.

"So it would appear," Frost says. "I have sent word that we wish to meet with him after the demonstration."

Willem is silent. The meeting with the earl is one he has sought since his arrival in England, but it will not be an easy one.

Jack has gone to look at Harry. He cranes his neck upward to inspect the damage to its face.

"Jack is a good lad," Frost says quietly, watching him. "I miss him. His innocence and honesty would make a refreshing change in Whitehall. A shame he cannot read or write, or I would request him as my permanent aide."

"He has certainly been a valuable assistant," Willem says. "Carving the heads was his own idea."

"Look out for him, Willem," Frost says. "Hew McConnell has been embarrassed today and I know him. He will seek retribution of some kind."

"I will do what I can," Willem assures him. He smiles as he sees Jack stroke the carved head as if it was a pet. "So where is Héloïse?"

There is silence for a moment.

"The Hospital of St. Mary of Bethlem," Frost says. He hesitates again. "They call it Bedlam."

RUNNING THE PASSAGE

The weather the captain predicted moves in much more quickly than expected. Before they have even passed the peninsula the ship is being rocked by blustery winds. The topsails are furled and the mainsails are quartered, slowing the ship as she leads the way across the mouth of the Baie de Douarnenez.

They are on the French side of the Channel, about five hundred miles southeast of London. By the time they reach the Raz de Sein passage, the ship is being lashed by squalls of rain and thunderous sheets of water that sweep across the deck. Footing is treacherous. The sun has risen but makes little impression through the thick black clouds.

Thibault emerges from belowdecks to find Captain Lavigne on the quarterdeck, shielding his eyes from the rain, peering through the darkness at the barge wallowing in the seas behind them.

"Any problems?" Thibault asks.

"All good so far," Lavigne replies. "How is your wife?"

"Nicole is not a great sailor." Thibault smiles apologetically on her behalf. "She remains in my cabin, tended to by the ship's physician, cursing me with words a sailor would waver to use for bringing her on this expedition."

"Already? It will get much rougher than this," Lavigne says.

Thibault smiles again. "Her airs began the moment she stepped on board. As I said, she is not a good sailor."

"But she will recover?"

"When we reach the British Isles, no doubt."

Thibault turns to the front, where the headlands of the Pointe du Raz protrude through the rain. Off the starboard bow, the Île de Sein is a ghostly illusion, shrouded by the rain and the mist rising off the water.

"It is a narrow passage," Lavigne says.

"It has been run before," Thibault says.

"That fleet lost one ship and the rest dispersed in confusion," Lavigne says. "And they were not towing battlesaurus barges."

"They ran the passage at night," Thibault says. "We shall have the advantage of the sunrise."

"What there is of it," Lavigne says.

The ship rocks even more violently than before, tossing and rolling on the increasing sea.

The sails are mostly furled; just enough are aloft to maintain steerage. It is still more canvas than would be usual in these conditions, but she is towing a heavy load. Sails flap in the gusts and ropes slap against the masts and stays. The sound of the wind through the rigging is a ghoulish shriek.

Waves batter the sides of the ship, erupting over the gunwales and drenching everyone and everything. The air is filled with spray and Thibault can taste salt. Occasionally the island to their right solidifies, breaking through the clouded mist. To larboard, white water breaks furiously against rocks. It seems close, too close.

"Safety lines, fore and aft," the captain instructs, and a moment later the sailing master shouts the same command. The ship plunges deep into furrows, lifting a moment later on huge swells of water. The passage is dangerous even in the calm; in these seas it could soon turn deadly.

There is a crack from overhead and Thibault looks up to see

a spar broken and dangling. Ropes hang loose and sails flap uselessly.

"Two points to starboard," the captain says, and the helmsman moves the wheel just so.

There are more instructions, and sailors are climbing the rigging, tossed and buffeted by the wind and the waves that reach well up the mast. Thibault watches as hatchets slam into loose ropes and the dangling, broken spar collapses. The final rope is cut and it disappears into a whirlwind.

"Four points to starboard," the captain orders.

The rocks to their left seem even closer now. The ship is being driven toward them, despite bearing well away from them.

"The barge is pulling our stern around. It is dragging us sideways." The captain's deep voice comes from close behind Thibault and he turns. Dandy or not, the captain is resolute in the storm, standing on the heaving deck as steadily as if it was dry land, unbothered by the rain and the driving waves that hurl themselves over the sides of the ship.

"If we cannot make way toward the center of the Channel, we may have to cut the barge loose!" The captain has to shout above the howling of the rigging.

"I would first cut you loose," Thibault says without emotion.

"If it drags us onto the rocks the ship will founder!" the captain shouts. "We will all be lost, along with your precious dinosaur."

"Then see that it doesn't," Thibault says.

The captain turns and storms off, without a word or a bow. He barks commands at the deck officers. Sailors run to carry out their orders. The helmsman works the wheel, fighting against the winds and the currents, but now the captain replaces him, his face a rigid mask as he feels his way through the turbulent sea.

More sails are unfurled by riggers high on the spars. A sudden gust of wind and the ship sways. There is a scream from above and a body falls, stopped only at the end of a safety rope.

The rigger spins and swings wildly at the end of the rope. The mast swings back, whipping the man through the air, smashing him against the mizzenmast. His struggles stop and he hangs limply at the end of the rope. Again and again the winds whip him back and forth, painting the mast in broad bright strokes of red before finally, mercifully, the rope breaks and he is gone over the side.

Thibault hears a crunch from behind, the sound carried on the wind. He is immediately afraid that it has come from the barge, but he turns to see it safe, if wallowing badly in the seas behind them. The crunch has come from another of the ships, its mainsails torn, at least one spar hanging loose. Its hull is broached on an unseen rock. It is leaning, almost horizontal, and men are falling from the rigging and the deck into the ocean.

"The *Sceptre*," the captain says. "She is lost!"

"The *Sceptre* is a troop ship, is it not?" Thibault asks.

"It is," the captain says.

"Those men must be rescued," Thibault says. "Signal the following ships."

"That would endanger those ships also," the captain says. "The seas are too rough."

"Captain, that ship carries over a thousand soldiers of the Imperial Guard," Thibault says. "Men who marched with Napoléon in Russia. Who held their ground against cavalry charges at Waterloo. Who defeated the famed Swiss Army at Zurich. Not to mention the officers and their wives."

"A terrible loss," the captain says. "But foolish action will only lose more lives. Sir, you are a soldier; I am a sailor. Trust me when

I tell you that to attempt this rescue will cost more ships. We will lose more of your men, and more of mine."

His lips compressed, Thibault regards him for a moment.

"Is there nothing that can be done?" he asks.

"You could pray for their souls," the captain says.

Only when the rocks of the passage are behind them and the ship has reached the safety of the open sea does Thibault again go belowdecks. His wife is in bed, a wooden bowl cradled in front of her. As he enters she quickly turns her face toward the window.

The ship's surgeon stands at her bedside, but leaves quickly at a glance from Thibault.

"How are you, my love?" Thibault asks.

"At the door of death," she says. "My stomach churns and my head spins. How long must I endure this torture?"

"A few days only," Thibault says. "And it will be much less arduous once this weather passes."

"It had better," she says. "I feel as though one of your creatures has laid its spawn inside me and it is trying to escape through my gullet."

"It is just the seasickness," Thibault says. "It will pass as soon as the ship steadies. A small sacrifice, my love, on the road to greatness."

"I am pleased for you, husband," she says, her eyes still fixed on the window.

It is as if she cannot bear to look upon his scarred and blackened face.

His anger flares.

"Then look at me," he says.

"I am ill," she says.

"And looking at me turns your stomach?" he asks.

"I cannot lie to you. It does," she says. He draws breath but before he can retort she says quietly, "And yet I am here."

"Why are you here?" he asks, anger still coloring his voice.

"Yours is not the face of the man I married," she says. "But you are still the man I married. The man I love. In the depths of my illness and misery allow me to turn away from you and listen to your voice, and thus see you as you still appear in my memory."

The anger dissipates immediately and he crosses to the bed and takes her hand in his.

"The road we are on is the path to our greatness," he says.

"I would rather it were you, not Napoléon, who was to lead the main attack," Nicole says.

"You do our emperor a grave disservice," Thibault says. "He is a brilliant tactician. Our landing will take the British by surprise. And that will open the front door to England."

"You speak admiringly of the man you plan to kill," she says.

"Napoléon is a military genius," Thibault says. "Even now, though he is old, tired, and unwell, I need his brain to conquer England. After that, he will hold no further use for me. He will be remembered as a hero and I will be hailed as emperor."

"And I will be the empress of France," Nicole says.

"Of the world," Thibault says.

NIGHTMARE

Willem wakes with a scream, unsure if it is aloud or confined within his own skull. He prays it is the latter. The walls of the officers' quarters are thin, and he often hears night murmurings, coughs, and snoring from the rooms on either side. For the British officers to hear him scream even once would be embarrassing. But this dream and the scream that follows happen nearly every night.

In the dream he is back in Gaillemarde, and everyone is still alive: Monsieur Lejeune; Father Ambroise; Madame Gertruda; the mayor, Monsieur Claude, and his stout wife. Everyone.

And the beast is back. The immense saur with the snout of a crocodile. The one that he and his friend Jean killed. But in the dream they do not kill it. As in real life, he freezes, but in the dream there is no Héloïse to break him from his rigidity. He is an observer, nothing more. In that frozen moment the dinosaur takes both Cosette and her father with a single bite as they cower amid the gravestones. The stone angel above them is misted red with blood.

The monster moves on to the church, where it feasts on the children who hide there and on the women who try to protect them. After that it turns to the rest of the villagers, one after another, who, like Willem, seem frozen in place, merely waiting their turn to disappear into the gaping maw, victims of the creature's insatiable appetite. Only then, when just Jean and Willem are left, does it turn toward them and those great teeth take Jean and now there is only Willem and that is when he screams. Because now the leaping flames from burning houses light up the great beast and he can see that it wears the uniform of the French general: Thibault.

Then he always wakes and in the first twilight daze of consciousness he remembers that Jean really is dead.

And so is almost everybody else.

Willem stands up from his bunk, shivering in the cold September night air. He lights a candle, which pushes back the darkness, and some of the demons that lurk there, but does nothing about the cold.

He uses the chamber pot although he does not really need to, then climbs back into the bunk, sitting up and drawing the bedclothes around him. He stares at the candle for a few moments, letting the intensity of its glow imprint itself on his eyes. When he closes them he can still see it, but reversed. Dark against the inside of his eyelids.

Facing the dinosaur at Gaillemarde was no dream. He and Jean slew the monster. But Jean is dead at the hand of his own cousin, and Willem knows that by himself he could never again face such a creature.

Even the gentle, innocent eyes of the herbisaurs chill him, and the microsaurs that sometimes skitter around his feet in the wooded lands of the artillery barracks seem to grow in his mind until they too are the terrifying monster of Gaillemarde.

He cannot return to the Sonian Forest.

And yet he must.

He pinches out the candle and darkness returns.

But for a long time, sleep does not.

BEDLAM

"I was told that Bedlam was at St. George's Fields," Willem says. "Here on the south side of the river."

The morning is cold and the Thames is covered with fog, a winter fog, even though it is autumn.

Willem, Frost, and Jack stand on the Woolwich jetty waiting for the ferry to return. Frost has requested Jack's services again today, as a guide, although Willem suspects that the real reason is to keep Jack well away from Hew McConnell.

"Héloïse resides at the old asylum," Frost says. "At Moorfields on the north side."

"The old asylum?" Willem asks.

Frost says. "The new building you refer to has only just opened at St. George's Fields. However, most of the patients, including Héloïse, remain at the old asylum awaiting transfer."

Willem nods in understanding. He looks out across the river. He cannot see the ferry yet and only knows it is there because of the regular warning call of "Hoy!" from the ferry master, alerting other vessels to their presence. The ferryboat is invisible in the thick yellow fog that suffocates the river in this early part of the morning.

Two oil lamps are suspended from poles at the end of the jetty. The sun has risen but the lamps are still lit, twin beacons to guide the ferry in the mist. Their light is dull and barely penetrates the fog. The new gaslights that illuminate many parts of London have yet to be installed here at Woolwich.

Willem does not like the fog, which makes his breathing heavy. He can see no farther than the length of his arm, and tries not to dwell on the thought of what might lurk, unseen, in the mist around them. His hand strays to the hilt of his saber, and rests there for a while, as a comfort.

The fog begins to glow and the regular splash of oars signals the imminent arrival of the ferry. A few moments later the blunt prow of the boat eases into the jetty.

The ferry master checks their papers before letting them on board. There are no other passengers and soon the sound of the oars resumes. Within seconds the jetty has gone. Here in the middle of the river they drift in a world of murky yellow, as if everything else has ceased to exist.

Willem becomes conscious of every sound. Every smell. The regular dip and splash of the oars. The sound of water moving past the boat. The voices of the guards on the jetty behind them. The ferry master's warning call. The fog has a strange smoky smell. The river too has its own odor: a sickly blend of mud and decay. Willem can taste the air, bitter on his tongue. He can feel its clammy fingers on the exposed skin of his face and hands.

He realizes this is what Frost's world is like. A world of sound, smell, taste, and touch, but no sight. He looks at the lieutenant. If Frost is nervous he does not show it.

Jack does. He looks as nervous as Willem feels. His eyes dart around like those of a rabbit or a bird.

"When we get to the asylum," Frost says, "do not be surprised and do not comment on anything you see."

"Of course," Willem says, although he feels these words were intended for Jack's ears.

* * *

A line of hackney carriages wait near the north-bank jetty as they disembark. Despite his lack of sight Frost seems aware of their presence and raises a hand. The first driver in line prods his horse forward until the carriage stops in front of them.

"Is it a long walk?" Willem asks. He is unused to riding in such a vehicle.

"More than two hours on foot," Frost says as Jack helps him to the step. "We would not make it back to Woolwich for the rocket demonstration and the earl's visit if we walked."

Jack opens the carriage door and Frost steps up inside. Willem follows.

"Where to, m'lud?" the driver asks.

"Bedlam," Frost says.

The driver nods as if this is a common request, and the carriage growls forward over the cobblestones.

"How did you know the carriages were there?" Willem asks. "I heard no sound that would give away their presence."

"I smelled the horses," Frost says.

The streets of London are narrow and the buildings are tall, topped by chimneys that claw away the sky. In places the brick walls rise so high on all sides that it does not seem real, but rather like the painted backdrop of a theater. The people seem no more than players in a convoluted drama on a busy stage.

The fog adds to the air of unreality. It is thinner here away from the river but still swathes everything and everyone in a ghostly gauze.

The roads are crowded in spite of the early hour. Chimney sweeps and charwomen jostle with flower sellers on the narrow pavements. Laborers wait on street corners. Vagabonds curl in doorways. Street sweepers are still at work, cleaning up the last of the dung of the previous day, dodging the carriages, delivery carts, and men on horseback that are already starting to fill the streets. The fresh fields of the artillery barracks seem like paradise compared to the grimy buildings of London. The air here is thick with the smell of soot and sewage.

Two mounted constables, "Robin Redbreasts," with their distinctive scarlet waistcoats under dark blue greatcoats, water their horses at a trough in front of a teahouse. One has dismounted, removed his top hat, and is energetically cranking the pump handle. The other glances idly at Willem as they pass.

Spread along the road by a small park, a row of costermongers in their colorful kingsman neckerchiefs are selling fruit, breads, fish, and other goods from wooden carts, while their donkeys graze on the nearby grass. One of them, a squat, ugly man with a long mustache and no beard or sideburns, is arguing with a dour-faced woman over the payment she has given him. He holds his hand out showing a single copper, while she indicates with her fingers that she gave him two. Willem wonders who is lying. He suspects it is the woman. Even back in Gaillemarde, a market vendor was very careful to avoid being labeled a cheat.

A little farther on, in dark alleyways running with rats and lined with straw to soak up the mud, Willem sees crawlers, old women who live on the street. They cannot, or perhaps choose not, to walk, and get around by crawling on their hands and knees. Willem thinks they look like animals, but he knows what his mother would say if she saw them. They are people too. They call out to the carriage as it passes and Willem tosses a few coppers from his purse, much to Frost's disgust.

"You should not encourage them," he says. "More will fill these streets if they find easy pickings from such as you."

"And yet those coins, which matter not at all to me, may mean that some of those women eat today," Willem says.

Frost shrugs. "I suspect that you do not think very highly of London," he says.

"It is what it is," Willem says. "I neither like nor dislike it. But it is vastly different to Gaillemarde."

That is an understatement. All his life, since he was old enough to remember, he had lived in a sleepy little village nestled on the bank of a river on the edge of the vast Sonian Forest. The houses were separate and scattered. The largest building was the church. Gaillemarde is a long way from London, in every possible sense.

He cannot think about his old village without thinking about two of the survivors of Thibault's massacre there, now held in Napoléon's prison. Cosette and his mother.

"You must help me convince Wellington to let me have my soldiers and my ship," he says.

"I doubt my word will carry more weight than yours," Frost says. "But I will certainly use all my powers of persuasion when we meet him."

"He must not back down from his promise," Willem says. When he closes his eyes all he can see is Cosette's lips, arcing into a smile.

Frost has an uncanny ability to read his mind. "Tell me about Cosette," he says.

"What is it that you wish to know?" Willem asks.

"Is she pretty?" Frost asks.

"She is," Willem says.

Even as he says it he feels guilty, suddenly conscious that prettiness is something the young lieutenant will never again experience. Lost to him forever are so many things, like the sight of a dancing field of flowers, the sun breaking over the hills at the start of a new day, or moonlight caught in the eye of a child.

"You have feelings for her," Frost says.

"I have spoken of no such thing," Willem protests.

"Yet when you speak of the rescue, it is always her name that you utter first," Frost says.

"You have been too long with the Intelligence Office," Willem says. "You find meaning where there is none."

"Are you betrothed to her?" Frost asks.

Willem shakes his head.

"Are you promised?" Frost asks.

"I am not anything to her," Willem says. He sighs. "Except a fool when I am around her and incomplete when I am away from her."

"I thought as much," Frost says with a smile.

"You see far and deeply without eyes," Willem says. "Jean would have laughed at me. He'd have said there are many maidens to woo before settling on one."

Speaking of Jean brings back memories of him, Willem's truest friend, murdered by his own cousin, François. It is a painful memory. Frost seems to sense his discomfort and they travel for a while in silence.

They skirt the old London wall, built by the Romans around the original city of Londinium to keep out wandering saurs. It is high and imposing, made of thick stone. Willem wonders if saurs were larger in those days, or perhaps more numerous.

Everywhere they see soldiers in small groups or marching in lines. They are a constant reminder that Napoléon's army is held back from London by just a short stretch of water. Not that the city needs reminding. Unease is everywhere: in the expressions on people's faces, on the pages of the newspapers, in the shop owners boarding up their shop windows in preparation for the imminent invasion.

They pass one news-seller with copies of the *Times*, holding up a hand-drawn poster of a dinosaur that looks more like a large rat.

"I heard that Napoléon is going to fly his battlesaurs over using giant balloons," Frost says with a smile.

"And I heard that the French are digging a tunnel beneath the English Channel," Willem says.

"Flying dinosaurs," Jack says. "Imagine if one did its bottom business. I wouldn't want to be standin' under that."

They all laugh.

The carriage finally turns into a wide tree-lined driveway on the grounds of an imposing building. It pulls to a halt outside a large gate in a curved wall, between two heavy pillars. On top of the pillars are statues, two reclining men with faces contorted by madness.

Jack seems immediately uncomfortable at the sight of this place. "I'll stay here and mind the carriage, if you please," he says.

"Come with us, Jack," Frost says. "I need your eyes."

Jack hesitates, then says, "Mr. Willem has eyes too, sir."

"Jack, I could use—" Frost begins.

"I'd rather not go in there, sir, if it's all the same to you," Jack says abruptly.

Willem is surprised by the outburst. "Do you know this place?" he asks.

"I seen it before," Jack says. "It's a bad place."

"It's a hospital," Frost says. "They help sick people."

"Bad things happen in there," Jack says. "I feel it."

"Héloïse is in there," Willem says.

Jack looks terrified. "Please, sir, Lieutenant Frost, sir," he says.

"But—" Willem begins.

"Jack, stay here," Frost says. He hands him some coins. "Here is the payment for our driver. Hold it for me and see that he does not leave before our return."

It is Willem's turn to be Frost's guide. He takes the lieutenant's arm and leads him through the gates toward a heavy stone wall, topped by four Roman pillars. Set into the wall is a narrow door.

"That was unlike Jack," Willem says as they walk.

"Decidedly," Frost agrees. "Something about this place has affected him deeply. Perhaps it is not entirely unknown to him. A family member, perhaps?"

They stop at the door, which is locked. A rope to one side pulls a bell and they wait as the sharp tones fade in the cool morning air.

"Not long ago, you could pay tuppence to visit the madhouse and laugh at the lunatics," Frost says. "It was considered a fine entertainment."

"That seems cruel," Willem says.

"Times have changed," Frost says without conviction.

A nurse greets them and invites them into a small waiting room, where she writes their names in a visitors' book. She is a sharp-faced but stout woman, with one eye that constantly weeps.

"I must ask you to remove your swords," she says. "No weapons are allowed inside, lest the lunatics take hold of them and use them to harm themselves or others."

Frost unbuckles his scabbard and hands it to the nurse, who places it in a cupboard. Willem follows suit, and the nurse locks the cupboard.

"We have come to see Antoinette de Forêt," Frost says.

This is the name by which Héloïse has been admitted to the asylum, to keep her real identity secret.

The nurse consults another large, leather-bound book, wiping at her damp eye.

"I am afraid Miss de Forêt is not available," she says.

"We have come a long way, and have only a little time," Frost says. "Might I ask that she be made available?"

"I'm sorry, sir, she is in treatment," the nurse says. "You can see her after that."

"Perhaps we can see her while she is in treatment," Frost says. "As I said, we are pressed for time."

"My apologies, good sir, she cannot be disturbed," the nurse says. "Therapy is not for spectators."

"I have tuppence if it is required," Frost says coldly.

The nurse sets her mouth and closes the book.

"Might we at least see the asylum?" Willem asks. He does not wait for an answer but steps past the nurse and opens a door into a wide gallery.

Asylum is the wrong word for this place, he thinks. This is clearly not a place of shelter. Nor is it a refuge or a sanctuary. *Madhouse* is the better word, for this is truly a house of chaos and madness.

As soon as the door is opened he can hear babbling, wailing, and the clanking of chains. The stench of human waste is like a solid hand pushing him backward.

As Willem enters—with Frost at his heels, holding the back of his coat for guidance—an elderly man with wide, staring eyes turns to see them. He has one look at Frost and begins to laugh, pointing at Frost's face. Perhaps it is the twin eye patches that he finds so funny. His laughter turns to cackles and is infectious; others around him also turn and snigger or giggle.

"What are they laughing at?" Frost asks.

"Nothing," Willem says. "They are just laughing."

The main hall is nothing but a stone-walled barn. The floor is covered with straw. The walls are lined with barred cells. Some of the inmates stand at the bars, staring out into the main gallery. Others lie on wooden beds, or are curled into balls in corners of their cells.

In the main gallery, men and women roam aimlessly with dazed expressions, others with melancholy eyes. One or two are crying. Some undertake small pastimes like card games or hand-knitting.

One man is completely naked except for a straitjacket. He stands facing a wall, gibbering like a monkey. Uniformed orderlies move among the inmates, separating those who seem on the verge of fighting, mopping up urine, and scraping vomit and feces off the floor. The orderlies wear wooden batons in loops on their belts. One is standing, baton raised, over a man who is curled into a ball on the floor. The patient's arms are bruised and bloodied.

"What do you see?" Frost asks.

"There are times when I envy your lack of eyes," Willem says. "I see things I would rather erase from my sight."

"You are free to wander anywhere on this level," the nurse says, behind them. "But the upper level is private. That is for our most dangerous—"

She is cut off by a scream that echoes down a stairwell. It is a shrill shriek that slices through the babble of groaning, moaning, and cackling.

"Héloïse?" Willem asks uncertainly, looking at Frost.

"You know her voice better than I," Frost says.

There is another scream and it does sound like Héloïse. Willem has heard her scream many times.

He finds himself moving toward the stairs without really thinking about what he is doing. The nurse moves to stop him but he steps quickly around her. He feels a touch on his arm and looks back to see Frost close behind him.

"That area is forbidden!" the nurse calls after them. When Willem looks back, she is scurrying away, to summon help no doubt.

Another scream comes echoing down the stone walls of the staircase. The steps are uneven, as if the building has shifted since it was built. On the next level the walls lean at strange angles and part of the ceiling is collapsed. At the top of the stairs is a long corridor, lined with cages, from which hands protrude, grasping and clutching at the two men. Moans and grunts from the cages are interspersed with laughter and shrieks, an unnerving cacophony of insanity.

Willem tries not to look in the cages, but when he does, he sees more things he would rather not have seen. A man standing at the bars, his arms outspread, his face turned upward and contorted with pain like Christ on the cross. Several of the patients are naked, their clothes strewn around their cells. Some are covered in feces. Some are crying, others snarling, some are silent, staring with hollow eyes.

Another turn, and the corridor changes in color and tone. There are no cages here, nor inmates. It is brighter, wider, and the doors are not barred. A sign above one door says COLD WATER THERAPY. Willem shudders to think what that might be. The screams do not come from here but from two doors down, where a closed door has a sign that says ROTATION THERAPY.

Willem shoulders the door open and Frost follows him inside.

In the room is a contraption from a bad dream. A large wooden frame, from the center of which is suspended a chair at the end of a rope.

A girl is strapped into the chair, unable to move, her arms

constricted by a grimy straitjacket. At first Willem is not even sure that it is Héloïse.

Her hair, once long and wild, is almost completely gone. Only short stubble covers her head. Her arms are blue with bruises and covered with black splodges. It takes Willem a moment to realize they are leeches. The chair is spinning and the girl's face is contorted in fear and pain.

Willem is speechless. It is Héloïse. He is sure of it. The girl whose life he once saved from a firebird and whom he will forever feel responsible for. The girl who repaid the debt by defending them all from the madness of François. A girl of the wilderness, happiest only in the sunshine, with the trees, birds, and small saurs of the forest. Yet here she is a prisoner in a straitjacket; locked in a lopsided, stone-walled madhouse; kept away from the sun and fresh air; forced into a contraption that spins her to such incoherent giddiness she can barely scream. Even her cave in the dinosaur lair beneath the Sonian Forest was better than this.

A large man in the uniform of an orderly stands by the side of the frame spinning the chair by turning a handle.

"Stop that!" Willem cries.

The man looks at him, but otherwise does nothing. He has a hooked nose and small, haunted eyes. His hair is pure white, although he seems no more than middle-aged.

"Stop that!" Willem cries again.

The man turns away and begins to wind the handle faster. The chair becomes a blur of movement.

All he has seen of this place suddenly explodes inside Willem and in a surge of anger he runs forward, pushing the orderly backward with two flat hands to his chest. The man stumbles and falls to the ground, knocking his head on a small wooden table behind him. The spinning chair starts to slow.

The orderly raises himself to a sitting position. He puts a hand to his scalp and it comes up bloody. He grins, a lopsided, unhinged smile. He stands and moves toward Willem.

Willem backs away slowly. There is a strangeness about the man's small eyes, as though something evil and animal lurks just below the surface.

Willem backs into Frost and stops. He is frightened, but he will not abandon Héloïse.

"What is it?" Frost asks. "What do you see? What has happened?"

"An orderly," Willem says. "A rather large one, and I fear I have angered him."

"Is Héloïse here?" Frost asks.

"She is," Willem says.

"You are an officer," Frost says. "Act like one."

And all at once Willem straightens his back and steps forward, seemingly unafraid.

"Sir, I am Major Johannes Lux of the Third Netherlands Infantry Division. I apologize for my anger, and the cut to your head, it was an accident."

"It were no accident," the orderly snarls, continuing to advance, drawing his wooden baton from its loop on his belt.

Frost pushes past Willem. "Sir, I suggest you back away," he says. "We are officers in the king's army."

"You need a blind boy to do your fightin'?" the orderly says, his eyes fixed on Willem.

"I choose to fight," Frost says. "Are you such a person as would strike a blind man?"

The orderly hesitates, then abruptly reaches out and pushes Frost to one side, the baton in his other hand swinging toward Willem. Willem ducks under the blow and dodges away from the

70

man, darting around the back of the apparatus, behind Héloïse in the still-turning chair.

The orderly smashes his baton against the wooden framework of the device. He does it again and Héloïse screams. Behind him Frost grabs at his arm but the man pushes him off easily, sending him crashing into a corner.

Willem moves quickly away from Héloïse. He does not want to put her in any more danger. He reaches the small table and puts that between him and the orderly.

The man grins and thrusts forward across the tabletop with the baton. Willem jumps to one side. The baton misses him by inches.

The man feints a couple of times, testing Willem's reactions, then lashes out with a sideways blow. Willem manages to dodge, but only just, circling the table.

Frost is shouting at the man, but neither Willem nor the orderly seems to hear him.

Now the man grabs one end of the table, upending it, removing Willem's meager defense. He steps forward, trapping Willem in the corner. He raises the baton and smashes it down. Willem can do nothing but block it with his arms and the sudden pain raises black spots in front of his eyes.

The orderly again raises the baton above his head and Willem braces himself for the next blow. But when the man's arm slashes down once again his hand is empty and there is a look of surprise on his face.

The orderly turns to face some unseen threat behind him, then collapses, stunned, as his own baton smashes down on his forehead.

The man stays down, blood pouring from a new deep cut on his head, as Jack hovers over him, the baton raised ready for another strike.

"I told you bad things happen in this place," Jack says.

"Thank you for coming, Jack," Frost says pleasantly, as though welcoming Jack to a party.

Willem cradles one arm with the other. It is not broken, he decides, but still the pain is intense. His forearm is throbbing and he feels dizzy.

"I realized I couldn't let you come in here alone," Jack says. "On account of something bad might happen to you."

"As it nearly did," Frost says.

The chair has come to a stop, bringing Héloïse around to face Willem. Héloïse's eyes are full of fear, but when she sees Willem her expression changes to one of hurt and anger.

Willem lowers his eyes, ashamed. He has left her to be tortured in this awful place. Caught up in the training, in his own importance, he has neglected her. He moves to unfasten her from the chair but stops at the sound of a new voice from the doorway.

"What is the meaning of this?"

Willem turns to see a stout man, stately and dignified, fashionably dressed in a double-breasted coat, tight pantaloons tucked into boots, and a high collar and cravat. He holds a cane topped with a silver lion's head. He is flanked by the nurse with the weepy eye.

"Who are you, and why are you interrupting this therapy session?" the man asks. He now sees the man on the floor. "Adams? What is going on?"

Adams tries to get up but stops as Jack waves the baton threateningly.

"He assaulted us," Frost says.

"Then I am sure he was provoked," the man says.

"Not unnecessarily," Frost says.

"He would not stop this torture when asked," Willem says. He still cannot look at Héloïse.

"Torture? You only show your ignorance of modern medicine," the man says. "The rotation is well proven to excise madness." He turns to Frost. "Lieutenant Frost, is it not?"

"You have me at a disadvantage, sir," Frost says. "I confess that I do not recognize your voice."

"We have not met," the man says. "But your fame precedes you. There can be few blinded artillery lieutenants who still wear the uniform. You are the saur-slayer. I am Doctor Thomas Monro, the principal physician of this asylum."

"Dr. Monro, I implore you to stop the treatment of this girl immediately," Frost says.

"I must not," Monro says. "For her own good."

"I insist," Frost says.

"You have no right to insist. Nor the medical knowledge to understand the treatment," Monro says. "I will ask you to leave."

"We will not," Willem says. "We urgently need this girl's assistance."

"I am afraid that she will be of no assistance to you or to anyone else," Monro says.

"This is a matter of vital military importance," Frost says.

"Even if it was life and death, it would make no difference," Monro says. "The girl cannot speak except in animal sounds."

"I am not surprised," Willem says, "considering the conditions here and the treatment you force on her."

"I take no offense at your ignorance," Monro says mildly. "I will advise you once again to leave."

"Advice that I cannot in good conscience take," Frost says.

"In which case I will send for the provost marshals, and you will all be arrested," Monro says.

"They will have to drag me from this room," Willem says. "I will not leave my friend to such barbarity."

"Barbarity?" Now Monro's careful calm threatens to break. "Barbarity? How dare you, sir?"

"Major Lux, we must leave," Frost says. "But this afternoon we will have the ear of the Duke of Wellington. Perhaps he will be able to sway the doctor's mind."

"The Duke of Wellington." Monro snorts. "A pompous fool. I will not be directed in medical matters by those with no medical knowledge."

"You will be hearing from us again," Frost says. "Jack, please guide me."

Jack releases Adams, who gets slowly to his feet, staring up at Jack with cold eyes. Jack takes Frost's arm and leads him from the room.

As Willem reluctantly follows he looks back. Adams has returned to the handle and is smiling at Willem as Héloïse once again starts to turn on that awful chair. Each time she turns her eyes meet Willem's. He sees nothing but loathing.

Willem waits until they are outside the main gates and approaching the hackney carriage before he risks speaking; his pulse is racing and his voice does not seem his own.

"A madman is in charge of the madhouse," he says.

"She must not stay in that place," Jack says, wiping tears from his eyes.

Willem grasps Frost by the arm. "How could you leave her in that torture room?"

"I would not," Frost says. "But if you and I are arrested, then there will be nothing more we can do for her. However, there are many ways to skin a gardensaur. The duke has great influence. Let us see if he can help."

Willem looks back as the carriage takes them away from the asylum. The last wisps of morning fog swirl around the building and the low sun strikes up under the eaves, creating hollows out of the window spaces. The asylum seems to radiate an evil presence.

"And if the duke cannot help?" Willem eventually asks.

"Then you will have to magic her out of that place," Frost says.

ROCKETEERS

The spinning, smoky tail of a rocket corkscrews straight into Lewis's mouth and explodes in a fiery burst, setting the head on fire.

Willem watches in silence. He has been silent for most of the trip back from Bedlam, his mind filled with the horrors of what he has seen. Of the degradation and humiliation of his friend. They have arrived back at Woolwich barely in time for the display by Sir William Congreve's rocketeers.

Lewis's head falls from its wooden neck and lies burning on the grass of the field. Willem glances sideways at Jack, who stands motionless and emotionless. Willem thinks of the hours of painstaking work Jack put into carving Lewis, and he thinks of the friend that it represents, lost at Waterloo. He sets his jaw, knowing what Jack must be feeling.

Fortunately for Jack, but unfortunately for Congreve, it is the only rocket of the first barrage to get anywhere near the five wooden trojansaurs dragged out by Congreve's horse crews to the wide-open training fields past the parade grounds.

The Duke of Wellington and Lord Wenzel-Halls, the Earl of Leicester, are seated on armchairs at the front of the viewing area. The chairs look out of place in the middle of a grassy field.

The duke is elegantly dressed in his red uniform tunic and his cockade hat. He wears a curved Mameluke sword and looks every inch the British nobleman, far different from how he looked in the plain gray coat he wore the last time Willem met him. The earl is a stout man, an old-fashioned one with a heavily powdered wig and stockings that would not have looked out of place in the previous century. He wears no military uniform. He dabs his bulbous nose regularly with a brown-stained handkerchief, a sign of a regular snuff user.

Next to the duke and the earl on simple wooden chairs are Lieutenant Colonel Sir George Adam Wood, the commander of the Royal Artillery, and Lieutenant Colonel Frazer, the commander of the Royal Horse Artillery, along with Congreve, the rocket master. Frost, Willem, Jack, and the other spectators stand in a roped-off area behind them.

The skies are clear and the whole event has the feeling of a gala. At least it did until the five trojansaurs were wheeled onto the field. It's all of them except Harry, who is in the workshop for repairs to his face. Any warmth in the day immediately evaporated as Willem realized what was about to take place.

Lewis's head still burns fiercely as the rocketeers reload their weapons. Gray smoke spirals into the clear sky.

"What is happening, Jack?" Frost asks. "You are to be my eyes, remember."

"Sorry, sir, I was just a bit shocked, sir," Jack says. "The rockets all missed, sir, except for one. That hit Lewis."

"Any damage?" Frost asks.

"He's on fire, sir," Jack says matter-of-factly. "And his head fell off."

As the rocketeers reload, Sir William Congreve stands and turns to face the audience. He has an object in his hands. A long, sleek rod with a barbed end. He gestures dramatically at the burning trojansaur with it.

"Welcome to the future," he says. "Napoléon fights with ancient animals. We will defeat them with modern military technology."

This earns light applause.

Congreve holds up the object. "If this is the first time you have seen our rockets in action, let me explain how they work," he says. "Like case shot, our rockets contain an explosive charge. Gunpowder also gives us our propulsion, with a range of well over three thousand yards. But today we are firing at a much closer range. We have lowered the elevation to simulate what might happen against dinosaurs on the battlefield." He points to the sharp barbed end. "We have developed a harpoon-like head to ensure that the rocket will penetrate and cling to a dinosaur's skin until it explodes, killing the beast. Not all the rockets will find their targets, of course, but even those that miss will disorient and frighten the creatures. A maddened, panic-stricken dinosaur would be equally dangerous to friend or foe."

He finishes to a loud round of applause.

"He has borrowed your words," Frost murmurs.

Willem shrugs. "It is a fact; it does not matter who says it."

Congreve retires to his seat and gives a signal to the rocketeers.

There is a series of small explosions from the field and smoke erupts from the ground, swathing everything in a light blanket of haze.

"They've let off some smoke bombs," Jack says quietly in Frost's ear.

"Yes, I can smell it," Frost says. "To simulate battlefield conditions, no doubt. Congreve clearly likes his theatrics."

From off to one side in the trees comes a low, reverberating growl. It has a flat, tinny sound to it.

"What the 'ell is that?" Jack asks.

"I imagine it is supposed to be the bellow of a battlesaurus," Frost says. "Probably just a man in the trees with a large speaking horn."

"I don't think he has ever heard a dinosaur roar," Willem says.

"Sounds more like a sick cat," Jack says.

"Or a cow giving birth," Frost says.

"Or a cat giving birth to a cow." Willem laughs.

The rocket-launching contraptions look like ladders, propped up with wooden legs, creating a triangular shape pointed toward the targets. The legs of the ladders have metal troughs. A rocket is placed on each trough.

The firing mechanism is a metal shape not unlike the stock of a pistol, with a frizzen, a firing pin, and a long lanyard. When all the soldiers are ready, they stand well clear of the tails of the rockets. Bombardiers wait for the order to fire.

Congreve raises his hand, holds it there for a moment, and then brings it sharply down. The bombardiers pull on their lanyards and there are puffs of smoke from the firing mechanisms, followed by sparks sputtering from the ends of the rockets. The rockets wriggle their tails for a second or so, then shoot forward with a loud hiss, leaving trails of smoke behind them.

"I do not hear the sounds of damage this time," Frost says after a few seconds.

Jack has been too relieved to say anything. Now he does. "They've all missed," he says, trying not to sound too cheerful. "Some has gone straight ahead, but not very near me wooden monsters. Others has gone all over the place, sir, up, down, off to the left or right. It's a right queer mess, sir, if you ask me."

"Just a little more quietly, if you please, Jack," Frost says.

Willem is aware of faces turning to look.

"Sorry, sir," Jack whispers. "Now the rocket men are reloading again, sir."

The rocketeers repeat the process of loading and arming the rockets, but this time do not wait for a signal from Congreve.

In twos and threes another barrage of rockets spark, sputter, and hiss through the air.

Jack keeps up his quiet commentary. He describes the scene as one rocket spirals into the ground just in front of its launch ramp. The rocketeers all dive to the ground as it explodes with a huge *thump*, throwing dirt and grass into the air.

The rocketeers stand up as if nothing unusual has happened and start to reload.

"Don't think I'd like to be a rocket man," Jack says. "Looks a bit dangerous to me."

"More dangerous to the troops than to the dinosaurs?" Frost asks.

"So far, sir," Jack says, but the words have barely left his mouth when the barbed nose of one of the rockets embeds itself in the wooden framework of Dylan. It protrudes from the splintered wood, still smoking.

"They've hit one," Jack says, trying to sound calm. "It ain't done much damage though, sir, it—"

The rocket explodes, destroying the neck of the creature in a shower of splinters and wood chips.

"What just happened, Jack?" Frost asks.

Jack has shut his eyes tightly. He opens them as the carved wooden head of the creature cracks into two pieces and topples, on fire, to the ground.

"They got Dylan, sir," Jack says.

Behind them somewhere McConnell calls out, "Good shot!" and there are cheers and applause from the rest of the audience. But the sounds quickly turn to cries of alarm, then horror, as one of the other rockets takes off almost vertically from its launcher, flying high into the air, then dropping in flames, a fiery falling star heading straight for the viewing gallery.

"Look out, sir," Jack cries. "It's coming right for us!"

"Don't be so dramatic, Jack," Frost says, not moving.

The rocket veers off at the last second and dives into the dirt just in front of the Duke of Wellington. The earl, seated next to him, cringes and raises his arms, but the duke does not move at all. There is an eruption of flame from the ground for a moment, but no explosion.

As the flame burns out there are more cheers and applause.

"We're all right, sir," Jack says. "The rocket didn't blow up."

"Well and good then," Frost says.

Barrage after barrage of rockets is fired. Still the three remaining trojansaurs are unharmed. Some rockets head skyward on twisted trails of smoke, others bury themselves into the earth. Some hurtle off sideways into the trees that line both sides of the field and one loops high into the sky, over the tops of the trees and into the town beyond. A rider is sent to check on any damage or casualties.

After half an hour of the barrage, a constant roar of hisses and explosions, another of the targets is hit: Ben.

Jack seems unable to speak for a moment as the rocket flies straight into the chest and explodes, tearing the structure to pieces. Behind him, McConnell celebrates with a whistle and the applause from the gallery is long and loud.

"They killed Ben," is all Jack can say.

Sam is next: a rocket lodges in the gun carriage and although it does not explode, it burns fiercely, setting fire to the framework, then the head. Thick smoke boils away upward. Douglas collapses when a rocket blows off one of its wheels.

There is applause and cheers when the demonstration finishes and the rocket troop gallops away. The trojansaurs—blackened, fragmented, or still burning—are left where they are.

"That'll show Bony," Jack hears Lieutenant Colonel Wood say. The duke nods and smiles but does not comment.

As they leave, they come face-to-face with McConnell, who smirks but says nothing.

"Thank you for your commentary today, Jack. You did a good job," Frost says as they walk back to the barracks. "You were a great help. Would you consider a transfer onto my staff?"

"Sir, I'd love that, sir," Jack says. "But what would I do, sir?"

"I'm sure we'll find something to keep you busy," Frost says.

THE DUKE

A late luncheon has been prepared in honor of the duke's visit. Willem attends in the role he is playing as a major of artillery, and Frost as a representative of the Intelligence Service.

To Willem's eye, the luncheon is a feast to more than rival even the best years of the spring festival in Gaillemarde. The table is loaded with soft, moist roast pork, golden potatoes, and fresh fruit. There are bowls of grapes, red, green, and yellow. Bread rolls are stacked in towers and jugs of sauce are full to overflowing.

The duke sits at the head of the table with the Earl of Leicester, along with the two commanders of the foot and horse artillery, Lieutenant Colonel Wood and Lieutenant Colonel Frazer. Congreve sits to the duke's left.

Frost draws Willem aside before they take their seats.

"The duke is a difficult man," he says. "He is fair and honest. But he does not suffer fools gladly."

"So you think me a fool," Willem says.

"Not in the least, and that was not my meaning. But you must take care what you say lest the duke forms that opinion."

"So the duke thinks I am a fool?" Willem asks.

Frost sighs. "I am privy to many things. Things that I cannot discuss with you. Regardless of what agreement you had with the duke, the world has changed. He will not honor an agreement with a peasant boy if it means losing a war."

"We will see," Willem says stubbornly.

"You must present him with sound arguments," Frost says. "Make him realize that what you suggest will help him, not hinder him. You—"

He seems to want to say more, but must stop as the duke sits, which is the signal for the other officers to take their seats. As the shuffle of boots and scraping of chairs dies away, Willem hears that the conversation at the head of the table has already turned to the rockets.

"A most able display," the earl says. "Let Bony come. Let him bring his blasted dinosaurs. We will kill them and then throw his Grande Armée back into the sea."

The duke does not seem to share his enthusiasm. "Frazer, you were in the thick of things at Waterloo," he says. "What is your opinion of the rocket display?"

Frazer, a fine-featured man with piercing eyes, takes a long sip of wine before answering and the table goes quiet, waiting for his response.

"My lord, I must defer," he says. "There was much smoke and confusion on the battlefield at Waterloo. It was all over in an instant and although I saw the creatures, I am not able to say how the rockets might fare against them."

"A shame," the duke says.

"Might I instead pass the question to the saur-slayer, the hero of Waterloo," Frazer says. "Young Lieutenant Frost, who was in the midst of the action and managed to kill not one battlesaurus, but two."

All eyes turn to Frost, who seems aware of it despite his blindness. He draws his handkerchief and coughs lightly into it before speaking.

"Your Grace, might I be permitted to speak plainly?" he asks.

"That is what we want," the duke says.

"And my plain speaking should offer no offense to Sir William, whom I regard as a genius and a personal hero of mine," Frost says.

"None will be taken," Congreve says, smiling politely.

"I think it was a wonderful demonstration today," Frost says. "Although I could not see it, I heard it well enough and Private Sullivan, who now acts as my eyes, described it vividly for me. I understand that all five of the available wooden dinosaurs were destroyed."

"Indeed they were, Lieutenant," Congreve says proudly.

"And the demonstration lasted what, an hour?" Frost asks.

"Less," the earl says.

"Merely fifty-two minutes by my timepiece," Frazer agrees.

"On the battlefield at Mont-Saint-Jean, it was all over in a fraction of that," Frost says. "From when the battlesaurs charged out of the Sonian Forest to when my ammunition caisson exploded could not have been ten minutes. The creatures are quick and agile. It was great skill on behalf of my crew that we were able to turn our gun rapidly enough to kill one of the creatures as it attacked. The second was pure luck. We had no time to reload."

"Then what happened to it?" the earl asks.

"It was killed by our exploding caisson, as nearly was I, and Sullivan, my spongeman, the only survivors from my team."

"Then you regard today as a failure, lieutenant?" Congreve asks, his eyes hard.

"I do not, Sir William," Frost says. "I regard it as neither a success nor a failure, but rather as a distraction. I fear that firing an hour's worth of rockets at stationary targets is so far removed from the reality of the battlefield as to provide no useful evidence as to their effectiveness."

"I am outraged, sir—" Congreve begins, but stops as the duke holds up a hand.

"You have no right to outrage," the duke says. "The lieutenant asked for, and was given, permission to speak plainly. He has a firm opinion, and quite frankly, as he has firsthand experience of these animals, I feel his opinion should carry some weight. I also was disturbed at the time it took to destroy the targets today."

"We are refining the weapons every day," Congreve says with a glance at Frost more dangerous than any of his rockets. "They grow more accurate and more reliable. In fact, we are already working on a design that would spin the rocket, like the rifling on a carbine, providing stability in flight."

"Then perhaps you should have waited until that design was ready for demonstration," the duke says. "In the meantime I am afraid our best hopes are still the mesmerization techniques and the pepper."

"Sparkle sticks against dinosaurs," Congreve scoffs.

"We still have time to perfect the rockets," Wood says. "Napoléon will not dare to invade anytime soon. The Royal Navy still controls the Channel. He will lose his ships and his precious battlesaurs, should he risk them in a Channel crossing."

There are murmurs of agreement, but Frost coughs loudly and in the quiet that follows says, "Napoléon is a cunning tactician."

"A fact we are all aware of," the duke says. "What is your point?"

"The man knows he cannot sneak past or defeat the Royal Navy, yet he still plans an invasion. Why?" Frost asks.

"He is delusional," the earl says.

"Let Frost speak," the duke says. "I want to hear his thoughts."

"Napoléon is a master of deception," Frost says. "The army at Calais could be a decoy."

"He still must cross the Channel somewhere," the earl says. "And the Royal Navy will not allow that."

"There is talk of a French fleet at Brest," Frost says.

"The fleet at Brest is nothing but a fancy," the earl says. "This is your decoy. Our spies tell us that the so-called fleet consists of nothing but freighters and barges, painted to look like warships. Their cannon are made of wood. Napoléon seeks to deceive us, to divert our ships to the south so he can cross at the narrow of the Channel. We will not be so easily fooled."

"A cargo ship can still carry a dinosaur," Frost says.

"Napoléon is at Calais," the duke says. "I know the man. He rides at the head of his army. If the attack was to come from Brest he would be there and so would his battlesaurs. Yet none have been spotted. They have, however, been parading around in open sight at Calais."

"All the more reason to think that it is merely a decoy," Frost says.

"Even if you were right," the earl says, "it would not matter. A powerful squadron blockades the port at Brest. That fleet, real or no, will never leave the harbor."

"It seems unlikely that Napoléon could make good his threat to invade the British Isles," the duke says. "But Frost is right. He makes his preparations. And so we must make our own preparations in case he should make land."

"My rocketeers will be ready," Congreve says pompously.

The duke does not quite manage to conceal a look of mild frustration.

"The trojansaurs destroyed today were modeled on those we encountered at Waterloo," Frost says.

"Of course. We had reliable witnesses to their size and ferocity," Wood says. "You and your man Sullivan foremost among them."

"It might interest Your Grace to know that those battlesaurs are not the largest in Napoléon's army," Frost says.

There is a shocked silence around the table.

"You jest, sir," Frazer says.

"I saw these creatures with my own eyes," the duke says, "albeit from a greater distance than you. You say there are larger ones?"

"I do, sir," Frost says. "A young man named Willem Verheyen, of Gaillemarde, near Waterloo, killed a much bigger animal prior to the battle when it escaped from Napoléon's men and attacked his village."

"Ah, yes," Congreve chuckles. "Willem, the Wizard of Gaillemarde."

"The saurs at Waterloo were taller than an elephant," the duke says doubtfully.

"And yet dwarfed by others in Napoléon's army," Frost says.

"Rumor and exaggeration." Congreve snorts. "I would question this Willem Verheyen myself, if he even exists."

Frost smiles. "He most certainly exists."

"Then bring the boy here," Congreve says. "Let us hear from his own mouth about this mythical beast of Gaillemarde."

"Indeed he is already here," the duke says with a smile at Willem.

Willem leans forward so they can see him.

There is complete silence at the table.

"Major Lux?" Congreve asks, clearly shocked.

"A necessary subterfuge," the duke says, "and one that I trust you will all treat with the greatest confidence."

"Willem, do you honestly expect us to believe that the saur at your village was larger than the ones we encountered at Waterloo?" Frazer asks.

"Much larger, I think," Willem says. "Although I did not see those at Waterloo."

"Piffle," Congreve says, and laughs. "What he saw grows larger in his mind's eye than ever it was in reality."

"The beast was tall enough to take a man from our watchtower in the church steeple while standing at its base," Willem says.

"The churches must be small in Gaillemarde," Congreve scoffs, but as Willem looks at the faces that surround him, he sees only horror.

"Yet you killed this giant?" Frazer asks.

"With help from a friend," Willem says.

"Using no more than mesmerization and a bolt from a cross-bow," Frost says. "Had Willem's village been armed with Sir Congreve's rockets I fear Willem would not be sharing luncheon with us today."

"We must find some answer to Napoléon's great beasts, and soon," the duke says. "Before the tyrant finds a way to outwit the Channel Fleet."

"What about the Ottomans?" Wood asks. "Can we rely on them to join a new coalition against the French?"

All eyes turn to the earl.

"We cannot expect any help from that quarter," the earl says.

"What was the response from Sultan Mahmud?" Frazer asks.

"The Ottoman Empire will not be joining any coalition," the earl says. "The sultan does not want to antagonize Napoléon."

"He joined us and the Prussians in the Second Coalition, why not this one?" Wood asks.

"He does not want to fight on the losing side," Frazer says. "He dreams that having conquered Europe, Napoléon will leave the Near East alone."

"He should learn from history," the duke says. "The Mongol hordes once controlled Europe from west to east. I am sure Napoléon has even higher ambitions."

"I also suspect that Mahmud conducts his own expeditions to the Amerigo Islands," the earl says. "In search of his own dinosaurs."

"That will do him no good," Frost says. "He does not know how to train or control the saurs."

"Nor how to fight them," Frazer says. "Which we do, thanks to Willem."

"Indeed," the duke says with a warm smile at the young man. "Thank you for your efforts to date, Willem."

"It has been my pleasure to serve," Willem says formally. "I . . ." He falters, unsure how to continue.

"Speak your mind," the duke says. "I presume you are about to remind me of my side of the bargain."

"That was my intention, Your Grace," Willem says uncomfortably.

"You are eager to rescue your mother and a young woman, whom the French have imprisoned at an abbey in the Sonian Forest near your village. Our agreement was two hundred light cavalry, if I remember correctly," the duke says.

Willem thinks the duke remembers perfectly well, but says only, "Yes, Your Grace."

"A well-conceived plan," the duke says. "Such a force would be very mobile. How long do you think it would take you to reach the abbey after you make landfall?"

"A matter of hours, your grace," Willem says. "Certainly before any sizable force could be mobilized against us."

"And if they unleash their dinosaurs?" Wood asks.

"It is a good question," the duke says. "Horses are no use against battlesaurs. We saw this at Waterloo. No matter how well trained, they will throw their riders and flee in terror."

"Napoléon's dinosaurs have already joined units in Calais or Brussels," Frost says. "There will be few, if any, left at the abbey."

"And the battle will be a short one, Your Grace," Willem says. "There are secret underground ways into the abbey. While the cavalry attack from the front, a small force, including myself, will emerge inside the abbey, rescue the prisoners, and retreat the same way. Even if there are still battlesaurs at the abbey, our entire force can withdraw, the battle over, before a single beast sees the light of day."

The duke sighs and steeples his fingers. He looks at Willem across the top of them. "Young man, you know that Bonaparte sits just across the Channel, teetering on the edge of invasion."

"Of course, Your Grace," Willem says, desperately afraid of what the duke will say next.

"Two hundred horses, in the right place at the right time, might be the difference between throwing Napoléon back into the sea or England becoming the newest state of the French Empire," the duke says.

"Your Grace, you made a promise—" Frost begins, but the duke stops him with a raised hand.

"An Englishman takes his honor and his promises very seriously," the duke says. "And you shall have your two hundred cavalry. But not just yet. Let us deal with this threat of invasion, and as soon as our isles are secure once again, I will give you whatever you need to rescue your mother and this girl."

"That may be too late," Willem protests.

"It has been three months," the duke says. "What is another three weeks, or another three months, if it comes to it?"

Willem stares at the table for a moment and there is silence. He slowly raises his eyes to meet the duke's.

"For many weeks I did not know where my mother was held," Willem says. "Or Cosette, the girl who has my heart. When I found out, I wanted to rush there immediately, but I stayed to complete the training of your men, as per my promise. Now I need you to uphold yours, so that I can free them before they are moved or killed. Who knows what indignities they are being subjected to by Napoléon's men? You cannot default on your agreement."

"Such insolence," the earl says.

"He is young and passionate, not insolent," the duke says. "And he is right, I made a promise. Willem, you will have your men, but not until I can release them. I am sorry, but that decision is final."

He drains the last of his glass and refuses with a flat hand when offered more.

"It has been a truly interesting day," he says, and stands. "In many ways. But now, unfortunately, I must return to Whitehall. Congreve, I look forward to a future demonstration of your spinning rockets."

"Of course, my lord," Congreve says.

The duke turns to the earl. "Lord Wenzel-Halls, will you ride with me back to London?"

"Thank you, Your Grace," the earl says. "But I have another matter to attend to. I will find my own way back."

"As you wish," the duke says with a short bow.

IN PRIVATE

"Lieutenant Frost, I am given to understand that you requested a private audience with me," the earl says. He pushes his plate away from him with an expression of contentment.

"That is true, my lord," Frost says, including Willem with a nod. "For both of us."

"The two saur-slayers," the earl says. "Is it anything that cannot be said in front of your fellow officers?"

"It is a private matter concerning your son," Frost says.

The earl's expression grows cold. "Come with me," he says. "We will adjourn to the smoking lounge."

The earl's aide, a hard-faced man, is the first to stand.

"A private matter," Frost emphasizes.

"There is nothing that Arbuckle's ears cannot hear," the earl says.

As they walk, Willem says quietly to Frost, "I did not get the chance to ask the duke about Héloïse."

"For the best, I think," Frost says. "However, the earl also is a man of great influence. We will ask him."

The smoking lounge is a plush room that reeks of cigars. Arbuckle closes the door and stands in front of it. He is more than an aide, Willem thinks. He is a protector, a guardian. Arbuckle is a dangerous-looking man. One of his sleeves rides up a little as he folds his arms across his chest, and he smooths it back down, but not before Willem has seen the hilt of a weapon, probably a small dagger, strapped to his wrist.

The earl settles himself into an armchair and produces a box of snuff. He takes a pinch and discards it before speaking, dabbing at his nose with a handkerchief.

"My son," he says. "I was blessed with only one. Therefore you speak of Dylan."

"We do, my lord," Frost says.

The earl lifts his head, as if raising himself above such conversation.

"Lost at Waterloo," he says. "His body was not found, therefore I still hold hope for his return. Unless of course he was eaten by one of Napoléon's monsters."

"Your son survived the battle," Frost says.

"He was not eaten," Willem adds.

The earl sits forward suddenly in his armchair. "You know this for a fact?"

"The British Army set up a field hospital in my village," Willem says. "It was there I met Lieutenant Frost. Your son was there, also."

"So you saw him, Lieutenant?" the earl asks.

"My eyes were lost before I arrived at the hospital," Frost says. "I did not see him, but I spoke to him."

"Then what became of him?" the earl asks. "Is he held prisoner by the French? There has been no ransom demand."

"He aided us in our flight from the village," Willem says. "But he had been wounded and was near death, even then."

There is a silence.

"You are sure this was the earl's son?" Arbuckle asks. His voice rasps like rough stones.

"I am an officer and a gentleman," Frost says. "You have no need to doubt my word."

"You were blinded," Arbuckle says. "And dependent on the word of the man you met. And I mean no disrespect, but you are still a child."

"As was Dylan when he was wounded in battle," Willem says. "And as he was also when he helped us escape, at risk of his own life."

"If it was my son," the earl says.

"He gave me this," Willem says, taking a leather cord from around his neck. On it is a ring, with a crown below a lion. "He asked me to return it to you."

The earl, who has opened his mouth to speak, now closes it. He reaches out and takes the ring, turning it over and over in his hands. His shoulders crumple and the whole man seems to deflate. Eventually he slips the ring onto one of his fingers.

"You really believe him to be dead?" he asks softly. "I have long suspected, but still, in my vanity, have held on to the idea that he hides somewhere in Europe, banded together with other survivors, or perhaps taken in by the Prussians."

"The amputation was a high one," Willem says.

He does not have to explain what that means. Dylan had little chance of survival.

"There was little life left in his body when we bade him farewell," Frost says. "I feel he used his last breaths to buy us time to escape."

"Which would explain why there has been no contact, no ransom demand," the earl says. He bows his head, all trace of arrogance now gone. A father grieving over a lost son. No longer a nobleman, just a man, suddenly old.

"Your son was a hero, my lord," Frost says. "Without him, we would not be here, and our army would not have the benefit of Willem's knowledge. Thanks to your son, we have a chance against the battlesaurs."

The earl nods. "He was a strong boy, in character and in body. He would one day have made a fine earl."

"I am sorry for your loss," Frost says.

Willem echoes the words but they seem trite and meaningless in the face of the earl's misery.

"I thank you for the return of this ring," the earl says. "And for your information about my son. If there is ever anything I can do, a favor to return, you need only ask."

"The rescue mission to the abbey in the Sonian Forest," Frost says.

"That will have to wait," the earl says. "The duke has made his decision."

Willem draws a deep breath. "I do not want to go to the Sonian," he says. "I am frightened of the place. I am frightened of what I might find there, of what I might have to face. I am secretly pleased that the duke has said no."

"Then we are agreed," the earl says.

"All I have lived for these past few months is the warmth of Cosette's smile and the sound of my mother's voice," Willem says. "Each morning I wake thinking of the day when I will see them safe from Napoléon's grasp. This is my only desire. I will go to the Sonian, despite what I may find there."

"You offered a favor," Frost says.

"I will speak to the duke," the earl says. "That is all I can do."

"Speak firmly," Frost says.

"There is something else," Willem says. "There is a girl in the lunatic asylum of St. Mary of Bethlem."

"Bedlam," the earl says with a sigh.

"She is a friend," Willem says. "She saved my life."

"And mine," Frost says.

"This untamed creature saved your lives?" The earl looks incredulous.

"In our escape from Gaillemarde she showed us secret ways through the forest," Frost says.

"And in Antwerp she outwitted a traitor," Willem says. "We would not be here except for her."

"Remarkable," the earl says. "But if she is in Bedlam, it is for a reason."

Willem shakes his head. "She is unwell, but not in the way they think. She is not mad. She is just . . . different. Someone beyond their experience or their ability to 'cure.'"

"Different. Beyond their experience." The earl repeats the words, not as a question, just sounding them out with his own voice.

"I fear they simply do not understand her," Willem says. "They cannot comprehend who she is or what she has suffered."

"Which is?"

"She is a child of the forest," Willem says. "For her, safety lies in the natural world, in trees and streams and caves. She cannot cope with a city such as London. She may not have been mad when she came here, but confinement in an asylum, in this city, will surely drive her mad if she is not released soon."

"It is true," Frost says.

"And I need her, if this mission is to succeed," Willem says. "We must again travel through the Sonian Forest, using the secret ways that only she knows."

"But I am not sure what I can do," the earl says. "The principal physician at Bedlam is Thomas Monro, a most single-minded man."

"We met him," Frost says.

"He has consulted on the sad case of our dear, demented king, and is held in high regard within his profession," the earl says.

"Surely he would listen to you," Frost says.

The earl glances over at Arbuckle and they smile at some private joke.

"Most unlikely," the earl says. "I have many times decried the conditions, and the treatment of inmates, at Bedlam. I have been a vocal supporter of St. Luke's Hospital, which makes me an enemy to Bedlam. I am afraid that Doctor Monro would probably do the opposite of what I say."

"Then tell him not to release her," Willem says.

The earl just smiles. "If I ask him and he refuses, then I feel it would take no less than an order from the king to obtain her release, and I fear such an order would be a long time coming, considering the king's current state of health."

"So there is nothing you can do?" Frost asks.

"Officially, no," the earl says. "Unofficially, if you were to somehow spirit the girl out of that godforsaken place, then I could find a place for her where Monro cannot reach her."

"Wenzel Park?" Arbuckle asks.

"My thoughts exactly," the earl says. "My country estate. It is not far from the city yet has wide stretches of forest. Perhaps she would feel at home there."

"It sounds wonderful, but if we cannot get Héloïse out—" Willem begins, but is cut off by Frost.

"A kind and generous offer," Frost says.

"I am sure you will find a way," the earl says. "The building is a collapsing morass of broken walls and uneven floors. Many doors do not even close, let alone lock. And most of the staff have already shifted to the new hospital, leaving only a skeleton staff at the old."

"Patients often escape and are found wandering in the streets," Arbuckle adds.

"That may be the case for ordinary inmates," Willem says. "But I fear that Monro will be taking special care with Héloïse."

"You mean he suspects our plans?" Frost asks.

"Yes," Willem says.

"Then he may move her sooner than we think," Frost says.

"You must not wait until she is transferred to the new asylum," the earl says. "The doors there are strong and it has high walls. Once she is inside, you will never get her out."

Willem thinks for a moment, then says, "Can you find out when she will be moved?"

"My man can make some discreet inquiries," the earl says, and Arbuckle nods.

"Not too discreet," Willem says, and for the first time that day, he smiles.

A PROUD AND LUCKY SHIP

"The little fish is about to see the hook," Lavigne says. "We shall watch her squirm."

Thibault does not reply, but he smiles, briefly.

A British frigate had appeared off their starboard bow just after dawn, materializing out of a rainsquall. She had probably located the French invasion fleet earlier but held position, undetected, until first light when she could gauge their course and the number of ships.

The dark and the weather could not conceal the frigate for long, and just after five bells she was spotted by lookouts on the *Magnanime*, a seventy-four-gun ship of the line on the French fleet's eastern flank.

The frigate had maintained her position, unaware of the trap that was already being laid for her.

There are eighteen ships in the French fleet. Nestled in the center are the three first-rate ships of the line, the *Duc d'Angoulême*, the *Montebello*, and the *Impérial*, each with a hundred and ten guns, each towing a heavy barge with its valuable cargo. They are protected by an outer screen of second- and third-rate ships.

At the rear are two sheep in wolves' clothing. The *Canard* and the *Mouette*: the duck and the seagull. These ships are freighters, lightly loaded and fast, able to fly across the tops of the waves, unencumbered by the apparatus of war. They are not weighed down by cannon, barrels of gunpowder, and racks of heavy cannonballs, nor by a large crew and all the necessary provisions that entails.

Each of the freighters is disguised as a heavy man-o'-war. The gun ports are merely painted on and the cannon on their top deck are made of wood, but on the heaving sea in the first light of morning it would take the eye of an eagle to tell the difference.

At the first sighting of the British ship, Thibault had ordered the fleet to bear away to the northwest.

The *Canard* and the *Mouette* dropped back, as if unable to keep pace, although in reality they are the fleet's fastest ships.

The British frigate followed the fleet, unconcerned about two lumbering men-o'-war fading away to the rear.

As soon as the rain and mist had closed in around them, the *Canard* and the *Mouette* had changed course, raising full sail, bearing to the northeast, invisible to the frigate, cutting off her escape route.

Now Thibault stands on the poop deck, steadying himself on the railing of the stern. He raises his spyglass and examines the British ship through the slowly easing rain. She seems a sleek little vessel, a twenty-six gunner, square-rigged on all masts: a nippy little dog with a sharp bite and an even sharper turn of speed. A trio of officers stand on the foredeck of the frigate, watching him watching them.

Showers and squalls, some heavy, have been with them since the French fleet left the port of Brest on the French coast. The rain at times is cold and hard, driving in on whiplike gusts of wind. But now it is fading and as it does, so the visibility increases and the *Canard* and the *Mouette* appear like ghosts, shimmering apparitions that gradually solidify into ships, to the stern of the frigate.

Thibault can almost imagine the shock on the British captain's face. The change in the frigate's behavior is immediate and desperate.

Sails swirl, ropes hiss through pulleys, riggers dance across spars. The frigate screws around to the northeast, spray flying from her bow as she slams into one wave, then another.

A cheer goes up from the sailors on the French ships as they see the frigate frantically trying to flee.

"She will try to outrun them," Lavigne says.

"She must not get away, no matter what the cost," Thibault says. "Or everything we have done is for naught."

"She is well boxed in," Lavigne says, standing next to the helmsman on the quarterdeck below them. "As long as she does not see through our subterfuge."

If the British captain realizes that he is being ensnared by two unarmed cargo ships he will aim straight for them, raking them with his own guns before fleeing to the east.

The *Duc d'Angoulême* and the rest of the French fleet now come about, chasing after the frigate, cutting off her avenues of escape.

The sea is a beast, a wild, rough-skinned animal. It snaps and growls at the ships, tossing them about on its white-flecked back.

The *Duc d'Angoulême* drops into a sudden deep trough and smashes her way out of it with a jolt that sends shudders through the ship and a hard spray across the foredeck.

The deck lurches beneath Thibault's feet. The ship tosses and shudders and slams into mounting waves that feel as solid as rocky cliffs. Heading northwest, they were sailing before the wind, and now they are bashing their way into it. Thibault thinks of his girls, Mathilde, Valérie, and Odette, chained in cages on the barges. He worries about them. He thinks briefly of his wife, unwell, in the cabin below. He worries about her also.

He steps lightly down onto the quarterdeck, holding the railing for support.

"Captain Lavigne," Thibault says, "if you commanded the British boat, what would you do?"

"I would strike my colors," Lavigne says. "There is no chance of escape."

"The British captain is not so timid, it would seem," Thibault says. "If you had his spirit, what would you do?"

Lavigne ignores the insult and stares across the heaving water for a moment, analyzing the course of the frigate.

"He has been fooled by the *Canard* and the *Mouette*," he says. "And so they have blocked his path to the east. If he turns south toward the *Magnanime*, she will rake the frigate from bow to stern before he can bring a single gun to bear. If he tries to skirt the *Magnanime*, he will come within range of our thirty-two-pounders, while we will still be well out of range of his little popguns. There is nothing he can do."

"He is doing something," Thibault says.

Another cheer has sounded from the crew as the frigate gives up the race with the *Canard* and the *Mouette* and comes about, heading back northwest.

"By now surely he is wondering how two men-o'-war can outpace his speedy frigate," Lavigne says.

"He may wonder, but he has not yet grasped the truth," Thibault says. "He turns from the imagined danger toward the real danger."

The frigate remains on port tack, a bearing that will put her almost on a collision course with the mighty *Duc d'Angoulême*.

"Surely he cannot think to challenge a ship of the line," Lavigne says. "We have a hundred and ten guns to his twenty-eight, and with a longer range and heavier ball. This little ship is David to our Goliath."

"David defeated Goliath," Thibault says.

"Not this time," Lavigne says.

"Nevertheless this British captain does not yet think to surrender," Thibault says.

The bow of the frigate, now running before the wind, surges through the waves, foam spraying into the air, at times almost concealing her hull. She veers slightly, heading directly across the bow of the bigger warship. On her single gun deck, the ports are open and the muzzles of the cannon protrude.

Already musketballs are cutting holes in the sails or embedding themselves in the deck of the *Duc d'Angoulême*. Puffs of smoke come from high on the masts of the frigate, obscuring the bright red uniforms of the British marines on the fighting tops. The crackle of musketfire is constant as French marksmen return the fire, as is the *thwack* of musketballs hitting sails, the *thwock* of them hitting wood, and occasionally a softer sound as the lead balls puncture human flesh.

"You should seek cover. As she crosses our bow she will rake us with her cannon," Captain Lavigne says.

"Can we not turn with her? Broadside her?" Thibault asks.

"Ordinarily, that is what I would do," Lavigne says. "But the barge is like an anchor at our stern. It stops us from turning quickly. The British captain has seen that, and intends to use it to his advantage."

"Here she comes," Thibault says.

"Everybody down!" Lavigne shouts, and the call is taken up around the ship. Sailors fling themselves to the deck, crouching or lying, seeking any shelter they can. To Thibault's eye there is no shelter sturdy enough to stop a cannonball at this close range. He remains standing, as does Lavigne.

The guns of the frigate belch flame and smoke as she crosses the bow, rippling from the front to the back. Wood shatters, canvas tears, blood sprays, and sailors scream as iron cannonballs tear through the length of the French ship's hull.

One high shot strikes the mainmast but it's only a glancing blow, veering off to the quarterdeck and decapitating the helmsman, not a meter from where Thibault is standing. The body of the man flies backward, an arc of blood spurting from his severed neck. A midshipman runs to take the wheel.

"I did suggest that you lie down," Lavigne reminds Thibault.

"Yes, you did," Thibault says.

Each cannon on the frigate has time for just one shot, then the British ship is past the bow of the French ship and turning to the southwest. Thibault looks to his left to see the *Montebello* close off the larboard side of the ship. The British ship will pass directly between them.

"This is suicide," he exclaims. "She will come under our guns as well as those of the *Montebello*!"

"Her captain is not suicidal but brave," Captain Lavigne says. "And damnably clever. We dare not fire lest we hit the *Montebello*. And the *Montebello* dare not fire lest she hit us. The frigate, however, can broadside us both as she passes."

"He is after my dinosaurs!" Thibault thunders.

"He cannot know what is in those barges," Lavigne says.

"He can guess," Thibault says. "And a single well-placed cannonball could do irreparable damage. Fire your cannon, captain. A full broadside, as soon as the frigate is under your guns."

"I cannot, sir," Lavigne says. "Not without hitting the *Montebello* behind her."

"Signal the *Montebello* to bear away," Thibault says. "And do your best to miss her."

"We can scarcely miss her at this range," Lavigne shouts. "It will be murder. I will not—"

He stops, staring at the muzzle of Thibault's pistol, now pointed directly between his eyes.

"Do I need to relieve you of command?" Thibault asks.

Musketballs swish as they cut holes in the air around them. A nearby sailor drops, clutching a hand to his chest.

"Captain?" Thibault demands.

Lavigne draws himself up and turns abruptly to the sailing master. "Signal the *Montebello* to bear away. Gun crews prepare to fire. Upper decks, chain shot, aim for her masts. Lower decks, aim for her cannon."

More musketballs cut splinters from the deck at their feet. A French marine tumbles from the fighting top and is caught up in the rigging, where he hangs, bleeding.

"That boat must not get near my dinosaurs," Thibault screams.

The *Montebello* begins to turn, agonizingly slowly, the gap between the ships widening as the frigate sails a path almost exactly down the middle between the two large French warships.

The British ship fires as she comes, swathed in the smoke of her own cannon, through which reach arms of flame. Fists that are iron balls punch holes through the hull of the *Duc d'Angoulême* on one side and the *Montebello* on the other. The frigate is smaller than the French ships, and some of her cannon are angled upward. Cannonballs erupt through the deck. One, just a few meters in front of Thibault, hits a seaman in the small of his back, ramming him up into the air and over the side of the ship.

But now the frigate is under the French guns.

Thunder comes from below Thibault's feet as the larboard cannon fire in a fearsome broadside.

Chain shot, two cannonballs connected by a chain, slashes through the rigging of the frigate, tearing ropes and sails, smashing through spars. The mainmast topples like a tree, collapsing back onto the mizzenmast. The rigging is a twisted spider's web of tangled rope. The ship's wheel is a pile of kindling and the helmsman just a puddle of red. Her gun deck is a shattered mess of splintered wood. Cries and screams sound from within.

With just a single broadside at point-blank range the frigate has been turned from a fighting ship into an unsteerable, unsailable wreck.

"Ha! She did not expect that," Thibault cries.

"Neither did the *Montebello*," Lavigne says.

The *Montebello*'s rigging is also badly damaged, from both British and French cannonfire. Her gunwales are shattered and men lie crying and dying on her deck.

"I warned you, sir!" Lavigne says.

"If you think I am pleased by this, you are mistaken," Thibault says. "It was the price to protect my dinosaurs."

The frigate slows to a drift, her sails in tatters, her masts in pieces, and her gun deck devastated. As the *Duc d'Angoulême*'s gun crews reload, the frigate strikes her colors.

The frigate is the HMS *Antelope*. Her name adorns the stern of the remains of the ship that now lies alongside the *Duc d'Angoulême*, secured by boarding ropes.

Her surviving crew are locked in her own brig, or hog-tied in long rows belowdecks, all except the captain. Under the muskets of the French marines, he climbs up onto the quarterdeck and stands before Captain Lavigne. He bows.

Lavigne returns the bow but points to Thibault. "You salute the wrong person," he says coldly. "It is General Thibault who has taken your ship. I merely steered the boat."

The captain turns to face Thibault, taking in the ruined arm, the garish scars, and the blackened skin. If he is shocked he does not show it. He bows again. Thibault is quick to return the bow.

"I am General Marc Thibault of the Imperial French Army," Thibault says. "Whom do I have the honor of addressing?"

"Lord Thomas Cochrane, captain of His Majesty's Royal Navy," the captain says.

There is a sharp intake of breath from Lavigne. "The Sea Wolf," he says.

"I should have guessed as much," Thibault says. "A British hero."

"You have heard of me?" Cochrane asks.

"Indeed," Thibault says. "I have greatly enjoyed reading of your exploits aboard the HMS *Speedy* and the HMS *Imperieuse*, even though many of them were at the expense of my own countrymen."

"I only do my duty to my God and to my country," Cochrane says.

"As do we all," Thibault says. "But some shine like the stars, while the rest of us can only bask in their radiance. It is an honor to make your acquaintance, sir."

"Thank you," Cochrane says. "And I congratulate you on your victory. I confess I had gambled that you would not fire on your own countrymen in the pursuit of my ship."

"A poor bet," Thibault says.

"I am pleased you think so highly of her," Cochrane says. "She will make you a fine prize. I have commanded the *Antelope* for less than a year, but she has been good to me. She has always been a proud and lucky ship."

"With a daring and wily captain," Thibault says. "And a plan that nearly worked."

"Not nearly enough," Cochrane says. "I confess I did not see your trap before you sprang it, and I am still confounded as to how you maneuvered those two warships onto my stern."

"The *Canard* and the *Mouette* are not men-o'-war," Thibault says. "Merely cargo ships, lightly laden. They carry no cannon."

"But . . ." The realization sinks in. Cochrane closes his eyes and lowers his head for a moment. "I could have escaped at any time, if only I had known."

"If only you had looked a little more closely," Thibault agrees.

"At risk of seeming discourteous, we must to business," Cochrane says. "I have many wounded. Our surgeon was killed. I trust you will allow your surgeons to treat my men."

"Alas, our surgeons are busy with our own wounded," Thibault says.

"Of course. Then I ask that they treat my men as soon as they are able," Cochrane says. "In the meantime, if you will release my ship's carpenters, I will have them start to repair the damage. I am afraid we will have to lose the mainmast, but she will sail well enough with the two remaining."

"She is badly damaged," Lavigne observes.

"Yet repairable," Cochrane says. "And as I said, a good prize."

"We have no need of prizes," Thibault says. "Not even a proud and lucky ship such as the *Antelope*. Had you struck your colors earlier and left your ship undamaged we might have joined her to our fleet. But we have no time to stop for repairs."

"You will scuttle her?" The captain looks sadly over the railing at the ship. "I will miss her." He sighs. "And you have my word as a gentleman that my crew will give you no problems when you bring them aboard."

"Indeed they will not," Thibault agrees.

Cochrane frowns as he watches two French seamen on the frigate emerge from belowdecks carrying gunpowder barrels. Other sailors are lashing shut the hatches to the lower decks. It is so unthinkable that it takes a few seconds for him to comprehend what he is seeing.

Finally the awful truth dawns and his face turns ashen. "You pirate!" he cries. "You blackguard! This is—"

He says no more as he has no air with which to do so. He looks down at the hole in his chest as the sound of Thibault's pistol echoes off the masts. Cochrane's eyes fix on Thibault's and remain there even as his body collapses to the deck.

Captain Lavigne turns away with a look of disgust.

"Captain Lavigne," Thibault says.

The captain turns back with gritted teeth. "Over the side with him?" he asks. "Or shall we let the captain burn with his ship?"

"Neither," Thibault says. "Send for the butcher. Let us see if the girls like the taste of British nobleman."

The rain has stopped and the sun strikes the sails of the French fleet, full and rigid with good wind, as the ships leave the wreck of the frigate behind. A fuse on board reaches its end and the gunpowder poured liberally over the decks ignites. Within seconds the wooden hull of the once proud and lucky ship is ablaze, the roar of the flames almost, but not quite, drowning out the screams from belowdecks.

SMALL JOYS

The sun is warm on her skin as Cosette takes the path to the spring, the source of the stream that runs past the abbey. The only other washing facilities are the troughs used by the soldiers, and neither Cosette nor Marie Verheyen will use those if they can help it.

It is a short walk through the forest to the jut of stone that forms a small rock pool. The water wells up on one side and escapes over a low lip at the other.

It would be so easy to run away, Cosette thinks whenever she is outside the old stone walls of the abbey. But if they caught her they would beat her and never let her outside the walls again. And if they didn't catch her, they would execute Madame Verheyen.

She is almost at the pool when she stops and turns, convinced that someone is on the path behind her. But no one is there. She examines the trees on either side of the path, but there is no sound, no movement. After a moment she continues on, not quite able to shake the feeling that someone is watching her.

At the pool she wets her cleaning cloth and washes her face and hands, glancing around one more time before undressing to take her bath.

She removes her dress and launders it in the pool, then lays it on a rock in the sun to dry. She does the same with her smalls, then steps up to her knees in the water, as deep as she dares. The spring water, from far underground, is icy.

This is a small joy. The fresh cold water, the heat of the sun on her skin. Such simple things, amid the terror and horror that surround her.

She washes the muck and mud from her skin and hair, and has almost finished her bath when she hears a cough behind her. Instinctively she plunges into the deepest part of the pool, crouching, immersed up to her neck. The cold burns like fire on her skin.

It is Belette. He has picked up her dress from the rock and is studying it with his one eye.

"My apologies, mademoiselle," he says. "I did not expect to find anyone here."

"But I am here, monsieur," she says. "And as you can see, I am not respectably dressed. I would ask you to leave."

Belette shakes his head. "That would be unwise," he says.

"Unwise?" It is freezing in the water. After just a few seconds Cosette is already shivering badly. Her teeth chatter so strongly she fears they will chip or break.

"Mademoiselle, you should have someone here to protect you," Belette says. "There could be wild animals or saurs roaming through the forest."

"This close to the abbey? I do not think so," Cosette says. "It is patrolled by your men."

"Who is to know what lurks in the forest?" Belette says. "It is not safe for you here alone. And our soldiers have not seen a woman for many months. What might they do if they found you alone and unclothed?"

"It is kind of you then, to have such concern for me," Cosette says. "Please turn around so I can come out. I have finished my bathing and am getting cold."

That is less than the truth. Her body is now shaking violently, as people do when they have been too cold, too long.

"Of course, mademoiselle," Belette says. He places the dress on the rock and turns to face the forest.

"You will not turn to look," she says.

"I give you my promise," he says.

Cosette remains in the water despite a growing numbness throughout her body.

"Mademoiselle?" Belette asks, without looking. "You will freeze if you stay much longer. Why do you remain in the water?"

"Because, monsieur, I fear that as soon as I stand up, you will break your promise."

"Mademoiselle!" Belette seems offended. "Have I ever given you reason to suspect I would go back on my word?"

"You have been watching me since I arrived at the spring," Cosette says. "I sensed you in the bushes."

"I swear I have not," Belette says. "I left the abbey only a moment ago. Perhaps it was someone else you sensed in the forest. Or some wild animal. But fortunately I am here now to protect you."

His hand drops to the hilt of his sword and he loosens it in the scabbard, still facing the forest.

Cosette is silent. She eases herself up out of the water as quietly as possible. She takes two quick strides toward the dress but he snatches it up before she can reach it, then turns to face her.

"You scoundrel," Cosette says, covering herself as best as she can with her hands. She is shivering violently and, although she wants to dive back into the concealing water, she knows she cannot; she is dangerously cold now. Besides, what is the use? He has already seen her unclothed. Her honor is already lost. Instead she crushes an arm across her breasts and a hand over her privates and spits at him, "You are a man of no morals. Give me my dress."

"There are many things that a young lady must learn in life," Belette says. "For example, that it is easier for a liar to pretend to be a truth-teller, than a truth-teller to be a liar. You should be grateful for this lesson. And of course I will let you have your dress back. If you earn it."

"I will do nothing," Cosette says, although Marie Verheyen's words now echo in her head: *This ordeal will end. Do whatever you have to do to survive.*

"But you will, if you want your dress back," Belette says. "Perhaps a kiss. Just a simple kiss. Would that be so bad? I have always been kind to you. Given you things. Protected you from the other soldiers."

"I will not," Cosette says.

This ordeal will end.

"That is all I ask," Belette says. "A kiss. After that you can have your dress."

"I cannot believe a man who confesses to being a liar," Cosette says. "I will scream, and other soldiers will come. You will be arrested."

"The walls of the abbey are thick stone," Belette says. "No one will hear."

"Give me my dress," Cosette says. "General Thibault will hear of this."

"General Thibault is probably in London by now," Belette says. "Dining at the royal palace. He cannot help you."

"Captain Horloge then," Cosette says.

"He is not here either," Belette says with a snort that shows exactly what he thinks of Horloge.

"He will hear of it on my return to the abbey," she says.

"So we have no agreement," Belette says. "A shame." He looks at the garment. "A poor dress for such a lovely girl. Just a rag really. And it will make a nice cloth for polishing my boots."

He finds the seam at the hem of the dress and bunches the dress in both hands. He pulls and the seam gives way a few centimeters with a tearing sound.

"One last chance," he says. "Or will I keep this rag and leave you to find your way back to the abbey clothed only in your own hands. A fine sight for the garrison, I would think."

Do whatever you have to do.

"I will not," Cosette says. Her eye falls on a large stone at the edge of the pool. She spins around and grabs it, turning back to see that Belette has moved even more quickly than she. His sword is drawn and pointed at her throat. She drops the stone and quickly regains what little modesty she can.

"Enough games," Belette says. "You will now do exactly what I say. Firstly I want you to place both hands on top of your head."

"I will not," she says.

"If you do not move your hands, then I will remove them from your arms," he says, laying the edge of the sword across her wrist.

"You are an evil man," she says.

Survive.

He smiles. She spits at him. The smile drops and he raises the sword.

There is a *swish* followed by a dull *thud*. Belette looks down to see a metal bolt protruding diagonally from his chest.

Cosette screams and clamps both hands over her mouth to stifle the sound.

"That's not right," Belette says. He sounds dazed. His hand releases the sword, which clatters to the ground. "Mademoiselle, I would have done you no harm," he says, but those are his last words. His eyes roll back in his head and he falls forward. Cosette has to jump out of the way. He lands at the edge of the pool, facedown in the water, his head slowly moving with the current.

Cosette screams again and snatches her torn dress out of his lifeless hand, holding it in front of her as she scans the forest.

A voice calls from the trees, "Please cover yourself, Cosette, so that I might come out."

She knows this voice, although in her terror and horror she cannot place the owner of it.

"Stand where I can see you," she calls back, still trying to arrange the dress in front of herself.

There is movement in the undergrowth.

François Lejeune emerges from the forest, fitting a bolt to a crossbow as he walks. He does not look in her direction, but only at what he is doing.

"François!" Cosette cries.

"Please cover yourself, Cosette," François says.

Cosette takes her still-damp smalls from the rock and puts them on before donning the dress, also damp. It is hard to clothe herself with hands that shake like leaves, not only from the cold. The tear in her dress is unseemly but not immodest.

She says, "You killed him!"

"I killed a sinner," François says. "An evil man who now descends to the place where he belongs."

He moves to the body while still averting his eyes from Cosette. He pulls on the bolt. It is stuck and it takes an effort. As it comes free, a gush of blood runs from beneath the body, down into the pool, mixing with the water and fading from red to pink as it washes away down the stream. He cleans the bolt in the stream, then returns it to a clip at the front of the crossbow.

"I would say I am happy he is dead," Cosette says. "But that would make me a sinner also, to rejoice in the death of another."

"The only sins were his," François says. "What he did, and what he planned to do."

116

"Thank you, François, for saving me," Cosette says. "I thought you were dead. I thought everybody from the village had been killed."

"Most, not all," François says. "Murdered by that devil Thibault. But I escaped. And so did many of the young children. I hid them in the church until the French soldiers left, then sent them to the church at La Hulpe."

"You saved the children," Cosette says slowly.

"As many as I could," François says. "I wish I could have saved them all."

"It is a miracle," Cosette says. "It is a miracle that you are alive, and what you have done!" She hesitates. "What about Willem? His mother believes that he escaped also, and the French have questioned us about him, which gives us hope. Do you know anything of him?"

François smiles. "On that subject I can give you good news. There are tunnels beneath the forest, caves. Like a maze. The French do not know their way through. Not even I, who has spent my life in these woods, knows these tunnels, but Willem and Héloïse were able to use them to escape."

"Where is he?" Cosette asks.

"I do not know that," François says. "He vanished as only a magician can, right under the nose of the emperor."

The shadows of the forest change as a cloud crosses the sun and a ravensaur calls high overhead. A breeze brings a deeper chill to her cold, damp skin, and she begins to shake again.

"You are certain that he is alive?" she asks.

"The French search everywhere for him," François says. "Does that answer your question?"

Manners and reason desert her and she steps toward him, throwing her arms around his neck, pressing her face to his chest, relief escaping in gasping bursts. Immediately reason returns, and she pushes away.

He does not let go, and his arms wrap around her. They are large and strong from years of swinging the ax, and they are warm like hearthstones.

"You are as though made from ice," he says. "Let me share my warmth with you for a moment. For the sake of your health."

Cosette stops her resistance and melts into his body, happy that there is no one to see the impropriety except Belette, and his unmoving eyes see only the rocky floor of the pool.

No words are spoken, but they stay like that as the heat of his lifeblood seeps into her and gradually the shivering stops.

François endures the embrace for a moment longer, then gently pushes her away.

"Come with me," he says. "I will take you away from here."

"They will track us and find us," Cosette says, wiping away tears.

"Pah! I know this forest better than a thousand French soldiers," François says. "I roam as I please."

She shakes her head. "Willem's mother, Madame Verheyen, is imprisoned with me. I must return. If I escape, they will kill her." She turns abruptly to look at the dead man by the spring. "But when Belette does not return . . ."

"I will dispose of the sinner's body," François says. "They will think he has fallen victim to a bear or a saur."

"Still, I must go back," Cosette says. "I will not endanger her life for mine."

"Then I must rescue you both," François says.

"This is not possible," she says. "They will not allow both of us out of the abbey at the same time. And even if they did, they still hold Monsieur Verheyen. She will never leave without her husband."

"I will find a way to rescue all three of you," François says. "How often do you come here?"

"Every few days. As often as I can," Cosette says.

"Look for me next time you come," François says. "I will be here."

"You are truly a miracle, sent by God," Cosette says.

"I do God's bidding, it is true," François says. "Now go, before anyone else comes."

Cosette touches his arm briefly, a more proper display of thanks and affection, before hurrying down the path back to the abbey.

Her heart and mind are conflicted. The relief of her rescue from Belette is tempered by her horror at the manner of his death.

But there are reasons for happiness also. François has survived, and thanks to him, so have many children from the village. She does not know who, but she sees faces. Pierre, the tailor's son; Sylvie, the orphan girl; bubbly little Veronique.

These are small joys amid great sorrow, like diamonds sparkling on a black cloth.

There is one thing that bothers her. How had François just happened to arrive at exactly the right moment? She remembers the feeling of being watched as she walked to the spring. Was it François, not Belette? Surely that cannot be true. François is pious and proper. He averted his eyes when she was unclothed. It is unthinkable that he would have spied on her bathing. His fortuitous arrival must have been just a coincidence.

Later, when it is too late, something else will bother her, but it does not occur to her now. When she mentioned Willem's father, François showed no surprise.

ESCAPE FROM BEDLAM

Thomas Monro is the third of his line to hold the position of principal physician at Bethlem Royal Hospital. His father held the post before him, and his father's father before that. In three generations they have made great strides in the medicine of lunacy. In this era of modern medicine the treatments are far more scientific and far less cruel than in his grandfather's time, when they would open a man or woman's skull to allow the supposed demons within to escape.

And if helping others should make Thomas Monro a very wealthy man, then so be it. There was money in madness, his grandfather had always said.

This third of the great Doctors Monro is a careful man, a cautious man. A man of thought before action. He walks with slow, deliberate movements, even when he is in a hurry—and this night, he is in a hurry.

He emerges from the side door of the hospital warmly and fashionably dressed in a fine horsehair coat. A carriage waits on the road that encircles Finsbury Circus. Despite the urgency of the situation he strolls to it at a measured pace.

The carriage looks like any other that plies the streets of London, without markings or insignia. But that is on the outside. On the inside, concealed from sight, is a sturdy metal cage. The carriage is used by the asylum to transport the most dangerous kind of inmates. Animal sounds come from within.

A night fog has come up in the unseasonably cold air. It moves through the trees of the park like a living, breathing thing, inhaling and exhaling with the vagaries of the breeze, gasping through the leaves and branches. A heavier ground fog whispers over the grasses of the greens.

Monro makes his way around to the front, and looks up at the driver.

It is Adams, the orderly, a large man with haunted eyes. He wears a bandage just below his hairline where he was cut while fighting with the young soldiers.

Adams had been an inmate himself a few years earlier, but was released, completely cured, according to Monro. Adams is eternally grateful for his release and his subsequent employment, and is therefore loyal, if troubled by occasional recurrences of the visions that had him admitted in the first place. But there are few others Monro trusts so completely, especially with such an important assignment.

"You have what I told you to bring?" Monro asks.

Adams nods and touches an oilskin on the seat beside him.

Monro climbs up alongside the driver, wrapping his coat tightly against the cold bite of the damp air. He opens the narrow shutter that allows him to see inside the cage, and shuts it again quickly to avoid a stream of spittle from within. The cage rattles and there is a howl so loud that he fears it will be heard by passersby. Fortunately there are none. The hour is too late and the park is avoided at night by Londoners. Inmates have been known to wander.

"It is the wild girl," Monro confirms.

"As you asked," Adams says.

Monro nods. Adams would have made no mistake. But still he had to check. This is his nature. Careful, methodical.

The wind whips around the carriage, making swirling patterns out of the fog, which is increasing by the minute. Adams unwraps the oilskin on the seat, revealing a pair of flintlock dueling pistols, accurate and deadly.

Monro takes one, tucking it into a large pocket of his fine coat.

"Might I ask the reason for the pistols, doctor?" Adams asks. "And the late hour?"

"Skulduggery," Monro says.

Adams nods as if this was the answer he was expecting. He flicks the reins to start the horses. The carriage bumps and rattles across the old, uneven cobblestones.

They have turned out onto the road that runs along the old London saur-wall before Adams speaks again. "What manner of skulduggery? I should know what to expect."

The wall exudes coldness, as if it sucks the warmth out of the air around it. It sucks the light as well and here in its shadow at this hour of night even the twin oil lamps that swing from the front of the carriage make little impression on the darkness.

"Nothing that we cannot handle," Monro says, patting the pistol in his coat pocket. "You remember the Dutch artillery major and the blind lieutenant who interfered with our treatment of this girl?"

"Of course," Adams says, touching his head bandage.

"Yesterday we had another inquiry. A man named Arbuckle. He wanted to know when we would be transferring this girl to the new hospital."

Adams steers the carriage expertly around a corner into Wood Street.

"This Arbuckle is known to me," Monro says. "A lackey for the Earl of Leicester."

"That old fool," Adams says. "Thinks he knows all about medicine and he ain't even a doctor."

"Exactly," Monro says.

"What would the earl want with the wild girl?" Adams asks.

"That was what I wondered," Monro says. "So I made some inquiries of my own. It turns out that the earl's son was badly injured at Waterloo. He was treated in a hospital in the village of Gaillemarde. The village of the wild girl. Lieutenant Frost was treated in the same hospital. I do not yet see all the connections, but that can be no coincidence."

"Very suspicious," Adams says.

"They think they are dealing with simpletons, but I see right through their contrivances," Monro says. "I fear they plan to engineer an escape, which would not be difficult from this creaky old madhouse. But the new asylum is far more secure and they must know that. Undoubtedly they wish to extricate the girl before she is shifted. But they are in for a surprise. We move her tonight. By the time they spring their plan, the girl will be safely inside the high walls of our new building."

"You are the master of cunning," Adams says.

"You flatter me," Monro says with a slight nod of his head. "But I am certainly more than a match for a simple artillery captain, a blind boy, and that befuddled old earl. If they—"

He is stopped by the jerk of the carriage as Adams wrenches at the brake. The horses rear up. A soldier has run right in front of the carriage, narrowly avoiding being knocked over.

"Look out, man!" Monro shouts, but the soldier runs on, turning back only to scream, "French ships sighted in the Thames!"

The carriage comes to a complete stop.

"Can that be true?" Adams asks.

"Napoléon's forces could not cross the Channel," Monro says. "It is well guarded by the Royal Navy."

Adams stares at him, uncertain. "Unless the French slipped a few ships past the Channel Fleet."

"It is nothing but hysteria," Monro says. "Balloons, tunnels, now French ships in the Thames! The talk of invasion grows more lurid and preposterous by the day. But regardless, let us hasten to our destination."

The cobblestones grind beneath the wheels of the carriage and the clack of the horses' hooves echoes off the buildings around them. Despite the darkness and the growing fog, they have no problem finding their way. Many of the houses have oil lamps hanging above their front doors, as is prescribed by law. The old saur-wall rises like a black ocean wave to their left, and more oil lamps hang from the battlements.

"What if it is Bony, sir?" Adams asks. He sounds nervous. "What with those stories of dinosaurs an' all."

"Then our troops and artillery would already be mobilizing to deal with them," Monro says. "Do you see any sign of that?"

Adams shakes his head. Other than the one panicky soldier, they have seen no other signs of the British Army. He seems reassured by this thought and flicks the horses toward Blackfriars Bridge.

The crossing is deserted and, looking left and right over the river Thames, Monro can neither see the lights of warships nor hear the sounds of battle.

They are over the bridge and traveling through the modern houses of Newington when they encounter the second soldier. An artilleryman. His face is a mask of blood and his uniform is disheveled. He is not wearing his hat.

"Battlesaurs!" he shouts, before running off into the darkness beyond the bright pools from the gas lamps that line the bridge.

Adams looks at Monro in alarm.

"Make all haste, Adams," Monro says, now badly unsettled.

"Whatever is happening, we will be safer behind the walls of the asylum."

Could the French really have landed a force at the mouth of the Thames? Could they even now be making their way to Whitehall? Every corner, every scrap of mist, now seems to be hiding something. In the distance he thinks he hears screams.

He withdraws the pistol from his pocket and holds it ready.

The streets are mostly clear until they approach the obelisk in the circle at St. George's Fields. Here there are odd irregular lumps on the side of the road, just visible in the lamplight from the carriage's twin oil lamps. Only when one of them stirs and moans does he realize that they are bodies.

Adams is obviously rattled by this and urges the horses on. The carriage leans precariously as he sweeps around the circle into Lambeth Road, barely two streets from the new asylum, only to find the road is blocked. A delivery cart and an artillery caisson, perhaps fleeing in panic, have collided. The lane here is narrow, part of the old village, and the two overturned vehicles have made it impassable. The men who were driving the cart and the caisson have fled.

Adams eases the carriage to a halt. Monro looks around nervously. Ahead of them, little more than a block away, he can see the high dome of the hospital. They are so close now.

"We will have to back up and take another route," he says, but even before the words are out of his mouth there is a scream from behind them, and another, and suddenly the street is full of people running: ladies in frocks; men in coats; beggars in rags; the people of Newington, terrified, panicked, screaming, some with blood on their faces.

"What the hell, sir?" Adams asks, now panicky.

"Dinosaurs!" comes a shout from the crowd.

"Great beasts from hell," a woman shouts.

The terrified crowd surges past them, rocking the carriage on its springs before clambering over the overturned wagons in front of them.

"Holy hell, sir," Adams says. He too has his pistol up now, and stares behind them into the fog and the darkness.

A roar comes from somewhere behind them, bouncing thinly off the brick walls on either side of the lane. Monro twists to look. More people run around the corner, screaming. He hears another sound now, a regular, recurring thump on the stones of the roadway, almost like footsteps.

When he turns back, Adams has gone, disappeared into the panic-stricken crowd.

"Adams!" Monro shouts. He climbs down and stands uncertainly beside the carriage. For a moment he thinks of the girl inside and he fumbles for his keys. But she will be safer inside the cage, he thinks. The fog swirls and seems thicker now, as if mixed with smoke. The roar sounds again and the footsteps are much louder. Then, the unthinkable: two eyes appear around the corner, glowing through the smoky darkness. Whatever they belong to is three times the size of a man. A twist of wind creates a sudden fissure in the fog revealing a long demonic snout and scaly skin surrounding a mouth of jagged teeth.

"My lord, protect me," Monro screams. He stumbles, the keys dropping from nerveless fingers as he grabs again for his pistol. He looks at it, then back at the head of the giant creature emerging from the corner behind him. He tosses the pistol away and runs after the crowd, squeezing between the wagon and the stone wall.

He runs madly. His coat is heavy and flaps around his legs, slowing him, so he rids himself of it and sprints. He loses his hat but does not notice, his hair wild to the wind.

He raps on doors as he runs, shouting for shelter, for refuge, but the doors remain closed. The windows are dark. Behind him, the footsteps get louder.

He sees Adams in the distance and follows him down the long driveway toward the asylum. The high stone walls and barred windows will be their best protection against what follows.

Adams reaches the asylum first, banging on the stone gates in the wall that surrounds the building. There is no answer. Monro arrives to find Adams pulling on the rope to the bell above the gates. The bell clangs loudly and after a moment the door opens. The orderly who opens it is clearly shocked to find his employer in a disheveled state at this time of night, but has no time to say anything as Monro and Adams burst past him, slamming the door shut behind them.

Monro's chest is heaving, his face dripping with sweat. He is hatless and coatless. His heart is pounding and his leggings are saturated.

But that is not sweat.

From outside they again hear the roar of one of the creatures, and it sounds closer.

But after that, nothing.

The city has gone strangely quiet.

IRELAND

The headlands at the entrance to the harbor are windy promontories, jutting into the Irish Sea. It is raining, an icy drizzle, and the red-coated British soldiers on sentry duty huddle beneath trees. They are cold and wet but dare not light fires for fear it will ruin their night vision.

The moon is curtained by heavy cloud and of no use, so the sentries do not see the unlit French ships holding position just off the coast. Nor do they hear the sounds of the ships' rigging through the hiss of the rain on the ocean.

The French longboat that enters the mouth of the harbor has been tarred to a deep black. Thibault's soldiers on board are covered by black cowls and the wooden cage at the stern is also black, as is what is inside. Two identical boats follow, also invisible on the dark ocean. The boats are not rowed, but sculled by a single oar at the stern. This is slow for a heavy longboat, but it is silent, and the current assists, sweeping them into the mouth of the harbor with the incoming tide.

The British sentries neither hear nor see the disaster that approaches.

The longboats slip past the headlands and keep to the center of the estuary, away from any curious eyes.

The lights of Fort Charles approach, and the longboats slow. Silence is more important than speed. They veer toward the shore, well away from the fortifications, and make landfall on a tiny sandy beach squeezed between seaweed-covered stretches of rock. The fort looms ahead of them, and on the other side of the estuary the smaller Fort James is a distant glow.

The eight soldiers on each boat now lift the wooden cages, nervously carrying them to the pathway that runs along the shore, trying not to listen to the scratching, slithering sounds and the strange rattles that come from within.

Three cages are set on the path and three saurmasters uncage three creatures, surely born in the smoky depths of hell.

Few men have ever seen such creatures and few of those who have, have lived. Even fewer know their name: demonsaur.

Each has a ridged and muscular hide the color of old burnt wood. Long, skeletal arms lead to bony fingers, jointed like a human hand, but ending in hooked claws. Protruding from their skulls and down their backs are thin spines that rattle as they move. Their hind legs have hocks like those of a horse.

With whips and low voice commands, the saurmasters guide the demonsaurs toward the fort, keeping to the darkest shadows.

The soldiers from the longboats, twenty-four in all, now creep over the rock and scrub of the foreshore to the roadway that runs past the fort.

The entrance to Fort Charles is via a drawbridge across a moat, leading to a set of heavy gates set in a stone archway. The drawbridge is down, in absence of any immediate known threat, but the gates are closed.

The soldiers take position on the roadway. They split into two groups, one to the left and one to the right of the bridge. They load and ram their muskets. They wait.

By the wall of the fort, the saurmasters release their hideous creatures and melt away into the safety of darkness.

The three saurs approach the great wall, sniffing at the air, their spines rattling with anticipation. They each place a foot on the wall, then another, the hooked claws of their so-human-looking fingers finding purchase where no man could.

They begin to climb, scaling the wall swiftly. They reach the top and disappear from sight. Almost immediately there are shouts of alarm and the clanging of bells from inside the fort.

Then the screaming starts.

There are gunshots, and the sounds of people panicking and running. A cannon fires within the fort, and the crackle of muskets is only overpowered by the piercing screams of the people.

On the roadway the French soldiers take aim as, with heavy creaking sounds, the main gates of the fort open and the inhabitants start to stream out.

The French muskets fire in volleys of eight, giving each group a chance to reload. On the drawbridge the bodies lie where they fall, or topple over the low wooden railing into the moat, gasping their final breaths in the cold, dark water.

Volley after volley sounds but even the roar of the muskets is lost amid the shrieks and cries from inside the fort.

The moon has finally found a gap in the cloud curtain as Thibault stands on the walls of Fort Charles and surveys the much smaller fort on the other side of the harbor entrance. They lost only two ships in the Raz de Sein passage, a stroke of good fortune considering the foul weather that had rushed in from the west. One of those ships was the *Sceptre*, a big loss, almost a fifth of his men drowned in one incident. The other ship was a supply vessel and that concerned him less. He can pick up food easily enough in Ireland, and if all goes to plan he will have plenty of gunpowder to replace that which he lost.

Montenot comes to stand with him to watch a British long-boat pull away from the rocks below them, the two enemy soldiers on board rowing frantically toward Fort James on the other side of the harbor. One of them is a captain, until recently the second in command of Fort Charles. Thibault would sooner have sent the commander, but most of his head is now missing.

"You think they will surrender that easily?" Montenot asks.

"I do not ask them to surrender," Thibault says. "The British captain will inform them that I have no interest in their fort, but if a single cannon fires on my ships, then every man, woman, and child within their walls will be fed to my dinosaurs."

As he speaks, the cruel sharp lines and the full sails of the *Redoubte* come into view at the mouth of the estuary, silvered by the moon. Behind it, as yet concealed by the headlands, a line of ships stretches out.

"Should we ready our cannon, just in case?" Montenot asks. Fort James is a bare half mile away and the big twenty-four-pounders of Fort Charles would smash it like a fist.

"They will not fire," Thibault says. "And I have no wish to see the fort damaged. It will be mine soon enough and I would rather not damage my own property."

On the other side of the estuary, the longboat reaches the shore and the two British soldiers run for the safety of the stone walls.

"And if they do fire?" Montenot asks.

"Then, as I have said, I will feed them to my girls," Thibault says. "But they will not fire."

A few moments later the *Redoubte* reaches Fort Charles, already furling its sails as it heads for the point. The captain salutes up at Thibault, who returns the gesture and watches with interest, but without concern, as the ship approaches the guns of Fort James.

There is only silence from the dark walls on the far side of the estuary.

The remaining ships of the French fleet now approach the shore. Ship after ship passes the fort, each lowering its sails as it turns past the point and moves on to the docks beyond.

Thibault turns to Montenot and permits himself a smile.

"Our first prize in the island kingdom. I want the ships unloaded as quickly as possible. We must make haste for Cork."

WENZEL PARK

Willem stands anxiously at the gates to the estate, under the lamps that adorn the huge pillars on either side. The first light of morning is just coloring the sky to the east. The earl's man, Ethan Arbuckle, stands with him. He holds a lantern in one hand and a leather tool case in the other.

Willem hears the carriage before he sees it. It is traveling quickly, from the sound, but not overly so, which would not be safe in the dark, in the mist, on a road of loose stone.

Eventually the curtains of fog peel back and the carriage emerges through them, as if arriving onstage.

Big Joe is driving, his face covered with blood. Frost sits next to him. The carriage slows as it pulls between the gates, then Arbuckle and Willem close the great metal gates behind it.

Willem runs to the side of the carriage and is horrified to find it still locked.

"She is still caged?" he asks.

"I am sorry, Willem," Frost says, stepping down from the carriage, feeling his way. "I did not know how she would react to her freedom. I did not want to lose her again in the streets of London."

"So you made her endure the cage even longer," Willem says.

"We did not have the key, Major, nor time to waste," Big Joe says. He climbs down also.

Willem calms himself. His nerves are tense, more than he had realized. "Of course. I was not thinking."

Arbuckle has already set to work with the metal saw on the padlock that fastens the cage. The rasp of the fine teeth on the steel of the lock makes a high-pitched grinding sound.

Willem climbs up onto the driver's seat and opens the narrow slot into the cage. "Héloïse," he says softly. "It is Willem."

A low animal growl comes from within.

"You are safe now," Willem says. "You will never go back to that terrible place."

Silence.

Willem waits for a moment, then steps down. He reaches for Frost's hand and shakes it, then shakes Big Joe's hand also. "Thank you, gentlemen," he says. "I am greatly in your debt."

"It was worth it just to see the look on that old doctor's face," Big Joe says with a laugh.

Willem laughs with him, then says, "You still have blood on your face. Best clean it before Héloïse sees you. She has been distressed enough."

Big Joe wipes some of the blood off his face with a finger, and licks it.

"And nice-tasting blood it is," he says with a grin. "But it is blood of the tomato, not of a man."

"Did you pay the city folk?" Willem asks.

"They all got their coppers," Frost says.

"And Harry?"

"Will be safely back in the barracks by now. Jack will have seen to that," Frost says.

"It was a well-crafted illusion," Big Joe says, wiping his face with a rag.

"A sight to be seen, Willem," Frost says, reminding Willem, whether he intends to or not, of the young lieutenant's affliction.

"What the eye does not see, the mind imagines," Willem says. "And the mind sees with a clarity that the eye can never hope to achieve. The illusion was only ever in Monro's mind."

"I wonder what will happen to him when he tells people of dinosaurs roaming the streets of London," Big Joe says.

"They will think him delusional," Willem says.

"Perhaps he will end up admitted to his own institution," Frost says.

"We can but hope," Willem says with a laugh.

There is a crack from the direction of the carriage and the padlock falls free. Arbuckle starts to slide the bolt on the cage, but Willem stops him with a hand on his arm.

"I would ask you all to step well back," he says. "Your presence may make her nervous."

The grins and excitement of the night's events fade rapidly as Willem opens the door to the cage. It is dark inside and there is no sound or movement. He gestures for the lantern and, when it is handed to him, eases it forward between the bars.

Héloïse is huddled in a corner, her arms entrapped by the same thick straitjacket that she wore on the spinning chair. Her head is turned away from him and her short hair is matted with blood. The side of her face is badly bruised. Willem suspects that their actions that day had earned her a beating.

"Héloïse, it is Willem," he says. "You are safe now." The words sound thick, heavy, and inadequate. His eyes run freely as he stretches out a hand toward her. Still she does not move.

He climbs into the cage with her and touches her shoulder. She shudders and pulls farther away.

"Héloïse, it is Willem," he says again. She must know him, he thinks. Whatever she has been through, she must recognize his voice, and know who he is, and what he once did for her. Can she have retreated so far inside herself that there is no way back?

135

He reaches for the buckles on the straitjacket and she does not pull away. One arm comes free, then another. The garment falls to the floor. Still she will not face him.

"Héloïse," he tries again.

Abruptly she launches herself at him, hissing like a wildcat. He stumbles backward. One foot catches on the edge of the doorway and now he is falling, landing on his back on the mercifully soft grass that adjoins the cobblestone driveway. He is winded and struggles for breath. She has fallen with him, straddling him, fingers clenched into claws, jagged fingernails ready to strike.

"Stay back!" Willem warns hoarsely as Arbuckle moves to pull her off him.

He lies still, making no effort to defend himself, breathing heavily from the fall and from what he is feeling.

"Héloïse, I'm sorry," he says.

Without warning the claws disappear. Her arms snake, lightning fast, around his neck. She pulls her face down to his and the next thing he feels are lips, soft and moist on his own. He has time to notice their warmth, and the heat of her body, cradling his, then she is gone in a blur of movement, disappearing into the forest.

The others approach and Willem wipes away tears before they become visible in the lamplight.

"Should we search for her?" Arbuckle asks. "The woods are unsafe at night. There are dragonrats in the undergrowth and pregnant adders near the pond. The stags too. They grow more aggressive as the rutting season approaches."

"The place she is safest is in the woods at night," Willem says.

"What would you have me do?" Arbuckle asks, looking at the trees where Héloïse disappeared.

"Please do nothing," Willem says. "Leave the girl entirely alone, and instruct all your servants and groundsmen to do the same.

Leave some food in a place where she will find it, but do not be concerned if she does not eat it. She can forage for herself."

"Willem, we should get back to the barracks," Frost says. "Before too many questions are asked."

Willem nods. "Mr. Arbuckle, please thank the earl for us. I will return tomorrow and wait for Héloïse to emerge from the forest, although I fear that may take some time."

"Your horses are ready," Arbuckle says. "And this terrible carriage will disappear into one of our stables." He smiles. "It will make a fine hay cart with a few alterations."

"Will she be all right?" Frost asks, staring at the dark trees. He does not mean in the forest.

"I pray that she will," Willem says.

He can still taste her on his lips and he thinks that the taste of a woman is not altogether unpleasant. That and the strange sensations in his belly make him wonder if there is more to their connection than that which is seen. Perhaps fate has bound their paths together from that day, when they were both so young and he saved her life.

He wonders if perhaps this half-crazed wild girl is the one he is destined to spend his life with.

His next thought is of Cosette.

THE ROAD TO CORK

The bodies of two British soldiers lie beside the road. One is face-down in a ditch in a jumble of contorted limbs, the other lies on his back, his eyes closed as if sleeping. They were messengers, sent by Fort James to warn the garrison at Cork Harbour. When they were intercepted by French troops, their warning died with them. Their fast horses are now in the service of the French Army.

The first of the artillery rumbles past the two bodies. A team of six horses pulling a gleaming twelve-pounder cannon, followed by three caissons of ammunition. These are followed by another cannon, and another, a seemingly endless train of men, horses, and weaponry.

The artillery is preceded by the cuirassiers, descendants of the medieval knights. The tallest, strongest men, on the tallest, strongest horses, resplendent in their shining armor, heavily armed with carbine, pistol, and saber.

Following the artillery, at a distance so as not to spook the horses, are battlesaurs—beasts such as have never been seen in Ireland before. Nearly twenty feet tall, lumbering along on two giant rear legs, with jaws full of jagged teeth that could swallow a man whole, controlled by riders using a contraption of cords and wires.

As dawn breaks, the teams of horses stop on high ground above the harbor. The invaders pull the cannon around to face the

British ships anchored below them and unlimber, making ready to fire. Linstocks are lit, gunpowder is rammed. Cannonballs are loaded.

Sailors on the ships of the British fleet below them awake to screams from Fort Camden, which overlooks the harbor, and a short time later are shocked at the sight of a French flag flying over its walls.

Scouts from the ships retreat under volleys of musketfire.

Suddenly the HMS *Bulwark*, anchored in the middle of the harbor, near the small second British fort on Spike Island, begins to unfurl its sails. A captain brave or foolish enough to make a run for the safety of the open sea.

Thibault smiles. He leans forward, resting his elbows on the heavy stone parapets of Fort Camden.

"Your gunners know what to do," he says, watching the British vessel's desperate dash for freedom.

Already the corporals in charge of the gun crews on the heights above the harbor are traversing and aligning their cannon. On a signal from the fort, the guns speak in unison.

Most of the cannonballs miss, but a few cut through the rigging and sails of the *Bulwark*. The French corporals are adjusting their aim, the spongemen are swabbing out the barrels, and the bombardiers are reloading the guns.

The cannon on the ships do not respond. They do not have the elevation to fire up at the hills.

The second cannon volley is more accurate and a deadly hail of iron balls smashes into the *Bulwark*. Twice more the cannon sound, then they fall silent at another signal from Thibault.

There is no need to waste any more shot. The crushed wreckage of what is left of the ship is already slipping beneath the surface.

"Raise the parley flag," Thibault says to an aide. "We will accept nothing less than their unconditional surrender. That includes the fort on Spike Island. And send a messenger to Napoléon. Tell him that England is ripe for the plucking."

He turns to Montenot. "Ready the saurs. As soon as the British ships strike their flags we will ride for Ballincollig. Let the battle-saurs lead the way."

"Lead the way, General?" Montenot asks. "You don't wish to hold them in reserve?"

Thibault shook his head. "When the cavalry at Ballincollig see my fine young ladies, they will melt away into the hills. The battle will be avoided. And if not, then my girls will have a fine feast of horse."

CONFINEMENT

Cosette waits as the guard's footsteps draw close by the door to their cell, then gradually recede. Since shortly after her return, the whole encampment has been in an uproar about the disappearance of Sergeant Belette. She and Marie Verheyen have been confined to their cell, a guard posted outside day and night. This is the first time they have been left unattended.

She had come under suspicion herself; however, nobody in the French camp seemed able to believe that a young, slender girl could have had anything to do with the demise of a tough old boot like Belette. She has dared say nothing that might reach the ears of the guard, although she has indicated with gestures to Marie that she has news.

When she hears the door at the end of the corridor open and shut, and the click of the lock, she moves quickly over to the square hole in the stone wall, the airhole that connects their cell to the one adjacent. Marie moves to stand next to her.

"I saw François yesterday at the rock pool," Cosette says.

Marie gasps.

"The son of the priest?" The voice of Maarten Verheyen, Willem's father, sounds hollow through the narrow airhole that leads to the other cell.

"Yes, him," Cosette says.

"So he escaped Gaillemarde?" Maarten asks.

"He did, and saved a number of the children of the village," Cosette says.

"God bless him," Marie says.

"Where has he been for all these months?" Maarten asks.

"I do not know, monsieur," Cosette says.

"Was he responsible for Belette?" Maarten asks.

"He was," Cosette says. "Belette attacked me at the pool. François saved me."

"Saved you how?" Marie asks.

"We shall see Belette no more," Cosette says. "But there are more important things to discuss before the guard returns."

"Did François bring news?"

"No news, but perhaps hope," Cosette says. She makes her own voice small, to conceal the excitement she feels.

"What did he say?" Marie asks.

"He confirms that Willem is alive," Cosette says.

Marie gasps and places a hand on the wall for support. "God is merciful," she whispers.

"I told you this was so," Maarten says from the other side of the wall. "Why would they keep asking you about him if he was dead?"

Marie seems not to hear him. "François is certain?"

Cosette looks around sharply at a noise from outside, but it is nothing but the breeze. "He says Willem, Héloïse, and some British soldiers escaped through passages, caves, underneath the forest, that the emperor's men do not know about," Cosette says. "Then Willem used some kind of illusion to vanish from under the emperor's nose."

Maarten snorts with laughter.

"The boy is his father's son," Marie says, with clear affection for them both.

"The boy is now a man," Maarten says. "And one to be proud of."

"It is true," Marie says.

"These passages," Maarten says. "Could we not also use them to escape? Can François help us?"

"Even he does not know the ways through the caves," Cosette says.

"We must let Willem know where we are," Maarten says.

"You must not involve our son in our plight," Marie says. "He is safe somewhere. Let him stay that way."

"Safe?" Maarten asks. "How can he be safe? The emperor's men hunt for him everywhere. They will not stop until they find him because they fear what he knows."

"He has sense," Marie says. "He was trying to reach England. He will stay there and be safe."

"He will not," Cosette says quietly.

She is conscious of Marie turning slowly to look at her.

"He will hunt for us," Cosette says. "For you, and for me. He has fire, your son. He will not stop searching."

"And England will not be a safe place for him," Maarten says. "The guards talk every day of the invasion. Soon England will be just another of Napoléon's conquests. Then where will Willem hide? We must get word to him. We must let him know where we are."

"But how?" Cosette asks.

"François," Marie says.

"He does not know where Willem is," Cosette says.

A cockroach crawls slowly along the small air passage between the two cells.

"Sofie Thielemans knows where Willem is, or at least how to reach him," Marie says. "I gave Willem her name when last I saw him in Gaillemarde."

"That was wise. But we cannot involve her in this again," Maarten says. "It is too dangerous."

"You fear for your old teacher, yet are prepared to risk the life of our son!" Marie says, and she weeps silently.

The cockroach emerges from the hole and begins to climb the wall. It crawls across Marie's hand, but she does not seem to notice. The wind stirs again in the corridor outside the cells. Cosette examines the sound for any hint of the guard returning.

"Can we trust this boy?" Maarten asks softly.

"François? Of course," Cosette says quickly. "He saw what happened at Gaillemarde. He has no reason to favor the French. And he killed Belette."

"But what if he is captured?" Maarten asks. "And reveals Sofie's identity? If she does know Willem's location, then that will put both of them in danger."

"He says he knows these woods better than a thousand Frenchmen," Cosette says.

"The risk is too great," Maarten says softly.

"My husband is right," Marie says. "Say nothing to François."

Cosette nods, but she thinks they are wrong. She thinks of the way Willem used to look at her. Of the flush in his face when she once kissed his cheek. And Willem would never stop searching for his mother. Not ever.

COUNCIL OF WAR

Of all the places that Jack least expects to find himself in his life, the War Office in Whitehall is probably at the top of the list.

This is a place for leaders and noblemen, not lads like Jack. But here he is, at an emergency meeting of the War Council.

Some faces he does know because he has met the men: the Earl of Leicester, and the Duke of Wellington. Others, such as Viscount Melville, the First Lord of the Admiralty, and Lord Liverpool, the prime minister of England, he knows because their portraits hang on the wall at the barracks.

Lord Liverpool sits barely ten yards from where Jack is standing, and just to be in the presence of these great men makes Jack nervous, afraid that he will do something wrong. That he will talk too loudly or say something stupid.

And of course the more he thinks about not doing these things, the more likely it is that one or the other of them is to happen.

He is grateful for Lieutenant Frost's presence by his side. Jack has been the lieutenant's official aide for just a few days. Not for writing or reading—Frost has an adjutant for that—but for helping Frost get around without his eyes. He *is* Frost's eyes, and the thought makes him proud.

He and Frost are in a raised gallery that surrounds the War Office on all four sides. It is packed with generals and admirals.

Jack whispers to Frost the names of those attending, at least those he knows. "But I can't see the king," he says.

"The king is unwell," Frost whispers back.

"I hope he is soon recovered," Jack says. "Long live the king."

"Our king will not live long," Frost says. "And he no longer functions as a king."

"I ain't sure what you mean, sir," Jack says after a moment.

"The king's mind has gone," Frost says.

"Gone where?" Jack asks.

"He is mad," Frost says. "But we must not talk of this. It could be considered treason."

Jack looks around quickly to see if anyone has been listening to their conversation. For the moment, the others all seem to be engaged in conversations of their own.

"I hope he's not at Bedlam," Jack says. "I didn't like that place."

Frost smiles. "The king is not at Bedlam."

The seat next to Jack has been empty, but now it is taken. Jack looks to see the earl's man, Arbuckle, who greets him with a nod.

There is a general quieting in the room as the meeting is called to order.

Jack looks around.

At one end of the room, in front of all the most important people, like Lord Liverpool and the Duke of Wellington, is a map on a large table. Small wooden markers are dotted here and there on the map.

The room is now completely silent. Lord Liverpool stands to speak. "The French have us on the bascule of a guillotine," he says. "And the blade is about to drop."

"The prime minister seeks to cause panic," Melville interrupts.

"Already the people of London see dinosaurs in the fog thanks to this kind of rhetoric. The French have landed a small force in Ireland. Let them keep it. It is full of Irishmen."

There is laughter at this remark, although Jack does not understand why.

"And just a stone's throw from the shores of England," Liverpool says.

Melville says, "They will never invade England. In the words of Lord St. Vincent: 'I do not say the French cannot come, I only say they cannot come by sea.'"

Lord Liverpool does not reply, but defers to the Duke of Wellington with a wave of his hand. Liverpool sits while Wellington stands and rests both hands on the map table. He gestures to the southern end of Ireland.

"The French have taken the harbor at Kinsale," Wellington says. "They marched overnight to Cork Harbour, took Fort Camden, sank the *Bulwark*, and forced the surrender of the rest of our Irish squadron, including the *Impregnable* and the *Hibernia*. Napoléon now controls the Irish Sea. He can invade from the west any time he chooses."

There are gasps from around the gallery.

"Worse is yet to come," Wellington says. "The French have taken the gunpowder mills at Ballincollig, along with a shipment of thirteen hundred barrels. Without powder our cannon cannot fire, and our ships are useless."

"We have inventory, surely," Melville says.

"Enough for a few weeks of sustained battle only," Wellington says. "Our stocks were depleted after Waterloo."

"What about the mills at Faversham and Waltham Abbey?" Melville asks.

"Their combined output does not equal that of Ballincollig,"

Wellington says. "Powder that we sorely need, but that the French now have."

"Our cupboards are bare, while theirs overflow," Liverpool muses. "Then we must retake Cork, and reclaim the mills at Ballincollig. What size is his army in Ireland?"

"He does not have a large force there," Wellington says. "A few thousand men at most, no more than a hundred cannon, and our spies have so far seen only three of his great battlesaurs."

"Then cannot the Irish Regiment throw him back into the sea?" Liverpool asks. "It is a short march from Clonmel to Cork."

"The Irish Regiment have no training in dealing with the battlesaurs," Wellington says. "They would be torn to pieces as we were at Waterloo. We must cross the Irish Channel and root those French weasels out of their burrow ourselves." He looks pointedly at Melville.

"The French have over thirty ships of the line patrolling the Irish Sea," Melville says, "half of them captured from us. The only way to retake Cork is to reclaim the harbor, and to do that we would have to divert our Channel Fleet."

"That is exactly what Napoléon wants us to do," Wellington says. "If we draw off the Channel Fleet to defeat him at Cork, then he will invade us from the east. He will cross at Calais and be in London within a week."

Liverpool steeples his fingers. "The man is a brilliant tactician."

"He would appear to have us at checkmate," Wellington says.

"Should we simply surrender and start teaching our people to speak French?" Liverpool asks.

"I hope he's not serious," Jack whispers, horrified. "I never was no good with French."

"He's not," Frost says. "Do you see the Earl of Leicester?"

"I do, sir," Jack says.

"Do you think you could catch his eye?" Frost asks.

The earl glances up at Frost and Jack at almost that exact moment, and Jack waves vigorously, drawing the eye of Liverpool and Wellington as well.

"With my lord's permission," the earl says.

Liverpool nods, and the earl stands, awkwardly, heavily, dabbing at his brow with a scented handkerchief.

"There may yet be a move left to us in this chess game that Napoléon has orchestrated," the earl says.

"We would all like to hear it," Liverpool says.

"The idea is not mine," the earl says. "Might I present Lieutenant Hunter Frost, formerly of the Royal Horse Artillery. The saur-slayer, hero of Waterloo."

There are murmurs around the room. Frost's name is well known.

"He is but a lieutenant, and a boy," Melville says. "He has no place to address this congress."

"A boy who killed two of Napoléon's great battlesaurs," Wellington says. "Our only success at Waterloo."

"A boy who now works for our Intelligence Service. Who correctly predicted Napoléon's plans at Brest, and his decoy at Calais," the earl says. "He asked that I should speak to his idea, but I would rather you heard it from his own lips."

"He predicted the escape from Brest?" Melville asks. "If this is true, then why did he not speak up about it?"

"He did," Wellington says. "But I was not willing to listen."

An uncomfortable silence falls over the room.

"Then perhaps we should listen to him now," Liverpool says.

Frost rises slowly to his feet. Without assistance from Jack he walks slowly to the front of the gallery, only occasionally touching the back of a chair to guide himself. He stands at the balcony.

"Napoléon's main force is at Calais," Frost says. "If we could distract or delay his army there, then the Royal Navy could sail to Ireland, defeat the French invasion force, and return to the Channel before Napoléon can cross."

"Distract? Delay?" Lord Liverpool asks.

"What would delay Napoléon at Calais?" Melville asks.

"A battle," Frost says. Jack cannot but notice the startled expressions of many in the audience. He hears the sharp intake of breath from those around him.

"Who would dare attack him?" Lord Liverpool asks.

"The Prussians," Frost says.

Jack glances at Arbuckle, who nods.

"The Prussians have surrendered," Liverpool says. "They have signed a treaty with the French."

"They may have surrendered, but Blücher still commands an army," Wellington says thoughtfully. "He hates Napoléon like a disease."

"They are too far away!" Melville protests. "It would take a week to march to Calais from Prussia, even if Blücher was encamped right on the border and prepared to mobilize."

"Blücher is not in Prussia," Wellington says. "His army is at Waterloo, only a few days from Calais."

"What is he doing there?" Liverpool asks.

"Since Waterloo there have been hundreds of British soldiers, those of other nationalities also, roaming the countryside and the forest," Wellington says. "All summer, Blücher has been tasked by the French with securing the area and clearing the battlefield."

"No matter how close he is, he would not dare attack Napoléon's forces in France," Melville says. "Not while Napoléon has his dinosaurs."

"Not even Blücher would dare go against dinosaurs," Liverpool agrees.

Jack can see that Frost has been waiting patiently to speak, and in the silence that follows the young lieutenant says, "However, the Prussians might consider the attack if Napoléon had no dinosaurs at Calais."

"What are you proposing?" Melville asks.

"We have men who have been trained in the art of mesmerizing and killing the great beasts of war," Frost says. "An army cannot attack Napoléon's encampment at Calais, but a small group of men dressed in French uniform might well be able to infiltrate the camp and slay his battlesaurs."

"That is disgraceful," Melville says. "Disguised in the enemy uniform? That is the stuff of commoners and spies, not of gentlemen soldiers."

"Napoléon is no gentleman," Frost says.

"The lieutenant is right," Wellington says. "He rewrites the rules of warfare as he goes. So perhaps should we."

"This is preposterous," Melville explodes.

"And if you kill his beasts at Calais, what will stop Napoléon from simply bringing more dinosaurs from his farm in the Sonian?" Liverpool asks. "It is barely a day or two's march from Calais."

"The lord speaks with intelligence and a clear mind," Frost says. "It would be a great disaster if Napoléon was to bring up more battlesaurs from his cave in the Sonian. We would need to find a way to prevent that."

"A cave, you say," Liverpool says.

"Indeed," Frost replies.

"And how many entrances are there to this cave?" Liverpool asks.

"Only one that is large enough for the saurs," Frost says.

"Then the answer is obvious," Liverpool says.

"Not to the rest of us," Frost says.

"A second team is needed." Liverpool's face flushes red with excitement. "While the first group attacks the dinosaurs at Calais, the second group will go to the Sonian Forest and destroy the entrance to the cave. Without risk of battlesaurs biting him in the rear end, Blücher will be free to attack the French and give us the delay we need to retake Cork."

"It is brilliant!" Frost says.

"I will write a letter to Blücher myself, imploring our former ally to use this opportunity."

It seems to Jack that Lieutenant Frost has somehow made Liverpool think exactly what he wants him to think. He is not sure how Frost did this.

"And if Blücher says no?" Melville asks.

"I know the man," Wellington says. "He would march at the head of his army if he knew that Napoléon had no saurs."

"I think you are mistaken, sir," Melville says. "Blücher will not attack Napoléon's Grande Armée to delay an invasion of England. Suppose this plan works, what then? Napoléon will attack Blücher with the full force of his arms. He will not rest until Blücher is dead, and Blücher knows it. He will not sacrifice his own army, his own life, to save England."

"Napoléon rules not by force, but by fear," Frost says. "He has not had time to put together the kind of *grande armée* that marched into Russia. His hold over Europe is a series of shaky alliances. Since the disaster at Waterloo, the Dutch, Prussians, Spaniards, and Italians are all technically his allies, but only because they fear his battlesaurs. The Russians signed a nonaggression pact; the Ottomans have shut their eyes and pretend they cannot see. But if it could be shown that Napoléon's dinosaurs are not invincible . . . that they can be killed, then might not the other countries rise up into a new coalition?"

Jack leans forward in his seat, awaiting the answer. A coalition of armies rising up against Napoléon. He likes the sound of that.

"That is a big assumption, and an even bigger risk," Melville says.

"I think Blücher might be prepared to take that risk," Wellington says.

"And if he is not?" Melville asks.

"Then what does it change?" Wellington asks. "We will still be in the same pot as before. If we follow Frost's suggestion, then at least we give ourselves a chance to leap out."

"Where will we find these teams?" Liverpool asks.

"The first team is ready to go," Frost says. "Six soldiers, all well trained in the techniques of killing battlesaurs. They were preparing for a different mission, which has since been postponed."

"And the second team?" Wellington asks.

"Would need to be people who know the Sonian Forest and the caves beneath it," Frost says. "We have but one choice."

"And that is?" Liverpool asks.

"Willem of Gaillemarde," Frost says. "And the girl from his village, Héloïse. They are the only ones who know the ways through the Sonian. I would volunteer to lead the mission."

He turns his head slightly toward Jack as he says this.

Jack keeps his expression blank, but inwardly he is overwhelmed with excitement, and a little fear also.

"I am no fool," Wellington says with a smile. "Let me guess that while attacking the cave, you would also be rescuing Willem's mother and the girl."

"A good likelihood." Frost returns the smile.

"Wait a moment," Liverpool says. "You volunteer to lead the mission?" He turns to Wellington. "Am I mistaken? Is this boy not blind?"

"I am, my lord," Frost says. "But the darkness in the caves below the Sonian is absolute. Since losing my sight I have developed a reliance on my ears and my nose."

"And you really think yourself capable of leading this mission?"

"I do, my lord," Frost says. "The caves below the Sonian are the kingdom of the blind, and in that place I will be king."

"I find myself, against all better judgment, quite liking this boy," Liverpool says. "But I cannot consent to a blind man leading such a mission. You may join the mission, if the others believe you will not be a burden, but you must find someone else to lead it."

"My lord—" Frost begins.

"Do not push your luck, young man," Wellington says. "It shall be as Lord Liverpool has said. Melville will find you a ship, something inconspicuous. I will provide you with fifty soldiers. From my own personal guard. Good men who shoot straight and true. They will go with you to your landing point in case you encounter any opposition there. After that they will return in the ship, and you will be on your own."

HÉLOÏSE

The rabbit twitches its nose as if sensing danger. The animal is an unusual color for a rabbit, a mottle of brown and gray. It does not know this but its odd coloring has served it well in the past, providing extra camouflage against predators. Its ears twitch also, picking up tiny forest sounds that only a rabbit can hear. Unsure, it takes a step backward. It is half-concealed in a patch of long river grass, the kind of grass that might also hide a snake, or a dragonrat. The rabbit is disturbed now, its head flicking around, seeking the source of what has spooked it, but unable to tell which way to run. A sudden noise by the edge of the stream causes it to turn and leap back toward the safety of the trees with panicky, jerky movements.

It does not make it.

The animal that rears up out of the grass takes it around the middle with two wiry hands and the rabbit's neck is broken before it even has time to lash out with its strong hind legs.

Héloïse retrieves her sackcloth smock from by the tree and puts the rabbit inside, with the fruit and roots she has gathered earlier. She is naked. Clothing smells, and it makes noise.

She makes her way silently back to the small cave she has found. The shelter is not even big enough to be called a cave, really. Just a jutting overhang of rock on a small tributary of the stream.

There she skins the rabbit with a sharp stone and strips off the flesh, pounding it with a heavy rock to soften it before eating it, raw, with burdock root. She rounds off her meal with a handful of blackberries.

She discards the carcass of the rabbit and places the rest of the meat back into the skin, wrapping it tightly and tying it with string-like reeds before placing it on the bed of the streamlet, secured by heavy rocks, where the water will keep it fresh. It may even attract some river fish, and she has a sharpened twig ready if it does.

Hunting, gathering, and fishing: these are second nature to her. She does not have to think, to decide. She just knows. It is just as well, because her thinking has not been clear for many days. Vague memories of the spinning and beatings have been fogged by black clouds across her mind. It is as if she is hiding in a deep cave and the world is somewhere at the mouth of it. But she does not want to go out there. There is only terror and pain. Here, in her cave, it is safe.

Yet still something draws her toward that light, and as the sun starts to go down she finds herself walking on one of the paths that humans have cut through the forest. Humans. She fears them. Animals, even the dangerous ones, can be trusted. Some can be trusted to attack you, others to run from you. But they are predictable. Humans are not. She does not understand them and she fears what she cannot understand.

She stops at the edge of the forest and stares toward the big house, where the humans live.

She is both drawn to it and terrified of it.

Eventually the force that draws her forward overcomes that which holds her back and she starts to walk, scurrying silently from shrub to shrub, seeking what shelter she can as she slowly makes her way toward the house.

THE MESSENGER

The day is clear and warm. The sunshine falls softly onto Cosette's skin as she makes her way to the rock pool.

For a week they have been confined to their cells, toileting only in the pail, unable to bathe. Food has been the most basic.

Finally, after six days of confinement, Cosette, and only Cosette, has been allowed outside.

She is especially careful. She waits in the trees outside the gate for a long time to see if anyone will follow her. Nobody does. Even after that she stays silent in the forest, listening for any noises that would indicate someone hiding in the trees.

Only when she is certain she is alone does she make her way up to the bathing pool. She washes quickly, and washes her dress also, putting it back on cold and wet, before sitting on a rock in the sunshine and waiting to see if François will arrive.

She is about to leave, not wanting the guards to think she has run off, when she hears a quiet cough and turns to see François standing on the other side of the stream.

"I am pleased to see you," he says.

"And I you," she says with a small dip of her head.

"And surprised," he says. "They have kept you locked away for many days."

"Because of Belette," she says.

He nods his understanding.

"Do you know how to contact Willem?" she asks.

"I do not," he says. "I have seen nothing of him since the escape."

"A shame," she says.

"If I knew how to contact him, I would," François says. "I am sorry."

"There must be some way to find him," Cosette says.

François shakes his head. "There was a lady and a man who I think was her son. They helped us when we got to Antwerp. Perhaps they know something."

"Can you talk to them?" Cosette asks.

"I do not know their names," François says. "Nor where they live."

"If I told you their names, could you find them?" Cosette asks.

"Perhaps." François shrugs.

"You must tell no one," she says.

"Do you not trust me?" François asks.

Cosette smiles. "I know you would not aid the French, but even if captured, and tortured, you must keep this a secret."

"If captured by the French, I would say nothing," François promises.

Cosette hesitates a little longer, then says, "I should not tell you this. I am going against the advice of Willem's parents."

"Then do not," François says. "You should not break their trust."

"I must," Cosette says. "The woman's name is Sofie Thielemans."

"Do you know her address?" François asks.

"I only know her name," Cosette says, without any idea what she has just done.

CHANGE OF PLANS

"You told them what?" Willem cries.

"Do you not want to rescue your mother and your beloved?" Frost asks.

"She is not my be . . ." Willem trails off, gritting his teeth. "You propose to send just four of us against an army. Perhaps you should have discussed this with me first!"

"The plan is different now," Frost says. "We no longer go in with great force, hoping to overwhelm the defenders. Instead we will use subtlety and quiet. We will sneak past the guards, extract Cosette and your mother, and blow up the entrance as we retreat. The French will not be able to follow us."

"And if we encounter dinosaurs?"

"Then you will deal with them."

Willem opens his mouth to retort but shuts it without speaking.

He sits in the small library, in an armchair that is far too big for him. He has been living in the earl's luxurious estate for four days, ever since what Frost calls the Night of the London Dinosaur. Frost thought it best to have him out of the way in case Monro came looking for him.

Frost has just returned from Whitehall, traveling separately from the earl, who stayed to attend another meeting.

The manor house, the largest building on the estate, seems a palace. The bedroom Willem has been given is just one of many on the second floor, yet it is larger than his entire house at Gaille-marde. There are maids to make his bed, draw his blinds, and empty his chamber pot. Every meal is a feast, prepared by a team of people in the kitchen. It is a world beyond anything he could have imagined.

But even that thought gives him pause. His own family was wealthy once. His father, Maarten, a magician, a darling of the courts of Europe, particularly Napoléon's. But that was when he was just a baby.

Had they lived in a house like this, with servants and butlers, and cooks to prepare their meals?

He thinks of his mother scrubbing in the kitchen bakery at their cottage in Gaillemarde, and he wonders what it must have been like to descend from comfort and luxury to a life of constant work and hardship. All because of the wrath of the French em-peror, once he felt Willem's father had betrayed him. The more Willem pictures his mother, up to her elbows in flour, soot from the oven blackening her forehead and lips, the more he misses her, the more he hates Napoléon Bonaparte, the more the waiting becomes unbearable. If facing the dinosaurs is the price he must pay, then he will do it.

That does not stop the fear that he will be found wanting.

But the dinosaurs he saw in the caves were chained, and no threat. If their little team is careful enough, then he will not have to face a saur.

"So be it," Willem says quietly.

The sound of carriage wheels on the cobblestones of the drive draws his ear and he stands, as does Frost. He guides Frost to the front entrance, arriving just as the earl's carriage pulls up outside.

"Idiots!" is the earl's greeting, booming out of the carriage as the door is opened by a footman.

"Your Grace?" Frost asks.

"Not you, Lieutenant, you were brilliant. And the way you induced Liverpool to think of the second team was quite masterful."

The earl, unsteady on the step with his large belly, is helped down from the carriage by the footman. Arbuckle follows. The earl makes no move to enter the house, so Willem guides Frost down the steps to him.

"The idiots I refer to are Liverpool and Congreve," the earl says. "Walk with me, and I will tell you the events of the meeting after you left."

"Walk?" Willem asks.

"Walk," the earl says. "It is good for the constitution and clears and calms the mind."

Willem wonders why he will need a clear and calm mind but does not ask.

The earl accepts a cane from one of the footmen, and using it as a support, leads them away from the house toward the garden, down a path lined with crushed seashells. Arbuckle walks ahead, scanning the bushes around them with a practiced eye. Jack seems very impressed by the earl's aide. Willem thinks that is good. He trusts Jack's judgment of character.

They pass through hedges, flower beds, and ponds, one with a fountain in the shape of a swan. They reach the forest and the earl follows a clearly defined cobblestone path between two dense hedgerows to an impenetrable wall of entangled creepers. The path splits here, left and right.

"My favorite part of my estate," the earl says, leading them to the left. "A good place for thinking."

Willem waits politely, but impatiently, for him to continue.

"We have a mad king, and now I suspect an even madder prime minister," the earl says.

Willem glances around at the others. Frost nods grimly. Jack, who is walking behind Frost, guiding him with an occasional touch on the arm, is visibly shocked. It is treason to talk this way of the prime minister, let alone the king, even if it is true.

"What is the problem, my lord?" Willem asks.

The earl calls out to Arbuckle, who has drifted farther ahead. "Slow down, man, it is not a race."

"The old hipposaurus waddles at a slow rate," Arbuckle says, but he stops and waits for the others to catch up.

"Such insolence," the earl says, but he is smiling. He gestures to Jack, who walks right behind Frost, ready to aid him should he step off the path. "See this young man following his master like a faithful dog," the earl says.

"You accuse me of faithlessnes." Arbuckle laughs.

"You? Faithful? You are a wild dog who roams as he pleases and pisses on treeses," the earl says.

Arbuckle laughs. It is clear that there is mutual respect and liking between them.

The earl turns to look at Willem. "There is to be an attack on the French forces in Ireland," he says. "Uxbridge will cross the Irish Sea and take command of the regiment at Clonmel."

"Have the Irish Regiment been taught how to fight saurs?" Willem asks.

"They have not!" the earl says. "That imbecile Congreve has convinced Liverpool to use his rockets! I told Liverpool they are not ready, and are more likely to do harm to our own men than to kill the battlesaurs, but Congreve has Liverpool blinded with his fiery rocket trails! Wellington has seen the demonstration, he knows the truth, yet he supports the idea!"

"Perhaps Wellington is not the fool you think," Frost says.

"He is a greater fool than you know!" the earl says.

"Consider this," Frost says. "If the rockets work, and the French force in Ireland is defeated, then Liverpool and Wellington will be praised for their daring leadership. If they don't work, then they will be regarded as wise and cautious commanders for retaining most of our trained saur-killers here, in readiness for the invasion."

The earl stops walking and regards him appraisingly. A gust of wind brings a spattering of raindrops and all faces turn to the sky. More raindrops follow and a hum from the forest is the sound of heavier rain on the leaves and branches of the trees.

"We will return to the house," the earl declares, and promptly leads the way.

"When do the Earl of Uxbridge and the rocketeers cross to Ireland?" Frost asks.

"In just two days," the earl says. "They plan to march on Cork within the week. Why do you ask?"

"It seems to me that Napoléon must be expecting this attack and will have planned for it," Frost says. "If the attack fails, and I think it will, then I fear this will precipitate Napoléon's main invasion of this country."

"In other words, your own mission now takes on added urgency," the earl says. "If you, with Liverpool's letter, cannot persuade Blücher to attack Napoléon at Calais, then I fear we will see the Grande Armée marching on London within a few weeks."

"Then we must leave immediately for Antwerp," Frost says.

"We cannot," Willem says. "Sofie and Lars do not expect us until Sunday night. Without their assistance we will never evade the French and Dutch lookouts along the Oosterschelde."

"Has there been any sign of the girl?" the earl asks.

"No," Willem says.

"A problem," the earl says. "And we have another problem. You still need a leader for your mission."

"I will lead it myself," Willem says.

"You may wear the uniform of a major, but that does not make you one," the earl says. "Wellington will not allow a civilian to lead a team of soldiers into battle."

"If I may, Your Grace," Arbuckle says.

"Arbuckle?" the earl asks.

"I would regard it as an honor if you were to release me for the duration of this mission," Arbuckle says. "As you know, I have traveled the old smugglers' routes in and out of the continent on many occasions. If anyone can get them to the Sonian undetected, I can."

"Are you not also a civilian?" Frost asks.

The earl shakes his head. "Arbuckle still holds his former rank. That of a captain of the infantry. However, most of his time in recent years has not been spent on the front lines, but far beyond them. Lieutenant, will you accept Captain Arbuckle as your commander?" the earl asks. "I can assure you that he is an extraordinarily capable man."

"It would be a privilege," Frost says. "It . . ." His voice trails off and he cocks his head, listening. Willem listens too, but cannot hear what Frost is hearing. All he can discern is the buzzing of the rain on the eaves of the big house.

The earl clears his throat to speak, but Frost raises a finger to his lips. He points to Willem, then toward the forest.

Confused, Willem begins to turn. Arbuckle moves in that direction also, but Frost holds up a hand to stop him. He gestures toward the house.

As the others, taking Frost's hint, disappear in that direction, Willem waits alone in the garden. The rain finds gaps in his clothing and water trickles down his neck. There is neither sound nor sight of anything notable. He has half turned to go inside when a movement by the large fountain that is a centerpiece of the garden catches his eye. He turns back to it and waits.

A figure emerges, female. At first he thinks she is naked but then realizes that she wears a simple brown smock that is rain-saturated and clinging to her body.

"*Bonsoir*, Héloïse," Willem calls.

She takes a few steps toward him, then stops, crouching by a tree next to the pathway, eyes darting around like those of a small, tense animal. This is not the Héloïse Willem knows. The girl he knew was a wildcat, unpredictable and dangerous. This is a timid fawn, trapped and trembling.

The rain thickens, yet she appears not to notice it. Willem's clothes are now fully saturated, clammy and noisy when he moves.

Still he waits, unwilling to spook her. Water droplets gather in the fur across her scalp that once was long, wild brambles of hair. They run down her face, dripping from the ends of her eyelashes.

A horse whinnies in the nearby stables and she jumps.

For the first time Willem realizes how much he and this wild girl have in common. They were both outcasts in their own village, now both cast out from that village. Both a little lost in a world that is foreign to them.

Slowly, so slowly, he raises a hand from his side, palm up and open, extending his arm toward her.

She does not move.

He extends his arm to the fullest, and leaves it there, an invitation, no more.

Her feet, he can see, are gray-brown with river mud, thick and gluggy, so that not even the heavy rain can wash it away. The mud has seeped up between her toes, and her toenails are black.

She scratches at an armpit like a monkey, then her other armpit, then her crotch.

She raises her head and sucks at the rain, never taking her eyes off him.

Still he waits.

She turns and looks back at the forest—*deciding*, he thinks.

He keeps his arm out although it is growing heavy and is starting to waver.

Then in a quick movement she is standing in front of him, her eyes piercing his, looking for answers to questions that he does not know.

He lowers his elbow to his side, keeping his forearm extended.

He feels a light touch on his hand, small, strong fingers wrapping around his. Withdrawing, then returning, interlacing with his. It is a feeling of warmth and connectedness that transcends the rain, the wind, and the mud on her skin.

At last she smiles.

He turns, and she turns with him, and together they walk toward the house.

AN UNEXPECTED VISITOR

In far-off Antwerp, the front door of a different house is opened, a centimeter, no more, and a huge shape blocks any light from inside. François stands patiently, without speaking, aware he is being scrutinized. It is almost dark outside and a sharp wind is gusting through the grassy park that is opposite number 25 Avenue Quentin Matsys.

Eventually the door is opened farther, revealing a huge man with a well-rounded stomach and a long, thick, and drooping mustache. It is the man who led them to, but not through, the Ruien, the underground sewer system, a few months earlier.

The man nods briefly in recognition but says nothing.

"I am François, from Gaillemarde," François says. "You remember me?"

The giant is silent and motionless.

"You helped us escape from Antwerp," François says.

There is a small noise from inside the room and François is surprised to see two eyes appear, as if from nowhere, in the darkness. It is a lady, very old. Dressed in an elegant dress of indeterminate color and constantly shifting shape. This must be Sofie Thielemans, François decides.

"Monsieur, we do not know you," Sofie says. "Nor do we know anything about the escape you speak of."

"I understand," François says. "I have come to the wrong

address and I apologize for disturbing you. I am searching for a friend of mine named Willem Verheyen. Do you know anyone by this name?"

"No," Sofie says. "But I wish you luck in finding him."

"You must leave," the man says, moving his head forward and checking both ends of the street.

"You are sure?" François asks. "I have an important message for him from his father."

The man does not react to the mention of Willem's father, but Sofie cannot avoid a slight widening of her eyes. Just the merest movement, a flicker of her eyelids, but enough to confirm to François that she knows Willem and the circumstances of his family.

"You have the wrong house," the man says.

"Again, my apologies," François says. "But should you, by any chance, happen to meet Willem, please let him know that his father has recovered from a long illness and is currently recuperating at the abbey in the Sonian Forest."

"I assure you, we do not know this friend of yours, and so are unlikely to meet him," Sofie says.

"Please do not come again," the giant says as he closes the door.

From the house to the tavern where Baston waits is barely a few hundred meters, but François walks a long, circuitous route that takes him past two or three of Baston's men, casually stationed in windows and doorways. If anyone was to follow him, they would see it. He cannot be too careful. Sofie Thielemans has eyes in all corners of the city.

What kind of signal they have among themselves is not visible to François, but it is there, for as he enters the tavern he is given a brief nod by a thin-faced French soldier standing just inside the door with a glass of ale that has not been touched.

François makes his way through the tavern, past a plump

woman in an indelicate dress and a moneylender engaged in a furious argument with a man who smells strongly of fish. A rear door leads to the alley behind and it is there that Baston waits, while more of his men guard each end of the alley.

"It was him," François says. "And an old lady who must be Sofie. They denied knowing Willem, as you predicted."

"And the message you gave them was exactly as I worded it?" Baston asks.

François nods. "If they can contact Willem, they will do so. I am sure of it."

Baston looks over François's shoulder and François turns to see the thin-faced soldier from the tavern, who still holds his untouched glass of ale.

"Use only your best men," Baston says to the soldier. "Watch them day and night."

Book Two

THE MISSION

October 6–October 14, 1815

THE SIEGE OF FORT CARLISLE

Thibault walks briskly through the courtyard of Fort Carlisle, his latest conquest in Ireland, and the one from where he intends to defeat the anticipated English counterattack.

Three battlesaurs are chained to huge bolts driven into the walls. Not one bolt, but four for each of the greatjaws. The idea of one of these creatures getting loose during the night is too awful to contemplate. They do not distinguish between French and foe. They can be controlled; that is all.

They are his girls, but they are not pets. They are not tame, nor tameable.

They growl and bellow at his approach, thrashing against the chains, but the links are large and the walls are resolute. The largest of the three girls, Mathilde, snaps at him as he walks almost within range. A meter closer and her great teeth would have taken his head off. She is his favorite.

Another cannon roars in the distance and the whistle of an approaching cannonball makes Thibault look up. There is a dull *thud* as the ball hits low on the outer stonework of the fort, where the wall is strongest and the cannonball will do little damage. The British dare not bring their cannon any closer as that would put them within range of the fort's cannon, so they content themselves with the occasional shot primed with extra powder for longer distance.

"They expect us to cower behind these walls while they besiege the fort," Montenot says, emerging from a doorway. He holds a letter and the canvas pouch it arrived in. Odette, the youngest of the saurs, snuffles and snorts at his presence.

"That would be the conventional approach for a smaller force protected by stone walls." Thibault smiles. "There are nearly six thousand troops out there, if our scouts are correct. We are vastly outnumbered."

"But we are not a conventional force," Montenot says.

"Indeed," Thibault says. "And tonight the green fields of Ireland will run red with British blood."

"And again I protest this decision," Montenot says. "Battles are best fought in the day. Darkness only produces confusion and disorder."

"Exactly what I am hoping for," Thibault says. "The saurs hunt better in the dark, and the British will not be expecting it."

"You risk the lives of our saurs," Montenot says.

"But not unnecessarily," Thibault says, looking back at the beasts, admiring their sheer size, their simplicity, their ferocity. "They are beautiful, are they not?"

"They have a raw power," Montenot agrees.

"Unhampered by emotion or sentiment," Thibault says. "Unafraid. The perfect soldier. If all my soldiers were as fearless no empire could stand against us."

"None will," Montenot says.

"You bring news?" Thibault asks, gesturing at the letter that Montenot holds.

Montenot glances down at it as if he has forgotten it. He nods.

"From the Sonian," he says. "We have the name of the collaborator who helped Willem to escape."

"Who is he?" Thibault asks.

"A she," Montenot says. "Sofie Thielemans, a resident of Antwerp."

"I trust that Baston is even now interrogating her," Thibault says.

"He is not," Montenot says, holding the letter out to Thibault, who ignores it and waits. Montenot continues. "He says she is old, and would die under torture. Instead he has set a close watch on her, in case Willem should make contact."

"A wise choice," Thibault says.

"And he sent François to her to see if she would reveal anything to him."

"That was foolish," Thibault explodes. "If he says or does anything to make her suspicious, we will lose our chance to catch the boy."

"There is more," Montenot says. "Sergeant Belette is dead."

"Belette? A shame. He was a good man," Thibault says. "How did he die?"

"By the hand of François," Montenot says. "Who 'rescued' the girl, Cosette, as planned, but killed Belette in the process."

"An accident?" Thibault asks.

"A crossbow bolt through the heart," Montenot says. "It was no accident."

"Then why?" Thibault asks. "Baston said François was under control and doing as he was asked. Baston is a good soldier, but caution and intrigue are not his strengths. I will have to return as soon as this battle is won."

There are other reasons why he must return, but they are not to be spoken in the light of day.

"If I may speak in Baston's defense," Montenot says. "There is only so much control with a zealot like François. His faith blinds him to all else. And . . ."

"What?"

"I think you should not trust him," Montenot says.

"Why do you say this?"

"We know that he regards Napoléon as being sent by God," Montenot says. "But once when I mentioned your name, behind my back he made the sign of the cross. One of my guards saw it."

"He thinks me the devil?" Thibault asks.

"So it would seem," Montenot says. "I believe that as much as he wants to help Napoléon, he looks for an opportunity to kill you. Be careful, General."

Thibault smiles. "This is his folly and his conceit, in thinking that I can be killed."

"Any man can be killed," Montenot says.

"The angel of death has already taken his chance and lost," Thibault says, gesturing at his scarred face with his mangled arm.

The lone British cannon sounds again and the whistle of the cannonball is followed by another dull thud in the distance. This shot has not even reached the walls.

Thibault turns abruptly and climbs a ladder to a wooden catwalk that has been erected around the inner wall of the courtyard. From the catwalk a wooden frame extends over the back of each battlesaur and he lithely steps out and onto the back of Mathilde. She stirs and growls softly but otherwise does not object as he settles into the saddle and takes hold of the thin leather straps that will guide the great beast. He ties one of the straps to a clasp on the stump of his arm, before taking the other strap in his one good hand.

"You will ride her yourself, into the thick of battle?" Montenot asks.

"The British troops know of me," Thibault says. "I am told they fear me even more than my battlesaurs."

"And if you should be killed in this inconsequential action?" Montenot asks.

"As I have already said," Thibault says. "The angel of death dares not touch me."

"As you say," Montenot says, lowering his eyes.

"Call the other riders, Montenot," Thibault pats the neck of his mount. "Night is falling."

SMUGGLERS

Willem is examining a metal cylinder when the boat lurches, dropping into what feels like a huge hole in the sea. He clenches his lips tightly together to stop himself from vomiting. That has been a possibility since they left London the previous day.

The River Thames was smooth and pleasant sailing, but once they reached the open Channel the waters turned rough and his stomach started to churn. He ate nothing and only took sips of water, trying to ignore the nausea, but with little success.

The boat is a sloop, unarmed. A smuggler's ship. She is nothing like the last ship he was on, a full ship of the line of the Royal Navy, although he remembers little of that after the explosion on the *Epaulette*.

Yesterday they rendezvoused with another Royal Navy ship, an eighty-gunner, and spent the night moored to her side.

That had not helped Willem's stomach at all, as the night had been one of rolling and tossing, and he had very little sleep. As sorry as he felt for himself, though, at least he could go on deck and take in fresh air. The fifty soldiers of the First Foot Guards on the deck below had no such opportunity; they had to remain out of sight and so had to simply endure what to Willem would have been insufferable conditions.

This morning they sailed to within sight of the Dutch coast and anchored there until the sun slithered below the horizon. Now, with light from only the stars and a slim, crescent-shaped moon, they are in the last stage of their journey, a perilous nighttime passage of the Oosterschelde, the northern branch of the Schelde River.

The boat heaves back up out of the hole and settles, and Willem replaces the cylinder in an oilcloth, then in a leather satchel he has brought to carry them.

These are devices of magic, what his father called a "thundercloud." But his father's were the size of a thimble, for use on a stage. Willem's versions are much larger. They are made from cut-down rocket casings, by the workshops of Sir William Congreve. He hopes he will not need them.

He wonders how Congreve has fared in Ireland, and fears it was not well.

Now he opens a wooden case and examines what lies inside. It is a red rocket, as is its twin next to it. A spare, in case the first one does not fire. A second case has two green rockets and a third case has yellow ones. They are in the hold, covered by bales of sheep's wool.

For all his doubts about Sir Congreve, Willem has to admire the speed at which he was able to blend Willem's colored powders with the gunpowder of the parachute flare rockets.

They tested them a few days earlier and the rockets produced a sizzling, colorful display that was visible for many kilometers, even during the day.

For his part, Congreve graciously took heed of some of Willem's suggestions. He seemed more amiable and amenable to the Calais plan once he knew his precious rockets would be put into action against the battlesaurs in Ireland.

Six rockets. Three colors.

If all goes to plan, then Blücher's army will have approached within sight of Calais.

When the dinosaurs in the city are dead, a yellow rocket will be fired, the signal for Blücher's army to attack.

Once Napoléon's Grande Armée is engaged in battle at Calais against the Prussians, without battlesaurs, a green rocket will be fired, a signal for the ships of the Royal Navy waiting off the coast. They will immediately set sail to Ireland. Once they arrive at Cork Harbour, they will engage the French forces there, defeat them, and then sail back before a saur-less Napoléon is able to disengage his army from the Prussians.

The red rocket is in case of disaster. If all goes wrong, it will be used to recall the Royal Navy. It will have to be fired before they sail out of sight.

Willem hopes he will not have to use that rocket. He closes the wooden case and heaps bales of wool on top of it, then climbs the narrow ladder to the deck.

The smell of the sea never ceases to amaze him, full of mystery. The thought that this water is deep and wide enough to swallow his entire village a million times over is hard to comprehend. The air here is different from that of the forest, which was full of leafy, earthy smells. This is a harsh tang, a bitter taste on his tongue, and yet it is a fresh smell, as though the world is new and he is witness to its birth.

The wind is also different at sea than on land. It brings spray from the front of the boat, a thousand icy needles in the cold cloth of this October night.

But most of all what he notices is the silence. London is a noisy place; the air is filled with carriage wheels rattling on cobblestones, vendors shouting out their wares, constant chatter of thousands of people. Here, apart from the sound of the hull burrowing through the water and the breeze rustling the rigging, it is silent.

He turns up the collar on his coat against the spray and walks forward. He passes Big Joe, Gilbert, and Weiner engaged in earnest conversation at the larboard gunwales. He nods and smiles, but it is a strange feeling seeing them in French uniform. He knows and trusts these men, yet the uniform makes him shudder.

He wonders what it is like for them, to be wearing the uniform of the enemy. It must not be a comfortable feeling, for more than one reason. If they are caught, they will be shot as spies.

He, Frost, Jack, and Héloïse wear civilian clothes for their journey to Gaillemarde.

He finds Frost and Jack seated at the bow, their backs to the railing, talking quietly. Willem joins them and finds himself in the midst of an uncomfortable silence.

"A private conversation?" he asks.

Frost shakes his head. "I was just asking Jack about Bedlam."

Willem glances at Jack, who shudders.

There is a touch on Willem's arm and he looks around to see Héloïse sliding down next to him. She puts her arm around his waist and rests her head on his shoulder. After a moment he decides that she must be cold, and he places his arm around her shoulders to keep her warm.

It is certainly not appropriate behavior for an unbetrothed young man and woman, but Héloïse, Willem reminds himself, is not privy to the usual mores and manners of polite society. And besides, she is cold.

"What did Jack say?" Willem asks.

Frost shakes his head. "It is, perhaps, a sensitive subject."

"It's a bad place," Jack says uncertainly.

"You had been to Bedlam before?" Willem asks.

"I didn't know what it was called until we got there," Jack says. "I recognized the statues out front. Nobody could never forget them, could they, sir?"

An image comes to Willem's mind of the contorted faces of the two reclining lunatics outside the asylum. He shudders also.

"I mean, who would put statues like that outside a place what's supposed to be helping people get better?" Jack asks.

"Why were you there, Jack?" Frost asks. "Did you live there for a while?"

"Oh no, sir, nothing like that," Jack says. "I was visiting me mum."

A bad memory seems to settle over him like a dark cloud. He shuts his eyes briefly.

"What happened, Jack?" Frost asks.

"It were after me dad died," Jack says. "He were at the Battle of Trafalgar. He got hit by a cannonball. In the . . . here." He pats his chest. "He lay next to Lord Nelson himself, so I heard."

"I remember you telling me," Frost says.

"He was on the *Victory*, that was Nelson's ship, sir," Jack says. "That's why he was in the ship's hospital next to him. I mean after Nelson got himself shot."

"That was 1805," Frost says. "You must have been about seven."

Jack holds up his hands, counting on his fingers for a moment, then gives up.

"Something like that," he says. "After that me mum went a bit odd-like. She wouldn't eat or drink. Wouldn't even talk. Not even to me. She just sat in the corner until the doctors came."

"What happened to you?"

"A family from the church took me in," Jack says. "They were good people. It was them what took me to see me mum."

The dark cloud that hovers over Jack has intensified.

"You don't have to talk about this," Willem says, but Jack does not seem to hear.

"I remember crying. There was an orderly, a big, fat orderly with piggy nostrils. He was shouting at me, shouting and shouting. I was running. There was a balcony. And an old man, with red, red eyes. There was someone screaming." He pauses. "Might have been me, sir. I remember falling."

"Then what, Jack?" Frost asks.

"Hospital, sir. I was there for a long time. The doctors were saying stuff about my head. Didn't make no sense to me."

"It must have been awful," Willem says.

"I was a clever little boy," Jack says. "Everybody told me that. Good with me letters, good with me numbers."

"I'm sure you were, Jack," Frost says.

"But nobody ever told me that after the accident," Jack says.

"A sad and moving story, but a half-wit is still a half-wit," McConnell says from the other side of the boat. Willem hadn't noticed him sitting in the shadows.

Héloïse snarls, baring her teeth.

"And a wild dog is a wild dog," McConnell says.

"You are aware, McConnell, that you are no longer in British uniform," Frost says with a smile that chills even Willem.

"I am still an officer," McConnell says.

"But not in your uniform," Frost says. "And Jack is a good lad, but if you push him too far, and don't have your rank to hide behind, I fear the consequences."

"I fear nothing from a simpleton," McConnell says.

"You should," Frost says. "Especially here, where a person could simply disappear."

McConnell's reply is stopped on his lips by a hushed whisper from amidships: "Sail off the larboard bow!"

Willem and Jack crane their necks to look.

From the square rigging it appears to be a small brig. Its sails are dull patches sewn on the dark cloth of the sky.

Their own sail is quietly lowering and as Willem scrambles back to the stern, Arbuckle greets him with a finger to his lips and moves closer, whispering in Willem's ear.

"Quietly, my friend. Sound travels a long way across water at night."

"What ship is it?" Willem asks.

"River patrol," Arbuckle murmurs. "Dutch flag."

"Dutch?" Willem asks hopefully.

"That will not help us if they see us," Arbuckle says. "The Netherlands are now allies of the French. We must hope . . ."

His voice trails off. Already it is too late. They hear shouted orders on the Dutch ship and the bow swings around in their direction.

"We must make a run for it!" McConnell says. He has joined them, as have the others, at the aftercastle.

"Outpace a brig in this little fishing boat?" Arbuckle asks. "We would have no chance. We will lower our sails and talk our way out of this."

"Are you mad?" McConnell asks. "You think to blind the enemy with your charm and wit?"

For answer Arbuckle merely glances at Willem.

"On this I trust Captain Arbuckle fully," Willem says, with emphasis on the man's rank.

McConnell stares at the approaching ship and fumes, but says nothing more.

"I am the only one who will speak to them," Arbuckle says. "Is that clear?"

"It is clear," Willem says, glancing around at the others, all of whom, with the exception of McConnell, nod their agreement.

"So you may say whatever suits your purpose," McConnell says.

"*Captain* Arbuckle is the only one who speaks," Willem says, starting to lose his composure. "Is that clear, *Lieutenant* Mc-Connell?"

McConnell reluctantly nods.

The sloop drifts to a halt, and the brig is soon upon her. It seems much bigger up close, although still tiny compared to the British man-o'-war on which Willem sailed to England. He counts six gun ports along the side of the ship. They were open, but are closed as the brig pulls alongside. Storm lamps are hung from the side of the brig, illuminating the smaller boat. A carronade, a small cannon, is mounted on the fo'c'sle to the right of the bowsprit. It swivels toward them. A sailor stands behind it with a lit linstock, making Willem far more nervous than he wants to feel.

Arbuckle does nothing to object when ropes are tossed down from the brig, stern and aft, and he instructs crew members to tie the ship up, even going to the trouble of making sure himself that the knots are strong and tight. He motions for Willem, Frost, and the rest of the crew to sit on the deck near the mast.

"Whose side is he really on?" McConnell mutters under his breath.

Muskets are trained on the sloop from the gunwales of the brig, and a few moments later a large, florid man appears at the railing. He glances around the deck of the smaller boat until his eyes fall on Arbuckle.

"Arbuckle, you scoundrel," he says in accented English, leaning over and resting his arms on the railing. He seems casual and relaxed.

"Captain Devilliers," Arbuckle says with a short bow. "I was worried it might have been some earnest young diehard, brave and intelligent. Thank God it is only you."

"Even with my muskets trained on your breast, you think to insult me," Devilliers says.

"That was barely an insult," Arbuckle says. "You should hear what I whisper about you in the taverns and bawdy houses of Antwerp and London."

"Arbuckle is an idiot," McConnell mutters. "He will do for us all."

"I am sure he knows what he is doing," Frost whispers.

Up on the deck Devilliers has adopted an expression of angry indignation.

"Your lies and half-truths will do you no good, sir," he says. "There are few who would trust the word of an Englishman, especially a rogue such as yourself."

"And yet all would believe such stories of a Dutchman," Arbuckle says. "Especially one as toadying, yet vain, as yourself. I do believe you would kiss your own arse if you could twist around far enough."

"What game is he playing?" McConnell whispers.

"I am wounded again," Devilliers says, with a smile.

Willem cannot tell in the dim light of the lanterns if the smile is one of good humor or of menace.

Devilliers continues. "Shall I ask one of my marines to return the favor with his musket?"

"Your marines could not hit the hull of your own ship were it docked and they on the wharf alongside," Arbuckle says.

"Let us find out if that is true," Devilliers says cheerfully. He motions to one of his marines, who steps forward and aims his musket directly at Arbuckle's chest.

"He should bribe his way out of this," McConnell says. "I know this type."

"Let Arbuckle handle it," Big Joe says.

"Arbuckle will shortly be dead," McConnell says. "And the Dutchman will only respond to money."

"Stay where you are," Frost hisses.

McConnell dismisses him with a haughty look and rises.

"Don't move," Willem says, but McConnell is rising and already walking toward the two men.

Arbuckle turns and his face is cold and hard. Devilliers stops smiling and raises an eyebrow at McConnell's approach.

"Sit down, sir," Arbuckle says.

McConnell ignores him. "Please excuse this fool. A man of no class or manners. He commands the vessel, but it is my cargo that we carry," he says. "Finest wool from my father's farm in the Scottish highlands."

"Highland wool," Devilliers says with an odd expression. "A valuable cargo indeed."

"Sit back down," Arbuckle says, granite-faced.

"Our captain does you a disservice," McConnell says. "My family is wealthy and this wool has good value. I am sure that a portion of that value would ease our passage today."

The captain makes a hand gesture and suddenly the musket that had been aimed at Arbuckle moves toward McConnell. The other Dutch marines raise their muskets again to cover the English crew, and Willem glances up again at the ugly snout of the carronade.

Arbuckle reacts instantly, swinging around with something hard in his fist, which smashes into McConnell's face, sending him flying backward. The Scotsman is dazed, crashing to the deck, blood splattering from a deep cut on his cheek.

"Arbuckle?" Devilliers asks, and his face has lost all joviality.

"A long story," Arbuckle says. "And one that is best shared over a glass of fine French cognac."

"Which you happen to have on board?" the captain asks, a smile returning to his lips.

"It so happens that I saved a barrel from Rémy Martin on my last trip," Arbuckle says. "If I may beg your indulgence, I will fetch it. Watch this stupid one while I do so."

He kicks McConnell's leg as he passes, eliciting a small, child-like squeal of pain.

Muskets remain trained on the crew when Arbuckle disappears belowdecks, and only lower when he emerges with a small barrel of cognac.

"We have known each other for many years," the Dutch captain says. "I hope you do not now abuse that friendship."

"I think you know me better than that," Arbuckle says. "Let us drink as friends and I will tell you my story. Then you can make whatever decision you will."

He hands up the barrel to a sailor who passes it to the captain. Devilliers uncorks it and sniffs. A smile spreads slowly over his face and he motions for Arbuckle to come aboard. A rope is tossed down to him and Arbuckle goes up quickly, hand over hand. He and the captain disappear belowdecks.

On the smaller boat, McConnell spits blood and wipes at his mouth with the back of his hand.

"If McConnell moves or speaks," Frost says to Big Joe, "hit him again."

"Gladly," Big Joe says.

Time passes. McConnell curses under his breath. The soldiers on the Dutch ship gradually relax. With no sign of opposition from what they believe to be a fishing boat, and the fishing boat captain clearly on good drinking terms with their own captain, they lower their heavy muskets, resting them against the gunwales.

An odd series of whistles and clacks comes from the stern.

"Dolphin," Frost says.

Willem nods. He has seen pictures of these wise men of the

sea, although he has never heard one before. He is a little surprised. For some reason he thought dolphins must sleep at night.

It surprises the Dutch soldiers too, and several of them go to the stern of the brig to look for it.

"You are too stupid to know when you are being sold," McConnell mutters, but softly so the Dutch sailors above them cannot hear.

"The stupid one is you," Big Joe says.

"Arbuckle is below with the Dutch captain right now, negotiating a price for our heads," McConnell says.

"He is taking a long time," Gilbert says doubtfully.

"And what would you suggest we do?" Frost asks.

"Most of the Dutchies have gone to look for that dolphin," McConnell says. "We could climb the side of the ship and overpower those left. Take their guns and seize control of the brig."

"Madness," Big Joe says.

McConnell bristles, but says no more.

A few moments later Willem notices something odd. Their boat seems to be drifting away from the Dutch ship, and glancing to the bow and stern Willem sees the cut ends of the ropes that had secured them.

A moment later a voice comes from the far side of the boat, Arbuckle's voice. "Get everyone down, now!"

"Everybody, lie down flat," Frost whispers, and Willem passes the whisper along, before easing himself into a prone position.

Héloïse lies next to him.

There is a shout from the ship; one of the marines has noticed the boat drifting away. More shouts, but the guards are clearly confused and unsure what to do.

In a rush of water, Arbuckle is over the side and running across the deck, hauling on the sheets of the foremast. It rises rapidly and a gust of wind from the stern fills it and suddenly the Dutch ship is behind them and the distance is growing rapidly. A few more seconds pass, then the first musketshot rings out and the port railing splinters. More shots, but the distance is growing all the time.

The gun ports along the side of the ship open, and the snouts of the cannon are rolled out, protruding like thorns on a rose stem. But the fishing boat is already well out of the line of fire. The bow-mounted carronade, inexplicably, does not fire. If it did it would slaughter those on the deck.

"They will chase us and sink us," Big Joe says. "They are much faster than us."

"Not with the water that is filling their ballast deck," Arbuckle says. "I stove in a plank in the hold. And if they try to chase us they will go only in circles. I also jammed their rudder."

"And the carronade?" Willem asks.

"Damp gunpowder will not light," Arbuckle says.

"That was the least convincing dolphin impression I have ever heard," Frost says.

"It fooled them." Arbuckle grins.

"What about Devilliers?" Willem asks.

The grin disappears.

"It was unfortunate, but he would not listen to reason," Arbuckle says with a long hard look at McConnell, who is only now stirring. "The Dutch are too afraid of the French and their great saurs."

"The brig will need a new captain?" Frost asks.

"He was a friend of mine," Arbuckle says in reply.

On either side of the boat, the dark shores of the Oosterschelde start to close in as the fishing boat surges forward on the incoming tide.

THE ATTACK BEGINS

Lightning flashes, a tumbling, roiling offshore thunderstorm. The headland is briefly illuminated, revealing thin wisps of mist curling around the rocky coastline. The flash is followed almost instantly by crashing thunder.

The seal stirs in her sheltered crevice on the foreshore. She checks her pup, two weeks old and still white-coated, then slowly raises her head above the enfolding rock. She peers through the darkness and sniffs the air to try to determine what has disturbed her sleep. Her whiskers, so sensitive underwater, are almost useless here on land. She must rely on her nose and eyes, but the darkness and the direction of the wind are not in her favor. Frightened yet unsure, and unwilling to leave the safety of their temporary home, she remains where she is. Her pup also senses danger. He whimpers and snuggles closer.

The harsh, inhospitable stretch of rock where the land meets the water is not flat, but ridged in long deep crevices as if some impossibly immense creature has raked its claws down the cliff to the sea. The seal's birthing place lies in the apex of one of those great rocky gashes.

Another flash of lightning reveals a number of dark figures passing the seal's sheltered corner of rock. Humans. They do not see her, or if they do, they give no sign of it. More lightning, a flickering sequence of flashes embedded in the clouds, briefly turning night into day. She watches the figures drop to the ground. The seal knows men and is wary of them, but they are not close enough to concern her and too quiet to have woken her.

The solid rock of the coastline vibrates beneath her. This is what has woken her. It is not from the thunder and it is not a sensation she is used to.

She continues to watch and to sniff the air, and another barrage of sheet lightning blazes through the clouds. For a moment the sea and shore shine in shocked white.

In that brief moment, the seal sees death, for surely that is what comes. A creature she neither knows nor understands emerges from behind a ridge of rock. At first just a giant head. An immense, jagged mouth capable of swallowing the seal in a single bite. Then the massive body and the tree-trunk legs. The rock shudders with its every footstep. The huge head sways with the animal's lumbering stride.

If she could flee from this, she would, even if it meant leaving behind her pup. But she cannot. She is frozen, no longer capable of movement as a massive clawed foot thuds into the rock on one side of her crevice. She mutely looks up at the stomach and undercarriage of the creature as it moves past, showing no interest in her or her pup. A heavy tail swings back and forth as the animal moves on.

More lightning, more crashing thunder, and the seal remains frozen as a second beast follows, then another.

Only when all three have passed do the seal's frozen muscles lose their rigidity and does she dare to turn her head, watching as the three, flash-lit in intermittent bursts of lightning, disappear into the rocky ridges and the curve of the waterfront.

The pup whimpers again and the mother seal draws him close

with a flipper. She shivers, aware that she and her pup were only a heartbeat away from a sudden and savage death.

Like the seal, the British sentry shivers, leaning against the boulder at the water's edge. But his shiver is from the bitter, offshore breeze.

Also like the seal, he is acutely aware of the possibility of a sudden and savage death.

He is young, thin-faced, a handsome young Irishman from Kilkenny, now three years in the service of His Majesty and three months betrothed to a pretty, freckle-faced girl he has lived next door to all his life. The soldier knows what he and his fellow troopers are up against here on this headland and it scares him. He is the outermost sentry, having drawn the short straw when stations were decided.

He watches the thunderstorm, praying it will not move toward the coast. He is cold enough without standing in the wet. He stamps his feet and wraps his arms around himself and thinks of his fair, freckled fiancée.

He raises his head at a sound, just on the limit of his hearing, an evenly repeated thud, dull and distant, from around the point of the foreshore. Or is it just a trick of his ears? The playful lightning reveals a curl of mist reaching around the point like the fingers of a hand, and he thinks there may be a shadow lurking in it. He cocks the hammer of his musket with a trembling thumb, holding the gun at his waist. He will have time for one shot, a warning to the other sentries and to the massed forces behind them. But he knows he must use that shot carefully.

Was that movement? A shape in the mist? Or was it simply a movement of the mist itself? He clenches the musket tightly and peers through the darkness. Every sense in his body is attuned to the rocky point.

Which is why he does not see the French soldier who creeps forward in the shadows. Not until it is too late. He hears a sound behind him, a pebble perhaps, clinking off a rock. He turns, raising his musket, seeing nothing, and turns quickly back to see a dark boulder in front of him erupt into movement. Lightning glints off a flashing, slashing blade and no sound escapes the throat of the young sentry, nor will any ever again. His musket is caught before it can clatter onto the rocks.

The next sentry, a hundred yards farther on, hears nothing. He is asleep, or close to it, and merely gasps softly as a dagger enters his chest.

MATHILDE'S CHARGE

Many times Thibault has sent men into battle on the backs of the great beasts from the Sonian but for him this is a first.

He has ridden the greatjaws on many occasions, but never in anger. Never wearing the heavy steel armor of the cuirassier. It is different somehow, as if the animal knows and relishes what lies ahead.

The battlesaur is the ultimate predator. It is a bringer of death and destruction under his guiding hand. He feels the surge of Mathilde's muscles under the skin of her sides; he feels her unfettered power. The rise and fall of the beast is unlike the smooth flow of a four-footed horse. When walking, as now, it is a lurching seesaw of a ride; running is a wild, exhilarating frenzy, but that is not yet. For now, it is about silence. Stealth.

He glances out to sea, where the storm shows no sign of approaching land. That is a shame. Rain dampens gunpowder and extinguishes linstocks. Muskets refuse to fire, artillery must be constantly sheltered and is hard to maneuver on soft, sodden ground. But the rain means nothing to the razor teeth of the battlesaurs, nor to the sabers of his cavalry, who remain just behind the gates of the fort, awaiting his signal.

Rain would have been a blessing, but it's not crucial. Dry weather will not save the British this night.

Thibault passes the body of the first sentry, a narrow-faced young man without a throat, lying in a wedge of rock. Ahead he sees a slight movement and he is glad that the skirmishers are paving the way.

The battlesaurs are great and powerful but not invincible, despite what he would like his enemies to believe. There have been casualties. Two at Waterloo, one at Berlin, and a rider killed at Rome.

The armies of Europe learned quickly to use canister shot against the greatjaws. It was not usually fatal to the mounts, although it was to the riders. But the canister shot is only of use at short range. The guns take time to turn, aim, and fire, and the battlesaurs, when on the charge, are surprisingly fleet of foot. If he can get in among the enemy artillery before they can fire, the guns will be silenced.

He guides Mathilde around another rocky spit just as the lightning makes an unexpected reappearance. There are glints of silver in the distance, a hint of light stabbing from a bayonet or from the blade of a sword. But this sentry is quicker, or perhaps just more nervous, than the others. The hard crack of a musketshot echoes off the equally hard rock of the shore before the body slumps to the ground.

Thibault curses. The gunshot reverberates through the sudden shocking darkness, a distinctive sound, far different from the rolling rumble of the thunder. There are shouts as other sentries take up the cry.

"The element of surprise is lost." Montenot's voice comes to Thibault from the battlesaur behind: Odette, the youngest of the three females. "We must retire or face their canister."

"If you turn back I will line you up in front of our own cannon and let you taste French canister," Thibault calls back.

Montenot says nothing, but when Thibault spurs Mathilde to

greater speed he hears the heavy footsteps of Odette and Valérie close behind.

They outpace the skirmishers, who move aside to let the battlesaurs through.

Then they are past the final point and no longer following the curve of the headland but rising up the rocky slope to the meadows and furrows of Ballytigeen Farm beyond.

The four British artillerymen were playing cards when the first musketshot rang out across the fields of the farm. Unable to sleep despite the exhaustion of the previous day's march, they were well into their third hour of three-card brag when the crack of the musket was followed by the cries of sentries, then screams.

Now they are at their gun, with the other members of their crew. Along the cannon battery all the crews are likewise occupied, loading and ramming gunpowder cartridges and canister shot.

They do not speak. There is no bravado. They know what has happened to other armies that have faced what they now face.

Some of them glance toward the wide trench dug in front of their position, filled with kindling and oil-soaked wood. Others glance backward, toward the new soldiers. The ones not of the Irish Regiment. The rocketeers.

Their guns still face the fort to the west. This is the direction from which an attack was expected to come. But now the danger, it seems, comes from the coast to the southwest. Lieutenants shout orders and gunners lift the trails of their cannon, swinging the heavy guns around.

"Rocket flares!" is the cry, from behind them.

The storm off the coast continues to rumble, but the lightning seems distant, concealed within the heavy clouds that hang low, almost to the surface of the sea.

The storm does little to help visibility on the land, then one last flash, a last gasp of lightning, and the British stir at what may have been movement at the brow of the hill where the land falls away to the sea.

It may be the result of an unsteady hand or a misheard command, but one of the cannon fires, sparking a barrage from the rest of the battery. The roar of the massed cannon is the curse of an angry god as flames belch from the cannon mouths. A pall of smoke drifts toward the ocean, mingling with the mist, intensifying it. The land remains in darkness, with no help from the sea storm.

Now the rocket flares hiss vertically, spinning and spiraling as they climb. Three bursts of light create three new stars, swinging beneath small silk parachutes, burning brightly as they fall slowly back to earth.

The British gunners are already in the middle of reloading. Worming the barrels, ramming the gunpowder cartridges and the canister shot. But there is no time. The flares turn the nighttime into a sinister, trembling twilight.

There is a scream from somewhere down the line and now raging up out of the low ground, wreathed in shadow, through the mist and the smoke, storm the devil's creatures. Great demons with armored breastplates and sinister hooded eyes.

"Retire!" is the order, screamed by their officers. The loaders drop their shells, the firers throw down their linstocks, the gun crews scatter, running back through the lines as the three beasts bear down on them, huge clawed feet tearing up the dirt.

A burning brand is thrown into the trench in front of the cannon and a flicker of flame spreads and grows.

Thibault pulls gently on one of the steering reins, guiding his huge steed a little to avoid a stunted tree in the middle of the farm field.

In front of him the ground has erupted in flames. It seems the entire field is on fire.

The cannon crews flee in terror, but the line of troops behind them remains.

"Why aren't they running?" comes a shout from beside him, Montenot's voice. The other two battlesaurs have caught up with Thibault's to form an assault line. Three battlesaurs, charging side by side. Thibault on the right, Montenot riding Odette in the center, and Major Campagne, their most successful battlesaur rider, on Valérie at the left.

In every battle since Waterloo the enemy has broken and run at this sight. But here a wide line of soldiers stand firm.

The leaping flames imprint on Thibault's vision, making it hard to see beyond.

Something is wrong here, but Thibault is not sure what. The soldiers should be running and screaming. It worries him and he briefly considers turning back, but dismisses the thought almost instantly. Victory is so close.

"Signal the cavalry attack," he orders instead.

"Why aren't they running?" Montenot shouts again.

Musketballs cut holes in the smoke and flames, peppering the armored breastplates of the greatjaws, ricocheting off the thick steel. Thibault crouches low, protected by the neck of his mount.

"Muskets against battlesaurs," he scoffs. "Old weapons against new."

A bright light behind the British lines is followed by a finger of fire stabbing out at them from behind the leaping flames of the trench. It hisses past Thibault's right ear, so close that he can feel the heat of its passage. It is followed by another and another.

"Rockets!" Campagne cries.

This is why the British did not run.

The battlesaurs slow, distracted by the streams of fire.

Still Thibault presses forward, charging into a maelstrom of fiery, crisscrossing trails. The rockets fly past him, around him, explode in the dirt at the battlesaurs' feet, in the air above them, but the fingers of fire do not touch him. Nor will they, he knows. Death cannot touch him.

They approach the flaming trench and Thibault narrows the blinders that control his beast, spurring her forward, past her own instinctive fear of fire, over the trench, into the line of deserted cannon. Mathilde knocks one aside with a casual flick of her head. Wooden wheels shatter. The heavy iron cannon embeds itself in the earth.

Still musketballs ring and zing off Mathilde's armor, and now before them Thibault can see the source of the rockets. A long row of metal frames. A troop of rocketeers, reloading, seemingly unafraid of the battlesaurs, focused only on their work.

Another rocket trail heads straight for his face at point-blank range. He twists to one side and it passes by, so close that it sears the skin on his neck, but he ignores the pain. Pain is to be savored later, when he has time to enjoy it.

Campagne is the first to reach the rocketeer line. He is firing one of his pistols as he approaches, although without result. He replaces the used pistol in its saddle holster and takes up another.

There are three pistols strapped to each side of Thibault's saddle also and he takes the first as he too approaches the line.

In the light of the parachute flares he sees a British rocketeer step forward, aiming a pistol at the head of Campagne's saur, Valérie. Thibault has time to laugh—a pistol against a battlesaur!—before the British officer fires. The sound is different from the crack of a pistol ball and a dark cloud envelops Valérie's head for a brief second.

Valérie screams and bellows, lifting and shaking her head.

Campagne is thrown to the ground and before he can rise he is crushed under a colossal foot. Valérie runs in a circle, screaming, shaking her great head from side to side, then charges off at an angle through the British ranks, which fall back or are trampled as she bursts through.

In front of Thibault another officer stands, pistol raised, and without thinking, Thibault hauls on his reins, slamming shut the leather blinders and nostril flaps on his battlesaur just as the man fires. The great saur, with neither sight nor smell, slows to a stop. A waft of bitter pepper drifts past Thibault, but already he is re-opening the blinders and the nostril flaps and has the satisfaction of seeing the mangled body of the officer tossed to one side as the battlesaur's great mouth closes once, then spits him out.

Another man with a pistol faces Montenot's saur and Thibault grabs for one of his own pistols, drawing it and cocking the hammer in one motion. He fires and the man drops just before Montenot comes within range.

Pepper! Thibault fumes. Another trick from the British and another saur-rider lost. In truth he worries less about losing Campagne than he does about his battlesaurs losing their reputation for invincibility.

Still the rocketeers load and light their rockets. The rocket frame in front of Thibault fizzles with just-ignited flame. He charges his beast into it, knocking it over just before the rocket fires. It skitters across the ground leaving a line of flame in the dirt, leaping up into an ammunition caisson loaded with more rockets. That explodes in a porcupine bristle of fire, rockets shooting in every direction, into the ground, into the sky, and into the massed squares of British infantry behind them.

Now the surviving rocketeers break and run, their last hope of defense extinguished.

Behind him, Thibault hears the cries of the French cavalry on the charge, and he spurs his own great steed toward the nearest infantry square. The greatjaw plows through it like a scythe through weeds and the cavalry are right behind him, sabers whirling.

Campagne's saur will be found the next day, red-eyed and indignant, resting in the muddy banks of a nearby pond.

AMBITION

Nicole waits at the castle gate for Thibault and covers her mouth with a hand as she sees the new blackened wound on his neck. Thibault waves away her concern.

"The battle for Ireland is over," he says.

"And if the British return?" she asks.

"They have been well beaten," he says. "They will not try again. I must leave now for France."

"Then I will come with you," she says.

"You must stay here where it is safe," he says. "The journey is risky. We must sail under the noses of the Royal Navy."

"Then you stay here also," she says.

"That I cannot do," Thibault says. "The battle for Ireland is over. The battle for Britain is about to begin."

"And what of Napoléon?" she asks in a hushed voice, glancing around to ensure nobody is within earshot. "You said he would meet his death on the battlefield, but I have heard that he is no longer the fearless leader, riding at the head of his army."

"It is true. He now commands from the safety of the rear, in Calais," Thibault says. "He is not the man he was before Elba."

"Then how can he die heroically in battle? You cannot be the emperor of France, and I cannot be the empress, while Napoléon still breathes!"

"Do not worry, my love," Thibault says. "I will take opportunity when I see it."

AMBUSH

The sentry post is a wooden tower silhouetted against the starry sky. Despite the appearance of their little fishing boat, there is no sign of activity at the tower. Lars and his men have done their job well.

The Oostershelde slips behind them. There are no more patrol ships and the last glimpse Willem had of the Dutch brig she was low in the water, bow down, and slipping lower.

Arbuckle had done a better job of stoving in the planks than he had realized. Willem can't help but feel a pang of guilt. The ship and her sailors were Dutch, not French. But war makes enemies of allies and there was little use in feeling guilty about it.

The estuary at night is a dark tunnel with no whitecapped waves to give contour to the shoreline. Just black land and black water beneath an almost-black sky.

He is glad of this. He feels the boat is exposed and vulnerable and it is true, as shown by the incident with the Dutch brig.

Another silent watchtower approaches and passes, blind to their passage. The Oosterschelde twists and turns, keeping the crew busy with the sails.

"Krabbendijke," Arbuckle says.

He points out a small beach, white sand glimmering dimly under the faintest of moons.

Willem stares at the beach intently. Krabbendijke was his

suggestion, although he has never been here in his life. It is only a few hours' ride from Waterloo, to the south, where he will try to gain an audience with Field Marshall Blücher. It is less than a day's ride from Calais, to the southwest, where the saur-slayers will find and destroy Napoléon's great battlesaurs. Krabbendijke is also far enough from Antwerp not to attract attention. It seemed like an ideal landing point and the others agreed. He hopes they are right.

A light glows briefly on the beach as a lantern is uncovered and waved back and forth. Then it disappears.

"Lars," Willem murmurs.

"I hope so," Arbuckle says.

Frost turns his head toward the beach, but his ears and nose cannot reach that far, Willem thinks.

The little sloop anchors as close as it can to the beach and Arbuckle motions to Willem to remain on board while he and a handful of men, armed with sword and musket, row ashore in the longboat.

All must be in order, for after a brief consultation with the figure on the beach, the longboat returns and Willem, Frost, Jack, and Héloïse climb on board and are rowed ashore.

More longboats start the job of ferrying the rest of the British soldiers and Willem thinks how daring this is. Landing a small army under the very noses of the French.

He climbs out of the longboat in the shallows, stumbling and almost falling, clutching desperately at the side of the boat while his other hand lifts his satchel and its all-important contents as high as he can. The satchel cannot get wet, no matter what.

"Willem!" A big voice sounds in front of him and he looks up to see the huge man, Sofie's son, Lars. Lars has a rope in one hand, looped through the reins of a number of horses. He grabs Willem with his other arm and crushes him in a hug that squeezes all the air from his lungs.

"It is good to see you, Willem," Lars says. "And good to see someone taking the fight to the French, instead of the other way around."

"It is a small thing we do," Willem says.

"But one that could have great consequence," Lars says.

"These are all the horses you have?" Willem asks. There are clearly not enough for all the men.

Lars laughs. "The rest are on a farm not far from here. I am afraid your men will have to march for an hour or so. But that is of little importance. I have news for you. It is of great consequence, if it is true."

"What news is this?" Willem asks,

"You should prepare yourself," Lars says with a great smile.

"I am as prepared as I need to be," Willem says, eyeing the big man curiously. "What is this news?"

"That your father still lives," Lars says.

Willem finds himself sitting on the sand. The collapse is unintentional; all energy seems suddenly drained from his body. This cannot be true. He has lived most of his life with the knowledge of his father's death. And yet . . .

Even the faintest hope that his father could be alive fills him with an excitement that he struggles to control. It cannot be true. And to raise his hopes only to have them destroyed once again would be worse than knowing his father is dead.

"I warned you," Lars says, extending a hand and pulling Willem back to his feet.

"Who told you this news?" Willem asks, wondering if it could possibly be true.

"Your friend, who escaped with you through the Ruien," Lars says.

There is a sharp intake of breath from Héloïse and a sudden stillness among the others.

"François?" Willem asks.

"The same," Lars says.

"François is no friend of mine," Willem says, his mind whirling. "This news is a lie."

"But he was with you when you escaped from the French," Lars says, narrowing his eyes.

"And then he betrayed us!" Willem cries. "François works for the French. But why would he come to you with this news, if it is even true?"

Héloïse has been looking around at the forest that surrounds them. Her every sense seems alert.

"Run!" she screams.

"It is a trap!" Lars curses loudly in Dutch. "Go, now! Back to the boat."

From somewhere unseen in the darkness, perhaps from the other side of the dike, comes a long, low, undulating roar, loud enough to shake dew from the leaves of the trees that surround them and to make horses rear and paw the air with their hooves.

"Too late," Frost says.

The unmistakable sound of a roaring battlesaur is followed by the sound of French trumpets.

Willem backs away toward the shore, unwilling to turn and thus take his eyes off the dark tree line. Frost is next to him with Jack beside him, guiding him as they move swiftly toward the boats.

Héloïse ignores Lars's instructions and Willem sees her heading to the side, toward the trees. That is where she will feel safe, he knows.

"Form a line! Form a line!" Arbuckle shouts, and the British soldiers are quick to form up into two rows, one behind the other, the front row kneeling.

"Fix bayonets," Arbuckle shouts.

McConnell is nowhere to be seen, but a glance behind reveals him already climbing up over the side of the boat, trying to push it off with one foot. It is too heavy for him, too firmly wedged onto the sand. Big Joe joins him, heaving on the front of the boat to dislodge it.

Whatever is coming is still unseen, hidden behind the high earthen mound of the dike.

Willem reaches into his satchel and extracts a stubby thunder-cloud cylinder, then another. He holds them close to his chest as he backs away toward the shore, unwilling to take his eyes off the dike. He hopes the British soldiers remember their training.

"Keep moving," Lars says softly, stepping in front of them. He releases the reins of the horses and slaps one of them on the rump. The horse too has heard the roar of the battlesaur and needs no further encouragement. It tosses its head and takes off toward the trees. The other horses quickly follow.

Lars produces a heavy club from somewhere within his coat and swings it from side to side. Willem thinks a wooden stick will be scant protection against what comes from behind the dike.

"Hold there," a voice shouts in French-accented English.

Now he sees the saur. His first glimpse of a real French battle-saur, not the wooden replicas at Woolwich, nor the gentle herbi-saurs that were slaughtered for practice.

The head of the creature appears above the dike, illuminated by the dawning sky.

It is not as large as the saur that attacked his village so many months ago, but it seems even more terrifying. Its eyes are deep-set and hooded. Its snout shorter and thicker than that of the crocodile-like creature of Gaillemarde. Its teeth are just as long and its skin is the same ridged hide that the men of the village hacked to pieces to hide the carcass of the beast.

A row of lights now appears along the top of the dike, like a string of glowing pearls. These are not jewels, however, but flaming torches, gleaming off the shiny armor of a line of French cuirassiers. In front of them appear soldiers on foot, low dark shapes before them, and now comes a sound that has given Willem many nightmares since his escape from Antwerp: the rattling spines and whispering grunts of demonsaurs.

Willem stops backing away as the French horses begin to move, descending the steep slope of the dike toward the wide clearing that is the boat landing.

"Get out of here, Willem," Lars shouts.

Willem shakes his head.

At the boat, Big Joe and McConnell wait, McConnell impatiently. Willem suspects he would have taken off by himself if he could have managed the longboat alone. The other saur-slayers have formed a semicircle in front of them, weapons at the ready, defending the boat landing.

"Hold!" the French voice shouts.

The cavalry wait at the foot of the dike. The battlesaur descends behind them. The French horses are well trained, Willem thinks, not to panic and flee. The flames of the torches now glint off the blades of sabers.

The French are within range of the British muskets, yet Arbuckle does not give the order to fire. Instead he says, "Protect the boy. All of you. With your life."

It takes Willem a moment to realize that "the boy" is him, and that all of these men have just been ordered to give up their lives, if necessary, for his. It is an uncomfortable feeling, yet there is nothing he can say or do. That is the order.

"Remember the magic," he calls out to Arbuckle, who nods.

He has not finished speaking when the French cuirassiers begin their charge, silhouetted in the glow of the flaming torches of the riders behind them.

In front of them, unleashed, race the evil, chilling shapes of the demonsaurs.

Willem twists the end of one of his cylinders, hearing the strike of the flint inside. He shuts his eyes and aims it high in the air, over the heads of the line of British troops. There is a sharp crack inside as a small gunpowder charge explodes and suddenly the air in front of them is filled with a fine-grained powder, finer than the finest flour. He drops the cylinder, now hot to the touch, and does the same with the second one, intensifying the soft, billowing cloud in front of the charging demonsaurs and cavalry.

"Now!" he shouts.

The British soldiers raise one arm, covering their eyes with their forearms. Willem is so busy watching that he forgets to do the same. Just in time he shuts his eyes as tightly as he can.

The first of the burning torches touches the edge of the cloud of drifting powder and as it does the sky explodes.

A bright flash, intense enough to make the insides of his eyelids glow bright red is followed by the sound of horses shying, rearing, and colliding.

He has closed his eyes only for a second but when he reopens them the air is on fire, terrifying the French horses and battlesaurs alike. A thick pall of pungent, white smoke is spreading, filling the clearing and filtering into the trees of the surrounding forest, hemmed in by the wall of the dike behind.

All is smoke and flames and confusion.

Now the muskets of the British soldiers sound and he hears the screams of horses and the shrieks of demonsaurs. It is the only volley. There is no time for the soldiers to reload. Instead he sees them present their bayonets at the men, horses, and demonic beasts that still tear through the thick smoke toward them.

As the smoke curls around him he drops to his hands and knees and scrambles on all fours like a dragonrat. The smoke is thinner at ground level, and he can see the legs of men and horses, their bodies ghostly shapes above.

A horse thunders toward him, but he senses its presence by the sound and sees its legs in time to dodge out of its way. The rider sees him at the last moment and stabs at him, but misses.

Above him now, towering over the men and horses, is the battlesaur. There is no time to try to mesmerize it. No time to thrust his hand into the small sack of pepper he carries. Time only to die, and yet he does not. The beast is distracted by a British soldier backing away from a cuirassier. Its head dips and for a moment the smoke turns red.

Willem runs past the battlesaur, out of its sight. He hears pistol shots, and more sounds of men and horses colliding. The darkness and smoke have turned the clearing into a chaotic circus. There are grunts, shouts, and screams. The constant rattle of demonsaur spines. It is a maelstrom of moving bodies and swirling smoke and in the midst of it somewhere is the huge dinosaur.

Through a momentary gap in the white curtain Willem sees Lars swinging his heavy club the way a woodsman swings his ax. A *thwack* is followed by the thud of a soldier hitting the ground, the clang of his armor. Then comes another *thwack* and Willem knows there is one less French soldier to worry about.

More pistol shots are followed by the scream of an injured horse. In the darkness, smoke, and confusion Willem thinks the soldiers are as much danger to themselves as to others. Always he hears the *thwack, thwack, thwack* of Lars's wooden club.

He thinks he sees a gap in the smoke in the direction of the trees and scrambles toward it only to find himself rolling over the ground, barely registering the sudden jarring pain in his right side, and above him is a French cuirassier, high in his saddle, pistol raised, aimed directly at Willem's chest. There is no time even to crawl backward and Willem can see, or thinks he sees, the man's finger move slightly on the trigger, then comes the flash of the muzzle, but the shot is wild, the pistol tumbling through the air as the man flies sideways off his horse and a dim shape moves over him.

The Frenchman convulses, then lies still, and the dim shape turns, becoming Arbuckle, a dark-dripping dagger in his hand. He hauls Willem back to his feet without a word, crouching low, pulling him along with him, and a second or so later they are moving swiftly along the base of the dike.

A harsh whisper comes from a clump of low bushes beside them. "Willem!"

They stop and Frost emerges, a French pistol in his hand. Willem cannot imagine how he got it, then remembers that in the absence of sight, Frost sees more clearly than most men.

Shouts, shots, and the cries of horses continue behind them as the three stumble as quietly as they can up the side of the dike. The earth of the dike is hard, claylike, and only soft grass grows on it. It is steep, but they are up and over it quickly.

On this side Willem can see the thatched roofs of a small hamlet, Krabbendijke. A windmill lies beyond that, its arms still and silent in the cool morning air.

"What about the others?" Willem gasps as they slither down the far side of the dike. Big Joe, Gilbert, McConnell, Smythe,

Weiner, and Patrick. His precious saur-slayers. Alive or dead? And what about Jack?

Héloïse does not concern him. He saw her reach the trees and in the forest she is a match for anyone.

"Those that can will find their own way to the rendezvous point," Arbuckle says. "There is nothing we can do for them."

"He is right," Frost says. "We will be lucky to get out of here ourselves. We must not stop. Not for anything. We must—"

He looks quickly back at the earthen mound of the dike.

"Take cover!" he cries, but it is too late. Willem hears the whinny of a horse and a moment later four cuirassiers charge up and over the dike, encircling them.

"Run!" Arbuckle shouts, drawing his dagger.

Willem grabs Frost's arm and darts for a hedge-lined lane that leads to the hamlet.

One of the soldiers spurs his horse toward Arbuckle while the others move to cut Willem off.

What happens next happens so fast that Willem is barely aware of it. The horseman raises his saber high and strikes down at Arbuckle, but the thin metal blade slices open only the air. Arbuckle has shifted like a breath of wind out of the path of the blade. He grasps hold of the man's sword arm and pulls himself up. The next thing, he is seated on the horse behind the soldier and there is a spray of blood before the Frenchman topples sideways, his saber now in Arbuckle's hand.

The other three cuirassiers wheel their horses around to face this new threat.

Willem grips Frost's collar and runs into the lane. They reach a crossroads and Willem glances back to see Arbuckle trapped in the center of a whirl of blades, then they round the corner and Frost and Willem are on their own.

The smooth dirt of the lane makes for fast going and the hedge-rows on either side are high enough to conceal them from the battle behind. They run, turning often, into a maze of narrow lanes. To stay on an eastern heading Willem keeps an eye on the windmill, the brooding shape of which is ever-present above the hedges.

They hear the sound of hooves in a nearby lane and press themselves into the hedge, but the horseman passes them without detecting their presence.

"Slowly," Frost says. "Slowly and silently from now on. They will only find us from our sounds."

He perks his ears up again, listening intently.

Willem does too, and somewhere in the lanes around them he hears the rattle of a demonsaur. It is close.

"This way," Frost whispers, leading Willem to the left. "We must put as much distance between us and that . . . thing . . . as we can."

They have just reached a lane that leads directly to the wind-mill when from behind them they hear the rattle of spines.

How it has found them, Willem does not know. It paces slowly toward them, making its harsh, whispered growl.

Willem grabs Frost's arm to guide him and they sprint away from the demonsaur, toward the bulk of the windmill.

"There's a windmill," Willem says, remembering that Frost cannot see it.

"Where is the door?" Frost asks.

"I can't see—yes!" Willem cries as a heavy wooden door comes into view at the base of the mill. If it is locked, they are lost. He risks a glance behind to see the demonsaur almost upon them.

They are in luck: the door is slightly ajar. He hits it with his shoulder and it is like hitting a rock wall, but the door opens and he stumbles through, sprawling across the dirt floor inside.

The door! He spins around, scrambling back to his feet to see that Frost has already thrown his weight against the bulky door. It is almost shut when there is a crash and Frost flies backward, but now Willem is there, putting all his weight against the door.

Frost recovers and they have the door nearly shut when a skeletal black hand reaches around, clawing at Willem's side. It snags on the cloth of his tunic, tearing it as he pulls away.

"Again!" Frost cries, and they both throw their weight once more against the door. The heavy door slams onto the wrist of the creature and there is a shriek of pain from outside. Again they slam it shut and there is a crack from the wrist but the creature does not withdraw its hand. Slowly the door starts to open despite all their efforts.

For a moment it seems as though they are winning, but it is just the creature drawing back. It slams into the door with all its weight and the door shoots open, sending Willem and Frost flying. Willem lands on a length of wood and picks it up, knowing how pathetic and useless it will be against the demonsaur.

Now it is inside, a snarl turning its mouth into an almost-human smirk. Willem backs away again and the creature follows, crouching back, then springing forward.

As it leaps there is the sound of a gunshot and the beast convulses in midair. Willem falls backward and rolls to one side as it lands right where he was standing. It reaches out its claws toward him, but feebly, and there is a spreading pool of black blood beneath it.

A French soldier stands in the doorway. A smoking pistol in one hand, a saber in the other.

"Come this way," he says. "And quickly."

Willem looks around desperately for a way to escape but the mill is a trap. He and Frost have nowhere farther to run.

"Come this way," the Frenchman says, only his accent is of the Netherlands, not of France. "If you want to live."

LIFE AND DEATH IN A MEAT CART

The boy lies in the reeds under the bridge, one eye closed, the other open, one leg in the water, moving back and forth in the current as though toe-fishing. Jack is tempted to try to close the other eye, but does not want to touch the body. Not because the boy is dead, but because it was Jack who killed him.

The boy was tall and strong, a little like Jack. Were it not for a different uniform and language it might have been Jack. Was this boy also a good lad? Jack weeps silently in the shadow of the bridge as the boots of the French soldiers march past on the road above.

The *clank* of chains comes from the road, then a curse, in English. It is McConnell's voice. Jack risks a look, parting the long reeds at the base of the bridge.

He sees prisoners in a caged wagon being led down the road by French officers on horseback. He looks to see if Frost or Willem is among them, but cannot tell.

A cart follows, on it a number of bodies in French uniforms.

Jack sits. He thinks. What should he do? The situation is confusing and his brain is as foggy as the night. What would Willem do? He would know what to do, but Jack is not as clever as Willem. He thinks of the time when they escaped from the village on the hospital wagon, Willem wearing the uniform of a nurse. That was the sort of thing that Willem would think of.

And that gives him his answer.

With whispered apologies to the dead boy, Jack strips him of his uniform. He undresses and folds his clothes, leaving them in a neat pile near the bridge support. He dons the French soldier's uniform, which, although small, fits closely enough.

He stares for a moment at the body, clad only in underclothes. *It is undignified*, he thinks.

He drags the young Frenchman up out of the water and dresses him in his own clothes, before laying him flat on the bank beneath the bridge, folding his arms across his chest.

He bids a silent farewell to the young dead man and slips quietly out from under the bridge, staying off the road, in the dark embrace of the ditch.

He moves quickly, but even so it is not until the column stops for a while at a crossroads that he is able to catch up with the cart. The soldiers are making cooking fires, probably their first meal of the day. They are relaxed and do not see Jack as he creeps up out of the ditch and crawls across the dark ground toward the cart.

When he is confident that no soldiers are looking in his direction, he clambers quickly up onto the cart. He is immediately immersed in a warm fug of urine, feces, and blood.

The bodies of the soldiers piled in the cart are still warm, evidence that in each of them a heart was beating only a short time ago. Most of the soldiers are French, but as he scans the faces Jack is shocked to find Lieutenant Patrick, the winner of the trojansaur race. His eyes are open but sightless. Jack tries to close them but they are frozen open. Next to Patrick, on his side, is Lieutenant Weiner, who had the constant smile. He is still smiling, a frozen rictus baring his teeth in a horrific grin. Jack keeps looking, lifting arms and legs and digging around to find more faces, eventually coming across Smythe. He sits back, exhausted. He is unsure whether he is happy or sad. Sad to see such a waste of such fine gentlemen. Happy because he cannot find Lieutenant Frost or Willem. Or Lieutenants Hoyes and Gilbert. Or Captain Arbuckle.

Voices sound nearby and footsteps are heading in his direction.

He lies flat and pulls himself forward over skin tacky with congealing blood. He rolls a body to one side and slides beneath it for concealment.

He finds himself face-to-face with another body, one not in French uniform. A huge head and a walrus mustache.

It is the big man, Lars.

There is a shouted order. Horses whinny. The cart creaks and begins to move. Jack and Lars stare at each other, in life and death in a meat cart full of dead soldiers.

Jack finds he no longer feels sorry for the French boy under the bridge.

SECRET REUNION

In the forest the lightening sky is only a distant thought, flitting occasionally between the branches. But the French lieutenant clearly knows the ways of this forest. He leads Willem and Frost through paths that do not look like paths, across streams, always knowing the best place to ford. Emerging finally onto a country lane with low stone walls. There they move slowly, not wanting to attract attention.

A few minutes down the road they come to an old, stone farm cottage. The lieutenant gestures they should enter, and it is with trepidation and reluctance that Willem pushes open the heavy, rough-sawn wooden door.

It is dark inside and when the door shuts behind them it is pitch-black.

Willem thinks he can hear breathing. A slightly labored wheeze.

"Who are you, old woman?" Frost asks, but as soon as he asks, Willem knows.

Sofie is there.

A flint sparks and a candle sputters into light, revealing a well-lined face shrouded by a black hood. Her clothing also is black, down to the lacy gloves that appear in the light of the candle, then withdraw into the darkness.

"Sofie," Willem says. "I am so sorry."

"You have nothing to be sorry for," Sofie says. "The fault was ours."

"It was François," Willem says.

"I do not understand what he does," Sofie says.

"He reveres Napoléon," Willem says. "François murdered his own cousin and tried to hand us to the French. We were lucky to escape him. Now I fear for Lars, thanks to our betrayer."

Sofie smiles. "Lars has been in worse scrapes than this. He is big, strong, and cunning. Do not fear for my boy."

"What now?" Frost asks.

"We travel from here to another farmhouse, farther north, where they will not think of looking for you. If you wish to return to England, we will try to arrange it in a few weeks when the fuss has died down."

"No," Willem says. "I did not come here to hide out in a farmhouse. My mother and my friend are prisoners of the French and are at risk of execution every day. I must find a way to rescue them." He pauses and thinks for a moment. "Perhaps also my father."

"I would not count on that news," Sofie says. "The information is only as good as its source."

"I know," Willem says. "But even so I cannot rest until I know."

"And my mission is not yet over," Frost says. "I must reach the Prussian Army at Waterloo on a matter of great importance."

"In both cases, I fear you face insurmountable challenges," Sofie says. "The offer stands."

"I must go," Willem says.

"And I will not safeguard my own life at the expense of others'," Frost says.

"Very gallantly spoken," Sofie says. "Such is the valor—and the foolishness—of youth."

"We escaped from the French ambush," Frost says. "The others may have escaped also. If they get to Calais and carry out their mission, to kill Napoléon's battlesaurs, what good will that be if Blücher and his army do not then arrive?"

"Indeed," Sofie says.

"Your concern is your mission," Willem says. "But mine is different."

"I understand," Frost says. "Your mother and Cosette are of course your first concern. Madame, I must travel to Waterloo. Might I ask your man to guide me there? As you can see, I would not be able to travel there alone."

Sofie shakes her head. "I apologize, young man, but Lieutenant Franke here has already been absent too long from his unit. He can use the confusion of the ambush as an excuse, but not for much longer. I would not wish to jeopardize his position in the French Army. It is too valuable to us."

"I understand," Frost says. "Then, Willem, I must prevail on you. Help me get to Blücher and deliver my message. After that we will together travel to the rendezvous point to see who else has made it, and then to the Sonian. I will do what I can to assist you in the rescue of your loved ones."

"I will do it," Willem says. "I hope we are not alone when we get to—"

Sofie's voice cuts over his. "I do not wish to know your rendezvous point. What I do not know, I cannot reveal."

"But you will help?" Willem asks.

She nods slowly. "I will give you horses. And French uniforms."

"To be caught in a French uniform is certain death," Frost says. "We would be shot as spies."

Sofie leans forward and looks at him. The flicker of the low candle makes shadowy crevices of the lines on her face. "For you and Willem, to be caught at all is to be executed. The uniform makes no difference."

"This is true," Frost acknowledges.

"Then leave immediately," she says. "Lieutenant Franke will

take you as far as the main road. After that you will be on your own. We must not know which direction you take."

"What about you?" Willem asks. "If Lars has been captured, then your life also is in danger."

"This wily old magician still has a few tricks up her sleeve," Sofie says.

A MAN OF GOD

François has a perch high in a leafy tree, from where he can see most of the comings and goings of the abbey. He has built himself a platform on which to sleep and strung unobtrusive ropes to neighboring trees that let him move around the forest without being seen by those on the ground.

Today he is sharing his perch with a bellsaur, a good-natured tree-dwelling saur that is harmless unless provoked. François knows not to provoke it.

He rubs absently at the scar on his head. He does not remember getting the scar. His cousin Jean told him it was from his own ax as they leaped off a waterfall to escape a firebird. He pretended he remembered, but he didn't. However, he remembers his cousin. More like a brother. It was a tragedy that Jean didn't have the faith, the belief in God and in Napoléon. That his sinning led him to the wrong path. It was an even greater tragedy that it was François who had to be the one to relieve Jean of his burden of sin, and help him on his path to heaven.

Cosette emerges from the gates and heads for the rock pool. François watches her walk for a moment, admiring the lithe confidence of her gait and the proud angle of her head.

After checking that she is not followed, he slithers along one of his rope walks to a different tree. There are two ropes, a low one to stand on and a high one for his hands. It was his uncle who taught him this. The memory of his uncle brings a smile until he remembers he is dead, and who killed him.

Thibault.

A quick climb down and he emerges from the trees just as Cosette reaches the pool.

"François," she says.

There is a depth of meaning in her voice. A raw emotion, and he wants to think that it is happiness at seeing him, he so wants to believe that, but there are many things that could cause that ragged edge to her voice and that sudden shortness of breath. Only time will tell if the heavens have more in store for the two of them.

"Cosette," he says graciously, with just the right touch of formality.

"Did you meet Sofie?"

"I did, but she could not help," François says. "I gave her the message regardless, in the hope that she will be able to pass it on."

"You were careful? Nobody saw you?" She looks nervous.

"Nobody," François says. This is true. Nobody saw him go to the old lady's house. It is not the whole truth, but at least it is not a lie.

Cosette breathes out slowly. "It was dangerous. It was stupid of me to ask you to perform this task. I am sorry."

"The smallest task for you brings me the greatest pleasure," François says, and immediately regrets it. Has he overstated things? Too much, too soon? It seems that he might have.

"Willem is my one true love," Cosette says, and her words cut like knives. "If my actions have put him in danger, I could not forgive myself."

"I was extremely careful," François says. "I would not want harm to come to him."

This, finally, is an outright lie, and he chastens himself for it, but he could not avoid it. More and more he is hoping that Willem has been killed and thus removed from the affections of the beautiful creature who stands before him. If that is God's will, if it is God's will that François and Cosette should be together, then surely He would ensure that Willem met a quick and painless end.

"And, besides, if Willem was captured or killed, Napoléon would have us executed," Cosette says.

François is shocked. Why would she say such a thing?

"That is not true," François says. "Napoléon is a man of God. A man sent by God. You speak perhaps of the devil, Thibault."

"I speak of Napoléon," Cosette says. "That is what I have heard. When he no longer needs us, he will have us killed. It is more important than ever for us to get away."

François shakes his head. She must be confused. Napoléon would not do such a thing. She is wrong, but he elects not to argue with her. Let her find out in good time what a godly man Napoléon really is.

"Come with me now," François says.

"I cannot—I will not leave the others," Cosette says.

François nods. "If you can find a way to get all three of you outside the main gate, I will get you to safety. Can you do that?"

"I can try," Cosette says.

THE ROAD TO CALAIS

Through a narrow gap between a dead man's arm and a dead man's leg, Jack sees the gates of a walled city slide past the cart. There are no signs, but he has heard the French soldiers speak of Calais more than once.

The trip has taken most of two days and he has not eaten in that time. He has toileted just once, at night, climbing down off the cart when the French soldiers were asleep. He tried to get to the caged wagon with the prisoners more than once, but there were always guards stationed around it.

He needs to urinate now, and does so, without shifting his position. The cart already carries the stench of excrement; a little more will make no difference.

The warmth of it is strangely comforting in the fabric of his trousers.

He has shifted around so that he won't have to face Lars's cold, sightless eyes. There is something accusatory in that gaze, and Jack feels responsible for the big man's death, although he does not know why.

It is easier to turn the other way and stare at the back of a balding Frenchman's head than to face those eyes.

They finally come to a halt outside a high-walled courtyard with a heavy, barred door. The clanking of chains comes from the front of the column and he hears McConnell's voice swearing at someone.

He eases himself over the back of the meat cart and slips into a shadowy doorway. He waits until the rest of the column moves off, then crosses the road to a stable where a pair of gray horses eye him incuriously as he nestles in the pile of straw between them, keeping an eye on the building across the street. It has high walls and barred windows. A prison.

It is warm in the straw and despite his best intentions, after being awake constantly for two days, he sleeps.

THE DEVIL'S RETURN

Thibault climbs carefully down the side of the French schooner into the unsteady belly of the flat-bottomed boat that has been waiting for him. He does it with seeming ease, despite having only one hand to grasp the rope netting.

It is not easy, but he will not look weak or crippled in front of others.

The shores of Berck are wide and flat, and only the flat-bottomed fishing boats of the village are shallow enough to navigate them.

The small, fast schooner that has brought him this far raises its sails the moment he is aboard the smaller boat. The schooner escapes to the north.

Napoléon may own the land, but the Royal Navy owns the sea, and the schooner's captain does not want to be trapped against the Berck shallows should a British warship appear.

The fishing vessel slaps and wallows in the wake of the schooner and Thibault sits, holding on to the seat, although the boat's master continues to stand, seemingly unaffected by the rocking. He is a surprisingly young man with skin brown from the sun and lined with salt from the sea spray. He does not look at Thibault. Not once.

The boat itself smells so strongly of fish, old and new, that Thibault has to turn his head to the side, toward the breeze, to be able to breathe.

The fisherman raises a tall sail and the boat is quickly tugged in the direction of the shore.

Along the shore Thibault sees carts lined up, waiting to receive today's catch from the school of boats, just like this one, that dot the sea off the coast.

When the flat bottom of the boat slides softly onto sand, Thibault climbs over the prow onto the shore, to avoid wetting his boots. He turns and tosses a small pouch of coins to the fisherman, who nods gratitude, still without looking at Thibault. He will probably make the sign of the cross, Thibault thinks, as soon as his back is turned.

A soldier is waiting with two horses on the beach. Evidence that his carrier pigeon message was received. The stench from the fishcarts is worse than that of the boat, and Thibault is glad to mount and follow the young officer across the hard sand up toward the land.

He smiles when they reach the road and head north. Ireland is taken. The invasion of Britain is about to begin.

He spurs his horse on, the lieutenant following close behind. It is a four-hour ride to Calais.

CONFUSION

"I have done everything you have asked, have I not?" François asks.

He has met Baston on the outskirts of Brussels. They ride together as if they're old friends taking the air. Baston's men ride a few paces behind them, just out of earshot.

"You have been a diligent and faithful servant of Napoléon," Baston says.

"And I have helped you capture Willem," François says.

"He eludes us as yet," Baston says. "But not for long."

"Then you have no longer any need for the prisoners you hold. Release them to me. I will take them far from here."

"Yes, you are right, François," Baston says. "When Willem is captured we will no longer have a need to keep the prisoners. But I will not release them to you. I cannot. I am under strict orders."

"What will happen to them?" François asks.

"That is military business, and not yours," Baston says.

"You are under strict orders," François says, "from General Thibault?"

Baston's face changes suddenly and he seems to be watching François closely. He chooses his words carefully. "My orders do not come from General Thibault. They are from a much higher authority."

"From Napoléon?" François asks.

Baston nods.

François lowers his eyes, turning away in case any of his private thoughts betray him and display on his face. Baston means to kill the prisoners. That is clear. The old man he does not care about, but the others are women. Innocents. Willem's mother, who has always been good to him, and the beautiful Cosette. God would not condone the slaughter of these two. But Napoléon is the instrument of God.

It does not make sense.

THE GOD OF WAR

The sun has long since dropped behind the stone walls of the prison, yet Jack waits, watching the deepening sky as the hard shadows of the buildings soften and darken. When the twilight ocher has faded and the stars have made their appearance, he slips quietly out the stable door.

He was not bothered during the day. His stall remained empty, and the stable workers did not see him in the rear corner, covered in straw. They did come in several times to attend to one of the horses, a small gray Arabian that bears the scars of battle. This horse belongs to someone important, Jack feels, and he wonders if it is the famous Marengo, the steed of Napoléon himself. He examines the ornate leather saddle on the bar at the front of the stall and decides that it probably is.

The street outside the prison is quiet. It is not a main thoroughfare. At this time, when most people are in their beds or at their dinners, it is deserted. Jack picks up a rock from near the stable door. Palm sized, it is smooth like a river stone. He pockets it as he sees an empty wine bottle lying in the gutter. He takes the bottle and fills it with water from the horse trough. He stoppers it with clay scraped from the side of the road, pressing it into the neck until it is as watertight as he can make it. He swings it in his hand, feeling the weight, then with a quick glance up and down the lane, crosses to the outer wall of the prison.

* * *

Inside the prison walls, General Marc Thibault sits in a chair in the corner of a room and watches the young British lieutenant who squirms under his one-eyed gaze.

"You are alive only by my grace," Thibault says at last. "Spies are to be executed immediately on capture."

"I am no spy," the lieutenant says. "I am a soldier on a soldier's mission."

"You wear a French uniform," Thibault says. "That makes you a spy."

"I am no spy," the lieutenant says, spitting on the ground in front of him.

Thibault stares at the spittle for a moment before continuing.

"A soldier," he says.

"I am Lieutenant Hew McConnell," the lieutenant says. "A soldier in the Fifth Artillery and the son of a nobleman."

"A soldier and a nobleman," Thibault says. He smiles, and it is clear that the British lieutenant misinterprets the reason for it.

"My father is Lord Byron McConnell of Inverness," McConnell says. "He will pay a handsome reward for my return."

"Yes, soldiers can be ransomed," Thibault says evenly. "But spies cannot. If you are a soldier, you must be a brave one, to be on so dangerous a mission."

"There is none braver," McConnell says, then pales as he realizes the trap he has fallen into.

"Convince me, then," Thibault says. "Tell me of your mission."

"I will not, sir," McConnell says.

"The mission is already a failure," Thibault says. "We captured or killed all of your men. What harm can it do to reveal details of a mission that will no longer take place?"

"I am a man of honor," McConnell says. "Surely you would not expect me to talk to the enemy."

"A spy has no honor," Thibault says.

"I am no spy," McConnell says.

"This becomes repetitive," Thibault says, standing and pacing. "There are two very simple possibilities in front of us. Either you are a soldier, which you can prove by revealing details of your mission, or you are a spy. I will give you exactly five seconds to choose which you are. At the end of the five seconds, if I have had no response, I will take you for a spy and have you shot. One."

"That is not enough time—"

"Two," Thibault says.

"I will tell you," McConnell says, his eyes darting desperately around the room as if looking for a means of escape. "I am no spy. But I want a promise that I will be ransomed back to my father."

"Of course," Thibault says, thinking how easy it is to lie to a desperate man. He crosses to a large table set against one wall and pulls back a cloth, revealing six long rockets. "You can start by telling me about these."

"They are rockets," McConnell says.

"I can see that," Thibault says.

"They are flare rockets," McConnell says. "Different colors. For signaling."

"Signaling what?" Thibault asks.

McConnell hesitates.

"Three seconds," Thibault says.

"Different colors mean different things," McConnell says.

"Of course," Thibault says.

"The yellow rocket was to signal that the battlesaurs were dead," McConnell says.

"The battlesaurs?" Thibault asks, holding in check a sudden surge of anger. "What battlesaurs?"

"Here in Calais," McConnell says.

"You were to infiltrate our camp and murder my saurs?" Thibault asks. "A foolish mission for foolish men."

"A desperate mission for desperate men," McConnell says.

"Who were you to signal?" Thibault asks.

McConnell sits mutely.

"Blücher," Thibault says. From the expression on McConnell's face he can see that he is right.

He smiles tightly. He looks forward to seeing Napoléon's reaction to this news.

At the rear of the prison is an open courtyard where prison carriages stop to unload. Jack staggers into it as if drunk. He has seen many drunk people and has no difficulty in copying their loose, graceless movements.

A guard leans against the wall by the rear door of the prison. He straightens as Jack wanders clumsily inside, and calls out something to Jack in French.

Jack smiles and waves the wine bottle at him.

The guard calls out again, angrily waving his musket at Jack.

Jack pretends not to hear and wanders over to the wall of the courtyard, making as if to urinate. He steadies himself with one hand on the wall, the other clutching the wine bottle tightly. He hears footsteps and more angry French, then suddenly there is a hand on his shoulder, twisting him around.

Jack spins in that direction, the wine bottle coming up as he turns, smashing into the Frenchman's temple. The bottle does not break, but the man's head does, blood spurting as he drops, his eyes rolling back.

Jack drops to one knee, a fist raised above the man's head, but he does not move. After a moment Jack relaxes.

The guard's uniform is similar to his, but with a different jacket and helmet. Jack quickly strips off the unconscious soldier's jacket and replaces his own. The helmet follows. He crosses to the door of the prison and tries it, but it is locked. Returning to the guard, he searches him for keys but finds none.

After a moment of thinking, he raises his fist and raps loudly on the wooden door. Footsteps sound inside and there comes the sound of a key in the lock.

The door opens and another guard peers out, confused to find Jack standing there. Jack waits only to check if there are other guards behind this one before the bottle again does its work.

The guard, with his mouth still framed in the beginning of a question, sinks to his knees before toppling to the floor.

This time the bottle has shattered and the sound of the glass on the floor seems like thunder to Jack, but there are no shouts of alarm, no running bootsteps.

When he is convinced that all is quiet, he closes and locks the door behind him, pocketing the key.

He is in a short corridor that joins a larger, longer corridor. A door is open halfway along, and through it he can hear voices, laughter, and the sound of glasses. The French troops are enjoying a meal and wine.

Without looking in he walks steadily, but as quietly as he can, down the corridor. He passes the open door without alarm.

The walls are made of rough-cut stone blocks, and lit only by lanterns every few paces.

This corridor leads to yet another. Glancing one way, he sees a number of guards and large doors that he presumes are the main prison entrance. The other way, presumably, leads to the cells.

There are footsteps now from that direction and a man approaches. Unable to avoid being seen, Jack puts his back to the man and raises the glass of the nearest lantern, as if checking the wick. This takes a moment, then he moves to the next lantern.

Now the man emerges from shadows into the light and it is all Jack can do not to run from the place. He barely manages to stop his knees from shaking so hard that he would fall to the ground.

The man is grotesque, a hideous, deformed, blackened thing, surely the devil that the rumors speak of. But now as the figure draws closer, Jack sees that it is not the devil. It is a man, and one Jack has met before, in the tunnels of the Antwerp sewers. It is Napoléon's general Thibault. But not as he was then. Part of one arm is gone and his skin is blackened and blotchy. His face has been mauled and scarred, and one eye is missing.

Jack clamps his lips together to prevent himself from crying out.

Thibault glances at him incuriously as he passes, a tight smile playing on his lips, his mind clearly on other things.

Only after he has passed does Jack step into the main corridor and walk quickly in the opposite direction from Thibault. Toward the cells.

Footsteps sound in the side corridor and he ducks through an open doorway into a darkened room. In it are a table and chairs. There are bloodstains on the floor and on the walls. Rusty iron shackles hang from the wall in a number of places. Jack does not like this place.

The footsteps outside draw closer, and there is a constant buzz of conversation. Jack cannot understand a word of it, and he hopes they do not intend to use the room he is hiding in. He has no weapon left but the stone. He has the guard's pistol, but he dares not use that for fear of attracting attention.

The voices stop, almost at the door, and the conversation

continues. Jack shivers in the darkness, staring at the blood-stained shackles, and waits.

"So the yellow rocket is the signal for Blücher to attack?" Napoléon asks.

"Yes, Emperor," Thibault says.

"To attack me?" Napoléon asks, steam building behind his eyes.

"An outrage," Thibault says.

"Treachery!" Napoléon thunders, kicking at the table before him, which crashes to the floor.

A ceramic box smashes and snuff disperses in a cloud.

"He will withdraw when he does not see the rocket," Thibault says.

"Perhaps," Napoléon says. He stands and paces. His breath seems short, and he stops, resting for a moment with one hand on the arm of his chair. "But even if he withdraws, what is to stop him from returning after my main force crosses the Channel? The man is a traitor. What is to stop him from attacking the re-mainder of my army here in Calais? They will have no battlesaurs to protect them. We take London while he marches on Paris!"

"You think him capable of such betrayal?" Thibault asks.

"I have no doubt about it. Blücher"—Napoléon spits out the name as though it were an insect that had flown into his mouth—"sits with his army on the fields at Waterloo professing loyalty to the empire, but the old warhorse is just biding his time. No, Blücher's army must be destroyed."

"The Prussians are our allies, Emperor," Thibault says.

"We are not allies. Blücher will never be our ally. We will turn this to our advantage. Prepare our armies, then fire the yellow rocket. Let him come. When he does, he will find the wrath of the man whom he betrays. Crush his artillery with my battlesaurs. Smash his army with the fists of my artillery. Surround him. Destroy him. When we are finished, his army will be nothing but bloody scraps on the battlefield and boys crying for their mothers."

"Blücher is no fool," Thibault says. "He will not uproot his army and march it here to Calais in the hope of seeing a yellow rocket."

"True," Napoléon says. "We must give him reason to believe the British infiltrators are still alive. Spread a rumor that they got away. Make it believable. That is sure to lure the old battleax forth."

"You are the god of war," Thibault says.

"And you are my devil," Napoléon says with a sly grin.

Thibault acknowledges the dubious honor with a slight nod of his head. Of course Napoléon would know what the men say about him.

"And here is the best part," Napoléon says. "Then we fire the green rocket. The Royal Navy will depart, believing my army to be engaged in battle, and thus their departure will open the front door to England."

"Genius," Thibault says.

Napoléon paces for a few moments, his hands clasped behind his back.

"Blücher knows of our battlesaurs deep in the Sonian," he says.

"Undoubtedly," Thibault agrees.

"He would not risk an attack if he thought he might face battlesaurs from his rear," Napoléon says.

"You think he plans an assault on the cave?" Thibault asks.

"If not Blücher, then the British," Napoléon says. "It is what I would do."

"I will order extra guards into the cave," Thibault says. "Enough to thwart the most determined assault."

Napoléon does not respond, but continues to pace.

"You are sure of these signals?" he asks. "If it is wrong, my plan will be a disaster."

"The information was gleaned from one of the captured soldiers," Thibault says.

"I will interrogate this soldier myself," Napoléon says. "I want to be sure he speaks the truth."

"He will not talk in the presence of the other soldier," Thibault says.

"Then we must remove him to a different location," Napoléon says.

"Of course." Thibault takes a pair of pistols from the table and places one in his side holster.

"Two pistols?" Napoléon asks.

"They are desperate and dangerous men," Thibault says. "I should not risk the life of my emperor."

As soon as the voices have faded, Jack is moving.

He uses his key to open a heavy iron door that leads into the cell block. Inside is a long row of cells, most of them with the doors standing eerily, rustily open. The cell block looks empty, except for two doors near the end of the corridor, which are shut. Close to those cells a guard sits on a wooden stool. He looks up as Jack approaches. He seems confused, and more than a little concerned. He says something in rapid French.

Jack opens his mouth as if to speak, then dissolves into a fit of coughing, hacking, and spitting, as if unable to get the words out, doubled over so the guard cannot see his face. He takes another few paces forward. The guard rises, reaching for his pistol. Jack coughs more and staggers forward a few more steps, now within range of the other man, who, still uncertain, has drawn his pistol but not cocked it.

Jack swings upward, the heavy stone he found in the street now clasped firmly in his right hand. It connects with the man's chin, knocking his head backward, stunning him but not knocking him out. The guard fumbles with his pistol, drawing back the hammer. Jack grabs his wrist, twisting it away from him, desperate to stop him before a gunshot alerts the whole prison. There is a crack and the man grunts in pain. He grunts again as the stone connects with his temple once, and then another time to make sure. The French soldier lies awkwardly across the cell-block floor.

He does not appear to be breathing. Jack checks for a pulse, but there is none.

He looks up to find Lieutenants McConnell and Gilbert standing at the bars of their cells, staring at him incredulously.

"Jack?" Gilbert asks.

"I think he's dead, sir," Jack says. "He ain't breathing."

"Good for you, Jack," McConnell says.

"I din't mean to kill him, sir," Jack says. "He weren't trying to kill me."

"Take his keys," Gilbert says. "Get us out of here." He stops, thinking. "Move the guard first. Drag him into an empty cell. In case anyone comes in."

Jack runs back to the main door and locks it. He returns and grabs the guard by the ankles, dragging him toward a cell farther down the row.

McConnell starts talking as Jack works.

"Jack, listen to me," he says. "Thibault knows everything. About the rockets, the colors, Blücher, everything. Whatever happens to us, you must get to Gaillemarde, to the rendezvous point. You must warn the others. Do you understand me?"

"Yes, sir," Jack says. He rolls the Frenchman into a corner and tries to make it look as though he is sleeping. He takes the keys from the man's belt. He is about to unlock the cell doors when the door starts to open at the end of the corridor.

He stops, unsure what to do.

"Sit down," Gilbert hisses.

Jack quickly seats himself on the guard's stool.

The door opens and he looks up, unable to stop himself gasping with surprise. There is no British soldier alive who does not know the shape and the face of the man who enters. Napoléon Bonaparte, the French emperor. He is followed by Thibault.

"Stand to attention," McConnell mutters under his breath, and Jack immediately stands, ramrod straight, as if he was being inspected by the Duke of Wellington himself.

He scarcely breathes as the emperor approaches, Thibault a menacing shadow behind him. They stop at McConnell's cell and Thibault says something in French.

Jack freezes, unsure what is being said.

Thibault speaks again, and still Jack does not move.

Both Napoléon and Thibault turn to look at Jack and behind their backs McConnell quickly mimes unlocking a door and points to the lock on his cell.

Jack fumbles with the keys. Fortunately there are only two on the ring, and only one that looks as though it would fit the cell door.

Thibault moves back, putting a little distance between himself and McConnell. He raises his pistol and aims it at McConnell as Jack unlocks the door and steps away.

McConnell steps out, now face-to-face with the French emperor. In English he says, "I'm not telling you anything."

"You don't need to," Thibault says. Then comes the crash of a gunshot, echoing crazily off the walls.

McConnell staggers, grunts, opens his mouth, but collapses to the ground before he can make another sound.

Jack stares in disbelief at the hole in McConnell's chest, just a dark circle on the white breast of his uniform. McConnell seems unable to form words. His lips move but no coherent sounds emerge.

"What the devil are you doing?" Napoléon shouts. "Are you mad? We were to interrogate this man!"

"In fact, that was never my intention," Thibault says calmly. "I have already learned from him everything I need to know."

He draws his second pistol and replaces the first one in the holster. He turns toward Napoléon and again the walls echo with the sound of a shot.

Napoléon stands still, his eyes wide in shock, but the expression is a falsehood. The fact that he is standing is another. He is a man dead on his feet, a bloodied hole in his forehead a clue as to the cause.

For almost a full second he stands, then all the muscles in his body seem to let go at once and he drops into an untidy pile of limbs on the floor.

Blood from his head wound pools and runs, mixing with McConnell's.

Jack stares. Napoléon Bonaparte, the mighty leader, the most powerful man in the world, has been reduced to this. A jumble of bones in a sack of skin, oozing dark red blood.

McConnell's lips are still moving and his eyes follow Thibault as he steps forward and places the still-smoking pistol in McConnell's hand.

"I despise a man who cannot keep his secrets," Thibault says. He takes a paper cartridge from a pocket and begins to reload the gun.

McConnell's eyes meet Jack's and his lips mouth a single word: *Run!*

Jack cannot. He is frozen to the spot, even as Thibault finishes ramming the pistol and the muzzle of the gun turns toward him.

From the corner of his eye he sees McConnell crawl forward on the cell-block floor, his hand curling around Thibault's boot, jerking him off balance as the shot rings out. Even so, it is so close that Jack feels the wind of the musketball as it passes his ear, and the crash of the shot against the stone walls of the chamber is enough to break him out of his rigidity.

"Get out of here, Jack!" Gilbert shouts, and now Jack runs.

WATERLOO

The ride from Antwerp has been largely uneventful for Willem and Frost. They have seen many people, but have not been challenged, just two French officers traveling on horseback. They skirted Brussels, keeping close to the Sonian Forest.

There were faster routes that would have taken them through the city, but there were too many people in a city like Brussels. Too many soldiers. Too many spies. Too many eyes.

A man on a horse, leading another, would be an oddity and would attract attention. So Willem lets Frost ride in front, the brim of his shako pulled low to hide his eye patches. Willem guides him with soft calls: "left," "right," "slow." The instincts of Frost's horse help, and so do Frost's other senses. He seems to know most of what is around him without seeing it.

They slept in the forest, preferring the risk of dragonrats and inquisitive microsaurs to the risk of discovery by French patrols.

Past Waterloo they begin to notice an odd smell in the air. A smell of rot and decay. Willem points it out to Frost, surprised that he has not noticed it.

"It has been in the air since Brussels," Frost says. "It is the smell of the battlefield."

He does not explain, and Willem is hesitant to ask further. He knows that Frost lost men on the battlefield on that June day.

They are within sight of the farmhouse at Mont-Saint-Jean when Frost stops riding. He lifts himself up in the saddle, listening.

"We have company," he says.

Willem looks around and can see no one, but he knows to trust Frost's heightened senses. "Where?" he asks.

"Ahead of us, on horseback, behind one of the farm buildings, I don't know which," Frost says.

Now Willem hears something that could be the snort of a horse. "Prussians?" Willem asks, preparing to turn and run if not.

"I don't know," Frost says.

It is too late. A group of six soldiers emerge from behind a barn. Two of them loop quickly around behind Willem and Frost to cut off any chance of escape.

They are big men, strong, and the sabers that hang from their belts are small and straight. Their uniforms are gray and forest green and they carry rifles, not muskets. Willem sees all this but little of it registers. All he really sees is the red plumes on their shakos, the insignia of the French emperor.

"Jägers," Frost murmurs.

Willem knows this word. Jägers, the elite of the Prussian Army. Scouts, skirmishers, and sharpshooters.

"Do you speak English?" Frost asks.

The leader of the troop looks around at the others, then shakes his head.

"French?" Frost asks.

Another shake of the head.

"Do you speak Dutch?" Willem asks, in Dutch, and this time one of the soldiers nods and moves forward.

"Tell them that we must speak to Field Marshal Blücher immediately," Frost says.

Willem repeats it in Dutch.

The man smiles and speaks in Prussian to the others, who laugh. He turns back. "I will pass on your message to my commander."

Willem thinks this is unlikely.

"Please tell your commander that I carry an important letter for the field marshal," Frost says, and Willem translates as he speaks. "Directly from His Grace Lord Liverpool, the prime minister of England."

Now the soldier raises his eyebrows and there is another discussion, which Willem cannot understand, although many of the words sound similar to Dutch. The soldiers laugh again.

Frost turns to Willem. "I fear they do not take me seriously," he says. "What I must do now is a big risk, but there is little choice."

"Do what you must," Willem says.

Frost moves his horse forward a pace. "I am Lieutenant Hunter Frost of the Royal Horse Artillery, G Troop," he says. He points back at Willem: "And this is Willem Verheyen, the saur-slayer of Gaillemarde."

Willem stops, a little uncomfortable, before translating the last sentence.

The Dutch-speaking Prussian stops laughing, a startled look on his face. He turns to the others, speaking quickly in a low voice. The others all turn to stare at Willem.

"Come with us," the leader says.

Two Jägers lead the way, while the others follow Frost and Willem, ensuring they do not try to escape.

The smell of death intensifies as they approach the town of Braine-l'Alleud. Cresting a rise Willem sees the battlefield in front of him.

The ground is covered with detritus of the battle of a few

months earlier. Broken helmets and muskets. Cuirasses with holes in them the size of cannonballs. Willem shudders as he thinks of what has happened to the men who once wore the armor. There are the tattered remains of drums and flags, piles of rags that are the colors of the French and British uniforms, mostly British, all stained dark brown with dried blood. There are no trees on the battlefield. There are only ragged stumps.

A man in a simple farmer's smock pushes a wheelbarrow, in which Willem can see five large cannonballs. A shot-collector. He will sell them back to whichever army will pay the better price.

In the distance a pyre smolders, sending up a long trickle of smoke to the sky. From that direction comes the smell of cooked meat. Man or horse. Probably both.

"They cremate the bodies?" Willem asks.

"With special permission from the bishop of Charleroi," one of the Jägers says. "To prevent disease."

A cry of excitement cuts across the silence of the field and Willem turns to see a man and a woman running toward a dog that is tearing at something in a ditch under a hedgerow. The couple chase the dog away with stones. They haul out a dead, decomposing body. It snags on something and they wrench the legs back and forth. The moment the body comes clear of the hedgerow they pounce on it, going through the uniform pockets, pulling rings from the fingers.

A pair of Prussian soldiers on horseback ride past, but barely look at the couple. The man forces open the mouth, then produces a pair of pliers from a back pocket. Willem turns away.

"It is criminal what they do," Willem says.

"I can't see what you see," Frost says, "and some days my affliction is a blessing. But think of this. Someone has to clean up the battlefield. Who else would do it but the locals?"

"But the looting of the dead soldiers," Willem protests.

"It is a small reward for an onerous task," Frost says.

On the other side of the road they pass a man with a hammer and a set of cutters, removing horseshoes from a dead mare.

Near the entrance to the village is a stream. A channel has been dug parallel to it. It seems to be full of congealed fat. Willem follows the channel backward and sees a long row of mounds of ash. This is where the fat has run from, he realizes.

His stomach churns.

LOYALTY

Marshal Ney is the first commander Thibault goes to see, backed by Baston and twenty loyal guardsmen.

Ney is seated in the commander's office of the fort. A narrow window gives a view of the harbor, and the sea beyond where the English warships prowl like hungry dogs.

Thibault enters without introduction or pomp, thrusting open the door and marching inside.

"General Thibault," Ney says. "I am busy, but if you would care to come back when—"

"I have assumed control of the army, and soon will be appointed emperor of France and all her territories," Thibault says.

His soldiers fan out around the room, their hands resting on their pistols.

"I think Napoléon would take a dim view of that," Ney says calmly.

"He would if he still drew breath," Thibault says. "He was shot and killed by a British prisoner not ten minutes ago. I have little time to waste. I need to know if you will pledge your support and loyalty to me."

"That is something I could take under consideration," Ney says. "We will certainly need a new leader if what you say is true. But you are a mere general."

"A general who commands the most powerful weapons in the

French Army," Thibault says. "No one will dare go against me. And no, I will not give you time to think it over. I will have your loyalty now, or I will consider you a traitor."

"Which means?" Ney asks.

"My girls are hungry," Thibault says. "As Marshal Suchet has already found out, to his cost."

Ney pales significantly.

"I have many people to visit and very little time," Thibault says. "Will you swear your loyalty now?"

He waits, his one good eye never leaving the stunned face of the marshal.

After a long moment Ney nods. He stands and kneels before Thibault, offering him his marshal's baton.

"Good," Thibault says, taking the baton and then handing it back to him. "Major Baston will remain here to ensure you do not reconsider in my absence."

With that he whirls and hurries out of the room.

There are many people to see today.

The politicians in Paris will be horrified and will oppose him; he knows that. But once he has control of the Grande Armée, they will have no choice.

MARENGO

The escape from the prison seems like a distant dream. Such was the confusion. The shouts, the people running, the screams from the cell block. Jack found himself caught up in a storm, just one soldier among many, whirling in a maelstrom of noise and horror. Everywhere he heard the cry, *"L'empereur est mort!"*

He did not have to speak French to understand what that meant.

He wasted no time. He left the prison through the rear door, and as soon as he was sure nobody was watching he crossed the street to the stables and hid in the back of the horse stall with the emperor's gray stallion.

This was not a calculated move. All he knew was that Napoléon was dead and Thibault would do anything to hunt him down. He was terrified. Gilbert by now would be dead. McConnell was dead. The only person who knew of Thibault's crime was Jack, and Thibault would come after him with every soldier he could muster.

Now Jack cowers under a pile of hay at the back of the stall, shaking so hard that he fears it will lead to his discovery.

He came here by instinct. Looking for a place to hide. A place he knew. But as the sounds of excitement gradually died away during the night, he started to think that maybe he had accidentally done something clever. Nobody would have expected him to hide so close to the prison. Just across the road. They will have spread out, searching the streets, blocking the gates. After many hours with no sign of him, hopefully they will have decided that he got away.

It is almost dawn before he risks climbing out from the back of the stall, soothing the stallion by gently stroking his rump.

He quickly saddles the horse. He will need to be quiet, he thinks. He finds some rags and ties them around each of the horse's hooves. He is not sure how he knows to do this, but it comes to him, as if in a dream.

Only when he is sure the street is empty does he mount the stallion and ride quietly out, heading to the north, keeping the lightening sky over his right shoulder. The frantic searches of the previous night have stopped and the searchers have gone to their beds. The city itself is not yet awake and the streets are almost deserted.

Still there are patrols, but he manages to avoid them by listening for horse hooves on the cobblestones. His own horse is almost silent.

Once he is nearly caught when patrols turn into the street ahead of him. But in the dim light and the shadows of the morning he is nearly invisible, and he ducks into a dark alley, waiting anxiously as the horses approach, then pass by without any shout or alarm.

Eventually he reaches one of the gates in the saur-wall and here he knows that his silent approach will no longer work.

He dismounts and removes the rags to give his horse a more sure footing. He watches carefully around the corner of a building.

There are four guards manning this gate. Two of them appear to be asleep, sitting against the wall with their heads lowered. The other two stand casually, their muskets propped against the guard hut.

Jack mounts the horse again. He takes a deep breath.

"Sorry, boy," he says. Then he digs his heels deeply into his sides. Marengo is not big, but he is determined and strong, a horse fit for an emperor. He does not whinny or complain. His iron shoes make sparks on the cobblestones and he accelerates to a full gallop in what seems like a heartbeat.

Now Jack is around the corner and riding straight for the gate. The soldiers see him and there is a moment of confusion, perhaps partly due to the early hour of the morning, then a shout in French.

Jack does not respond, nor does he slow. He spurs the stallion to even greater speed.

At last the guards realize that something is wrong. Those on the ground spring to their feet; all of them grab for their weapons. But Jack is already upon them, bursting past them before any can bring their muskets to bear. The barrier in the center of the gate is merely a low hurdle for a horse like this and Marengo soars over it, racing up the road away from the city.

Now comes the first musketshot. It is too quick and poorly aimed and although Jack hears the crack of the musket, he does not hear the passage of the musketball. The next shot is closer, and the next two closer still; he hears both of them fizz past his ears.

Now the guards are reloading but by the time they finish he will be well out of range.

He hears their shouts of alarm and he knows that a pursuit will follow. But this is a fine horse and Jack is not stopping. Not for anything. Not for anyone.

He rides hard, for Gaillemarde.

BLÜCHER

Field Marshal Gebhard Leberecht von Blücher is an aristocratic-looking man, with a bushy but well-groomed mustache. His face bears the marks of recently healed wounds. His eyes are dark and piercing but his smile is warm. He has the demeanor of a friendly uncle.

The field marshal's headquarters are in the Caillou farmhouse, near the Waterloo battlefield. It was where Napoléon made his headquarters during the battle, Willem has learned.

Blücher is seated behind a table, one of three pushed together in the center of the dining room, on the ground floor of the two-story brick farmhouse. He sips from a glass of brandy as he eyes Willem up and down, barely glancing at Frost.

"So this is the little saur-slayer," he says in excellent English. "We have been looking for you for many weeks."

Willem looks at Frost, confused.

Blücher sees his expression and interprets it correctly. "We were told to be on the lookout for a boy of your description," he says. "You had pulled off some kind of vanishing act and Napoléon was very keen to have you unvanished. I wondered then why the French emperor had such an interest in you, and it did not take long for me to discover why. You are the boy who can control saurs. And now here you are. And again I wonder why."

"May I speak, Your Excellency?" Frost asks.

"You may," Blücher says, turning his gaze to the young lieutenant.

"As you have been looking for us, so we have been looking for you," Frost says.

"Fascinating," Blücher says to his aide-de-camp. "The boy Napoléon fears more than any man alive wants an audience with me."

"We seek an alliance with you in an attack on Napoléon's forces," Frost says.

Blücher throws back his head and laughs. It is a meaty sound. He points to his face. "The scars of my last encounter with Napoléon have yet to heal, but you come seeking more misery for this old man."

"We do not fear Napoléon," Frost says. "The last time, we did not know of his battlesaurs. We will not be surprised in this manner again."

Blücher's face grows serious. "My horse was killed beneath me, and I was nearly killed beneath it. For hours I lay trapped, thought to be dead, while cavalry from both sides used me as a doormat. I would be dead if not for Count Nostitz here." He nods and smiles at his aide-de-camp. "Yet here I am. I tell you this so you will know that I am no coward. I have seen things that would turn most men to jelly. I have faced death. And I am afraid of Napoléon. Perhaps you should be too."

"You have perhaps noticed that I have lost the use of my eyes," Frost says calmly.

"Of course I have noticed and I am sorry for your loss," Blücher says. "But . . ." His voice trails off and he looks at Frost with an entirely new expression. "You are the one."

"One of many," Frost says.

"You are the one who faced a battlesaur and brought it down

257

on the battlefield," Blücher says. "I find myself in the rare position of needing to apologize. You are the other saur-slayer. You have my admiration and respect."

Frost bows his head slightly.

Blücher turns to Count Nostitz. "A British lieutenant and a Flemish boy, not even a soldier, seek an alliance with this old warhorse. The world grows more mad by the day."

"May I explain?" Frost asks.

"You may try," Blücher says.

"Napoléon is poised to invade England," Frost says. "If Britain falls, then all of Europe will soon follow."

"There is a certain inevitability to it," Blücher says.

"Perhaps not," Frost says.

Willem sits back and examines the room as Frost explains the situation with Ireland and the Royal Navy to Blücher.

The floor of the kitchen is paved, a rich orange color, well polished. The walls are whitewashed stone.

Frost finishes and Blücher lowers his head, glowering at them from beneath bushy eyebrows.

"You think me foolish enough to take on battlesaurs?"

"With luck they will be dead," Frost says.

Blücher nods. "My spies have heard stories that your men have indeed escaped. So perhaps, with luck, cunning, and courage, they will be able to complete their mission. But what about the rest of the French dinosaurs? In the cave beneath the Sonian? Or do you expect me to attack the abbey also? If so, I must teach you a lesson about fighting a battle in a forest, where artillery is useless, especially in a forest protected by creatures that are most at home among the trees."

"This matter was also of grave concern to the Duke of Wellington," Frost says. "So much so that he tasked Willem and myself with the job of sealing the entrance to the cave, to ensure that no other battlesaurs are brought into the battle."

Blücher laughs again. "Now I see why you are not afraid of Napoléon. How you held your nerve on the battlefield and brought down a battlesaur. You have an old heart for a young man."

"Thank you, Excellency," Frost says.

"But my answer is no," Blücher says. "Even without battlesaurs Napoléon is a formidable enemy. His Grande Armée is bolstered by the Dutch, the Bavarians, and the Italians. It is a battle I fear I could not win."

"You would not have to win it," Frost says. "You may not even have to fight it. Just the presence of your army on the outskirts of Calais would be enough to force Napoléon to delay the invasion. He knows your reputation."

"That is true," Blücher says. "But Napoléon is no fool. He would call my bluff and bring the battle to me. I would have to withdraw and the repercussions against Prussia for breaking the alliance would be savage."

"Your Excellency," Frost begins, but he is stopped by a raised hand from Blücher.

"I must decline your offer and my answer is final," he says.

"And what if Napoléon was dead?" A familiar voice comes from the doorway and Willem looks up to see Arbuckle, his hands bound, escorted into the room by two Jägers, swords at the ready. He is almost unrecognizable. His face is a mask of dried blood and his clothes are bloodied and torn. He is limping.

"Captain Arbuckle," Blücher says, rising. "I might have detected your hand behind all this." He motions for Arbuckle's hands to be untied. "A glass of brandy for this man."

Willem is greatly surprised to learn that Arbuckle is alive, and somewhat less surprised to find that he knows Blücher personally.

259

As soon as his hands are free, Arbuckle salutes, and Blücher returns the salute, then takes Arbuckle's hand and shakes it warmly.

"It is good to see you, you young rapscallion," Blücher says.

"And you, you old scoundrel," Arbuckle says. He turns to the others. "I apologize for my delay. I was held up somewhat after we were attacked at Antwerp."

Willem looks again at the blood and the torn clothing. He thinks that Arbuckle's "delay" has been a costly affair.

"What of the others?" Willem asks. "Jack and the saur-killers?"

"I know no more than you," Arbuckle says. "I can only hope that they got away and are on their way to Calais."

Brandy is duly poured and Arbuckle drains the glass in a single gulp.

"If Napoléon was dead, that would change everything," Blücher says. "But the gods would not smile on us so brightly."

"Perhaps the gods favor you more than you think," Arbuckle says. "The emperor is indeed dead. Such is the word and it is spreading like flame in dry powder. I am surprised it has not yet reached your ears."

Blücher looks startled and motions to an aide, who hurries out of the room.

"Is this one of your tricks?" Blücher asks.

"If I am wrong or right, you will find out soon enough," Arbuckle says. "I am sure you have eyes of your own in Calais. But the man who told me believed it to be true."

"Napoléon dead!" Blücher rises from behind his desk, crossing excitedly to a map pinned to the wall of the kitchen, if a big man of advanced years could be said to move excitedly. "If this is true, his army will be in turmoil. Forget the invasion. Bring your ships to Calais. The French Grande Armée would be a firebird without a head."

"The army still has its battlesaurs," Nostitz says. "And Thibault, who commands them."

"And I will not send my men up against battlesaurs," Blücher says. "But on the other hand, if your saur-slayers have succeeded, then there will be no better time to smash the Grande Armée."

"You will know when you see the yellow rockets," Arbuckle says.

Blücher ponders this a moment longer. "If the rumors are true, and Napoléon is dead, then I will move my army to Calais. If we see the yellow flares, then we will launch an attack."

"And if not?" Frost asks.

"Then I will have no choice but to swear my loyalty to whoever now leads the French Army," Blücher says. He turns to Nostitz. "Give the order. We move at first light."

To Frost he says, "Wellington wanted you to seal the entrance to the cave. I am interested to know how you intend to do that."

"It will not be easy," Frost admits. "There are secret ways into the cave system. Willem and I have used them once before, but then we had a guide. A girl who had lived in the forest for a number of years. She came with us, but was separated from us when we were attacked."

Blücher frowns. "A small, feisty girl? With very short hair? Looks like a boy?"

"Yes!" Willem cries. "That is Héloïse! What do you know of her?"

"I know that my guards will be very pleased if you take her off their hands," Blücher says.

BREAK OUT

The brute, Private Deloque, comes to the door of the little church, blocking the meager sunlight that folds its way in through the thick trees of the forest and over the high stone walls of the abbey.

Cosette and Marie are mending uniforms for their captors. It is a choice, not a duty forced on them. Marie suggested it a few weeks earlier and Cosette agreed. *It does not hurt to be on good terms with our captors*, Marie had said.

And it passes the time.

They have been given needle and thread to do this, along with an old blunt pair of dressmaker's scissors that Cosette has sharpened by unscrewing the blades and scraping them on the stone walls of the church. She has paid particular attention to the points of the scissors.

Marie and Cosette both look up when Deloque arrives at the doorway. Cosette shudders a little. Deloque always makes Cosette uncomfortable. His eyes linger on parts of her body where a gentleman's eyes should never linger.

Today Deloque has a big dumb smile on his face. He grins stupidly at them for a moment, then turns to leave.

"Something is going on," Marie comments quietly to Cosette.

"Private Deloque," Cosette calls out.

Deloque looks back, but just grunts.

"Do you have something to tell us?" Marie asks.

"Nothing you will not find out soon enough," Deloque says.

It is the most words Cosette has heard him string together in a single sentence.

Deloque turns again to leave.

"Don't be silly," Cosette says loudly. "If there was anything worth telling, they would not entrust it to someone as stupid as Deloque."

Deloque turns back again and scowls. "I know things that nobody knows. They thinks I don't listen but I do."

Cosette turns to Marie. "I am not interested in what he has to say. Even if he did overhear something, I doubt he would have understood what he heard."

"Laugh all you like," Deloque says. "You won't be laughing soon."

"He knows nothing," Cosette says.

Deloque sneers. "They found that boy," he says. "They killed him."

"What boy do you mean?" Marie asks carefully.

"The one who killed the saur," Deloque says, and he gives a short laugh.

Cosette is unable to breathe. Her heart seems to have jammed in her chest. Her feelings must show on her face and it makes Deloque grin.

"The one they all been looking for," Deloque says. His words seem to be coming from far away. "He came back from England on a boat and they caught him and killed him. Put his body on a cart and paraded it through Paris."

Now he is grinning broadly. Cosette forces a smile to mask the horror that she is feeling. "We don't even know who that is," she says.

Deloque laughs. "So you say," he says. "I say different."

His shape leaves the doorway, but Cosette can still see him outside, tending the plants in the central garden.

"Pray God that it not be true," she says.

"Come," Marie says. She seems distant. "We will talk as we walk."

She gathers up the dressmaking tools and Cosette follows her out of the church.

"There are things to do," she says.

"Madame, if the news is true, then your son is dead," Cosette says, dumbfounded. "Do you not wish to mourn him?"

"Do I wish to mourn him?" Marie asks, without stopping or looking at Cosette. "Of course. But we have no time to mourn him."

"What do you mean?" Cosette asks.

"If Willem is dead then so are we," Marie says. "He was the only reason they kept us alive."

"We are no danger to them," Cosette says. "If Willem is dead they will have no reason to keep us here."

"Foolish girl," Marie says sharply, and in her tone Cosette finally hears the depths of her anguish. "We know what happened at Gaillemarde. We are witnesses."

"We did not see it," Cosette protests.

"We did not need to," Marie says. "Thibault will never allow us to leave. Not alive. You must escape and it must be today."

"But we can't . . ." Cosette trails off, realizing what Marie has just said.

"Three of us cannot make it," Marie says. "Cosette, you must take your bath today, and slip away. If François is there he will help you."

"We must all escape," Cosette says.

"That is not possible," Marie says. "You must go."

"No," Cosette says. She turns back. "Private Deloque," she says, and her voice is strong and formal. "Please inform Lieutenant Horloge that I require an audience with him immediately. I will be in my cell."

"I'm not your errand boy," Deloque says, looking up from his hoe.

"Then I will find him myself and tell him that you refused to pass on my message," Cosette says.

"I ain't afraid of that little flower," Deloque says, but he turns and heads off in the direction of the officers' quarters.

Lieutenant Horloge stops in the doorway of the cell, knocking on the door with a quick tap of his fingernails, no more.

Deloque towers behind him.

"This is for your ears alone," Marie says.

"It does not matter what the private hears," Horloge says, sniffing at a handkerchief stained with snuff.

"It matters to me," Marie says.

Horloge looks at her haughtily, then at Cosette and back.

"Are you afraid?" Cosette laughs lightly. "An armed soldier, an officer in the French Army, afraid of two unarmed women?"

"Lock the door," Horloge says to Deloque. "And wait at the end of the corridor. I will call you when I am finished."

Deloque looks sullen, but complies.

Horloge watches to make sure he leaves and starts to turn back but stops as he feels the sting of a sharp point at his throat. One blade of the scissors. Deadly sharp.

"Call out and I will sever your artery," Cosette says. "No surgeon will be able to save you. You will be dead in thirty seconds."

"And you will be dead in sixty," Horloge says.

"That is true, but you will still be dead," Cosette says.

Horloge is silent and she takes that as a sign of compliance. Marie steps close and reaches for his pistol. Horloge drops a hand to his holster to stop her.

Cosette presses the blade harder into his throat, drawing blood. He gasps and moves his hand away.

"You will die for this," Horloge says.

"We were to die anyway," Marie says, withdrawing his pistol slowly, silently. She cocks the hammer with her thumb, checking the frizzen for powder. "Those were your orders, were they not? Once Willem had been found?"

Horloge is again silent. Cosette produces the other blade of the scissors and weaves a delicate line down the front of his tunic, to the region of his navel, then below.

"Perhaps! Perhaps," Horloge says. "But your son has not been found."

"That is not what we have heard," Cosette says.

Horloge glances at the door, in the direction of Deloque. He sets his jaw angrily.

"What you have heard is only part of the truth. Your son and a group of other soldiers and spies landed near Antwerp. Most of them were killed or captured. But your son got away."

"You lie," Marie says.

"I tell the truth," Horloge says.

"It does not matter," Cosette says. "What has been started cannot be stopped. Call Deloque back in. Call him now."

"I will not," he says.

"Because of your duty? Your honor?" Marie asks. "Do as we ask and we will leave here, and you will have your life. Refuse, or try to fool us, or alert the guard, and you will die. There may be honor in dying on a battlefield, but there is none in dying in a prison cell at the hands of a woman."

266

Horloge is quiet for a moment, then calls, "Guard!"

"A wise move," Cosette says. "Perhaps you deserve a kiss for your trouble."

She moves in front of him, embracing him, turning him away from the door, the blade pressed again into his neck. Marie slips quietly behind the door, the pistol in her hand.

Deloque, as Cosette has anticipated, is shocked at the sight of Horloge and Cosette locked in a romantic embrace. He unlocks the door and enters without a thought for Marie's whereabouts, until her voice sounds quietly behind him.

"Give me your musket or I will sever your spine and if you live, you will spend the rest of your days as a cripple," Marie says.

Deloque spins around, seeing the pistol aimed steadily at his midriff. He starts to raise his musket.

Cosette presses the blade even deeper into Horloge's throat. He squeaks with the pain. "Do as she says. Don't be a fool," he says.

Deloque hands his musket to Marie.

"Against the wall," she says, stepping back from the big man, the pistol steady.

Deloque obeys, crossing to a wall of the cell.

"You join him," Marie says to Horloge, who also obeys.

"Now strip off your uniforms," Cosette says. "And give us no trouble."

Horloge stares at her for a moment before starting to comply. "Mademoiselle," he says, "you may not think much of me, and I am not as much of a man as the soldiers that surround me. But I am no coward and I am no animal. I do not agree with women being used as pawns in this game. In all honesty I shall be pleased to see you free. You shall have no trouble from me."

Cosette bows her head in thanks. His response seems genuine.

"I believe you are a good man," she says. "I am not so sure of your companion."

"I am still the commander of this garrison," Horloge says. "The private will do as he is told."

"Bind them tightly," Cosette says to Marie.

A DESPERATE ACT

Deloque's uniform is far too big for Maarten—Marie's husband and Willem's father—who seems much older than his years. A withered stalk of a man, brutalized by so many years in the stone-walled confines of his cell. Captured by the French and forced to teach them his secrets of mesmerizing dinosaurs. He seemed unsure when they released him, unready to step outside the cell that had been the boundaries of his world for so long.

Still, with quick application of needle and thread, Cosette and Marie manage to stop the trousers from falling down and tuck up the sleeves. The tunic is so long it looks like a woman's dress, but there is nothing they can do about that.

Cosette fits more easily into Horloge's small uniform. The chest is tight and she feels squashed and short of breath, but it will be only for a short time. She will cope. She studies his face, thinking of all the shows she has performed in back in the village, and how features can be brought out with a little application of makeup.

She has no makeup here, and the application would have to be much more subtle to pass inspection at close quarters. She mixes a little dirt from the floor with dust from the walls, dampening it with spit.

Using the shiny blade of Horloge's dagger as a mirror, she does the best she can to transform her face into his.

The first guard they must face is outside the door of the cell block. She might pass inspection but Maarten will never pass for Deloque.

She practices Horloge's voice. It is deeper than hers, and his accent markedly different. However, he has a soft way of speaking that is easily imitated.

Maarten checks the bindings and the gags that secure Horloge and Deloque before he and the two women exit the cell, locking the door behind them.

Followed by Marie, then Maarten, who is clutching Deloque's musket, Cosette marches to the end of the corridor and raps on the door to be let out. Maarten and Marie hang back, hiding in the doorway of one of the cells.

The guard checks through the barred hole in the door, as he is supposed to, before there is the click of a lock and the door opens.

Now is the moment, Cosette knows. Everything depends on this. She knows this soldier.

She coughs, covering her mouth with her hand. So far the guard shows no sign of alarm or recognition that she is anyone other than who she pretends to be.

"You are relieved, corporal," she says, in her best approximation of Horloge's voice. Even to her, it does sound like him. "Private Deloque will take over guard duties."

"Yes, sir," the corporal says. "What is my new assignment?"

"You may take your rest," she says.

"Thank you, sir," the corporal says. He salutes and leaves.

The walk across the main courtyard of the abbey is a gantlet of potential danger. They pass by the huge doors of the storeroom, which is really a cover for the entrance to the caves beneath. One of the great doors is open and she can hear the grunts and smell the stench of the big animals in the cavern far below.

There are many soldiers in the courtyard. Any one of them could put an end to this charade immediately, noticing something odd about the captain, or the ill-fitting uniform of the guard who walks in front of him.

Out of the corner of her eye Cosette sees an adjutant approaching. This is a man who works every day with Horloge.

The other soldiers see Horloge mainly at a distance, but this man knows him personally. She panics momentarily, her hand straying toward the pistol in her holster.

She moves it away, thinking quickly, and pulls out Horloge's handkerchief.

She waits until the man is quite near and turns to him, sniffing at the silk cloth.

"Sir, a letter from Calais," the man says. "It just arrived. Most urgent."

"Thank you," Cosette says. She holds out a hand and the man hands her the letter, then salutes.

Cosette knows she has to return the salute but to do so would involve taking the handkerchief away from her face.

Again panic rises in her throat but at that moment Marie swoons, falling into the arms of her husband, the "guard" behind her.

The distraction is enough.

"See to your duties," Cosette says. "I have matters to attend to."

The man looks at Marie, and realizes. He pales.

"Of course, sir," he says, spinning sharply on his heels and walking quickly away.

"Thank you," Cosette whispers, as Marie stages a not-quite-miraculous recovery.

"Your performance is superb," Marie says out of the corner of her mouth.

From his perch in the trees François sees three figures leave the main gate of the abbey and a cold sensation runs through him as though Satan has run his fingers down his spine.

The three figures leaving the abbey are a woman, followed by a guard, followed by the temporary commander of the abbey, Lieutenant Horloge. François has met Horloge and does not like him, finding him to be a weak, insipid excuse for a man.

The reason for François's chill is the identity of the members of the party. The woman has to be Madame Verheyen, Willem's mother. For her to be taken out in this manner can mean only one thing.

The last time François saw such a party it was to deal with a deserter. He was shot and his body dumped in a ravine, left for the saurs and other wild animals of the forest.

He slings his crossbow across his back and takes one of his rope walks to a different tree where he can get a better view.

From his new perch he can clearly see Horloge, his manner and gait are unmistakable, the angle of his head, the way he holds his hands. He is too high to see the face below the peak of the helmet, but he does not need to.

The guard is a new one. François has not seen him before. He is surprisingly old and frail for a soldier and François cannot imagine how he got posted here.

He lets them pass by, almost directly beneath his tree, then lines up his crossbow on the back of Horloge.

He almost fires, but stops himself. There is no point. If it was Cosette being marched to her execution, then yes, he would kill. He would take out the guard first, then the officer as he ran for help.

But this is not Cosette, just Willem's mother. He has no

feelings for her. None other than pity and that is not strong enough for him to want to cause the kind of ruckus that the disappearance of the commanding officer will cause.

He moves into another tree, no ropes needed here because the tree canopy is so thick that he can simply step from branch to branch.

It occurs to him that if Madame Verheyen is to be executed, then Cosette will surely be next. Unless the soldiers keep her to use as a plaything.

He shudders at that thought. It is against God.

He has feelings for Cosette and they have taken him a little by surprise. He sees her face when he closes his eyes for the night, and again when he wakes. Her shy smile, her lazy eye, they are the imperfections that make her perfect. Her wit and inner strength are also qualities to be admired.

Madame Verheyen marches to her death courageously, François thinks. Her head held high, her gaze proud and defiant.

He climbs easily down the knobbly trunk of an old oak and follows the trio, surprised when they do not turn off the path toward the ravine.

They reach the water hole and wait, while François watches, confused.

Then Horloge softly calls out, and it is not his voice but Cosette's.

"François?"

And now he understands.

For caution he keeps the crossbow loaded and aimed as he emerges from the tree line.

The girl in the French officer's uniform turns toward him and for a moment he thinks it really is Horloge. A little shading has been applied to her cheeks, and to her top lip to simulate Horloge's embryonic mustache. With the helmet low over her eyes it is a good disguise.

"Cosette," he says, and lowers the weapon as she takes three quick steps toward him, embracing him, tears now flooding.

"François, thank God," she says.

"What has happened?" he asks.

"They say that Willem is dead," Cosette sobs.

François looks quickly to Madame Verheyen, who nods. "Horloge denies it, but I think he would have said anything to appease us."

François thinks carefully about what to say. To lie is a sin, but he has lied before, for the greater good. He knows that Willem has escaped, but the French hunt for him constantly. It is only a matter of time before he is found and put to death.

It would be cruel to so raise their hopes now, only to have them dashed later.

And the softness of Cosette's skin feels so good against his.

"They are all dead," he says. "An ambush near Antwerp."

He does not explain how he knows this.

Now the man talks. This must be Willem's father. The prisoner whom François has never seen.

"His death will not go unavenged," Monsieur Verheyen says darkly. He seems weak and his wife quickly puts her arms around him to support him.

"Come," François says. "We must hurry, before they discover you are gone."

He strokes Cosette's hair lightly. A gesture of sympathy, nothing more.

"Where are you taking us?" Maarten asks.

"To La Hulpe," François says. "The priest there will hide us."

"No," Cosette says. "We go to Gaillemarde."

"That is too close," François says. "It will not be safe there."

"After Gaillemarde we can continue to La Hulpe," Cosette says.

"There is nothing at Gaillemarde to see," François says softly.

"And that is what I must see," Cosette says.

François considers this for a moment, then nods. "The search for you will be savage and thorough," he says. "Perhaps Gaillemarde is for the best. There is a priest hole in the rectory. I used it to hide the children of the village when the French troops . . ."

He does not finish the sentence. He cannot. The massacre at the village is still a red raw scar across his heart, not least because he still wonders if somehow he was partly responsible for it. He has prayed to God many times about what happened at Gaillemarde, but God, so far, has chosen not to answer.

"The church was left alone," he says. "We can hide in the priest hole while they search."

GAILLEMARDE

The ride into Gaillemarde with Frost, Héloïse, and Arbuckle is perhaps the hardest thing Willem has ever done in his life.

Héloïse shares his horse. She was offered her own but declined. He knows why. She has never learned to ride. He feels her arms around him now, clinging, and he thinks it odd that a girl who is afraid of no wild thing is afraid of something so tame.

As they round a corner of the river and the gates of Gaillemarde come into view he eases his horse to the slowest walk and would stop, maybe even turn back, if not for the presence of the others.

He knows this place. He knows every stone in the road, every stunted shrub on the riverbank. He knows the loops and coils of the water in the river alongside.

He knows what he will find across the bridge and behind the saur-gates of the village. He can picture every house, every flower in every garden. Every face that will turn and smile to see him arrive.

And he knows he will not find this at all.

When they reach the shallow indentation in the ground where Cosette's sister, Angélique, was taken by the greatest of all the saurs, he does stop. Staring at the rocky depression, still stained rusty red with her blood, he thinks, *This is where it all started*. If not for the monster, then the soldiers would not have come with their swords and their muskets.

When he gets to the bridge across the river he stops again. Unable to go on, unable to turn back. Caught in a kind of limbo between the world as it is and the world that once was.

This place is where his every memory was forged. Where almost everybody he ever knew lived their lives, making a living in the tranquillity of a country village, far from the intrigue and the politics of the capitals of Europe.

Just not far enough.

"Come, Willem," Frost says. "They may be waiting for us."

There are others who will surely be waiting for us, Willem wants to say, but does not. The spirits of all those who died. Will they blame him, staring with hollow endless eyes? Does he blame himself for what happened here? He has still not decided.

He glances back at Héloïse. Her gaze is fixed on the gates of Gaillemarde and he thinks she too is wrestling with memories and emotions. Arbuckle is nowhere to be seen, which is strange as he has been with them the whole way from Waterloo.

Willem nudges his horse forward, across the old stone bridge.

The saur-fence looks to be intact. The gates are shut but are blackened and burned, almost to the ground. The horses step over the remains.

Inside, it is worse than he feared. The pretty little village is a wasteland. A burnt-out hulk, swarming with weeds and vines. In just a few months the land has started to reclaim this village and no one has been here to stop it.

The lovely river cottages are still there. Their thatched roofs are gone but their stone walls have been unaffected by the fires that destroyed much of the village.

Frost stops riding. He lifts himself up in the saddle, listening.

"There are people here," he says.

Willem looks around and sees no one, but he knows to trust Frost's heightened senses. "Where?" he asks.

"I am not sure," Frost says.

"Our people?" Willem asks, preparing to turn and run if not. Running into a French patrol at this stage would be disastrous.

"I don't know," Frost says. "But they don't smell French."

Willem has no time to ask what he means by this.

A trio of soldiers emerge from the remains of the tailor's house near the gate.

Their uniforms are British, but so torn and muddied that they are almost unrecognizable. They carry a variety of weapons: muskets, pistols, swords. One has dark skin, almost black.

"Kill them," an unshaven man says. He wears the uniform of a corporal. His expression is sullen.

Héloïse snarls at him and he draws back uncertainly.

Willem is suddenly very aware of the uniforms that he and Frost are wearing.

"We are not French!" he blurts out. "We are British soldiers."

"More spies," the man says. He raises his musket toward them.

"We are British," Frost says.

"That's what the last one said." The man spits on the ground after speaking.

"Easy now, Noah." The dark man steps forward. "They have not the accent of the French. Let us hear what they have to say."

"I do not care to hear their lies," Noah says.

Willem dismounts and helps Héloïse down, then steps toward the men, holding out his hands to show he means no harm.

The dark man moves forward. He is a large, strong man, and the others seem to respect him. He carries a Prussian cavalry saber. He places a hand on Noah's shoulders and steps in front of him.

"Who are you?" the man asks. "What are you?"

He towers over Willem, who takes a step backward.

"What are you?" the dark man asks again.

"Mogansondram?" Frost asks.

The man steps closer, scrutinizing Frost. "Who are you and how do you know my name?"

"Corporal Mathan Mogansondram, if my memory serves me correctly," Frost says. "I know your voice."

The soldier studies Frost for a moment, then his face breaks into a huge smile. "It is I, sir. I know you also. You were the lieutenant that night. On the battlefield. After Waterloo. I did not recognize you straightaway, sir. You had rags around your eyes that night."

"You would not leave your captain," Frost says.

"He died, sir," Mogansondram says. "I did what I could for him after that, then I left."

He lowers his weapon and the others follow suit.

"A wise decision." Arbuckle's voice comes from behind the group of soldiers. He has a pistol in one hand and a saber in the other, inches from the neck of the unshaven soldier. Willem did not see him arrive and it is clear that nobody else did either. Arbuckle holsters his pistol and sheathes his sword, then offers his hand to the men, who reluctantly take it, one by one.

"How did you end up here?" Frost asks.

Mogansondram lowers his eyes. "I hid out in the forest for a while. I could not find the rest of my unit. I did not intend to desert, sir."

"I know that you did not," Frost says. "There was chaos after the battle."

"Then I found this place," Mogansondram says. "The others wandered in over the next few weeks. We hide when the French and Prussian patrols come."

"How long have you been here?" Willem asks.

"I don't know, sir," Mogansondram says. "Perhaps a month. It is difficult to keep track of the days. What are you doing here, sir? And in French uniform?"

"That is a matter of great importance, and great secrecy," Frost says.

"You said 'more spies,'" Arbuckle says. "Have there been others?"

"Just one," Mogansondram says. "He arrived this morning. He is tied up in the remains of one of the river cottages while we decide what to do with him."

"Did he give you a name?" Frost asks.

"Hoyes," Mogansondram says. "He claimed to be a lieutenant but his accent was not that of an officer."

"He is indeed an officer," Frost says. "And a very worthy one. I would ask you to untie him and fetch him here forthwith. Then I would like to enlist your help."

"We would be honored, sir," Mogansondram says.

THE SWAMP

The forest is alive with French troops. Many times the small group have had to duck into the undergrowth, frantically concealing themselves as soldiers on horseback, in twos and threes, prowl the tracks and pathways of the forest.

Each time they encounter French patrols it is only Frost's exceptional hearing that gives them the warning they need to escape the oncoming danger. And it is Héloïse who is always able to find the best place to hide.

"Something is up," Mogansondram says needlessly after a foursome of cuirassiers gallop past. "I have never seen so many patrols."

"What are they looking for?" Willem wonders.

"Us," Arbuckle says.

"But how? Why?" Willem asks.

"Word of our mission has clearly reached French ears," Arbuckle says. "That will complicate things."

They wait in the shelter of a thick bush while Frost listens carefully to ensure that the riders are not coming back, and that no more follow.

After a moment Frost nods and they ease out of their hiding place. In the distance they hear dogs barking.

"Do not fear the dogs," Héloïse says. "They do not know our scent."

"That is good news," Willem says.

"It is the demonsaurs we must be afraid of," Héloïse says.

They reach the river and track along the stony bank for a while, walking in the edge of the water to hide their scent. They cross at a shallow ford and continue on the other bank. Several times Frost hears soldiers but Héloïse shakes her head. "They do not come this way."

They pass the remains of an old jetty that Willem remembers from his last trip up this river. That time in a boat, hunting for a firebird. The river is exactly as he pictures it in his mind. A row of old rotten posts and collapsed timbers lined with ravensaurs staring at them with unblinking eyes, shaking dew off their long, leathery wings.

They are almost at a patch of giant, flowering ferns when Frost again pauses, pointing upriver. With an effort, Willem can hear it, too. The *swish* of a boat through the water and the sounds of oars.

"This way, and hurry," Willem whispers. He takes Frost's arm and pulls him toward the ferns, pushing through them, mindful of the edges, which from experience he knows are sharp and hard. He holds back as many of the ferns as he can as the rest of the soldiers swiftly pass through the opening.

On the other side is the swamp, just as he remembers it, and on the far side of that is the old shack. Crumbling stone walls with bushes and tall weeds sprouting up through the collapsed chimney. The roof and door are long gone, merely rotten remnants decaying in the humid swamp air.

The swamp buzzes with insects and burps with gas. It was here that they found Angélique's body, if you could call what they found a body.

"I remember this place," Frost says. "We came here when we escaped from the village."

"We did," Willem says. "It is easy to miss, and a good place to hide."

"The entrance to the caves is close to here," Héloïse says.

There are voices now on the other side of the ferns. French voices, speaking quietly, just loud enough to be heard over the wash of the boat through the river.

Then the boat is past, the voices fading as it drifts downriver.

"We stay a little longer," Frost says. A few moments later he adds, "More footsteps."

They wait, motionless on the edge of the swamp. Even Willem can hear the sound of military boots on the rock of the riverbank. The sounds stop and there is a rustling in the ferns. There is a muted exclamation of pain, no doubt from the sharp edges of the ferns.

Willem curses and draws his sword. They cannot be caught again. Not here. Not now. Not by French troops. Some of the British troops raise their muskets, but Arbuckle motions them away. They don't want gunshots.

Willem is the closest to the cave entrance as the ferns are parted and a man pushes through. He carries a weapon, not a musket or a pistol, not even a sword. It is a crossbow, and that is how Willem knows him before he even looks at his face.

François sees Willem in the same instant and spins toward him, the sharp point of the crossbow bolt swinging around in an arc.

Willem rushes at him, aware that he is too far away, that there is not enough time. He stumbles on a root at the edge of the swamp and this saves his life as he falls; he only hears the sound of the crossbow and feels the bolt tug at the cloth of his garments at his shoulder.

Then he is back on his feet, rising to meet François, who has no time to reload and just swings the crossbow in front of him like a club to fend off Willem's sword.

The clang of metal on metal is loud, reverberating through the trees that surround them, and Willem's thrust is knocked away. He lifts the sword high and slices down but again the stock of the crossbow is there to meet the blow. Now it is François's turn to stumble, one foot slipping on the mud at the edge of the swamp. He falls backward into the slimy water. The crossbow falls from his grasp and he has only his arms to defend himself, raised in front of his face, flesh and bone against the hard, cruel steel of Willem's sword.

But Willem hears Héloïse's voice, an urgent warning: "Willem!"

He flicks his head around, aware of the flash of a French uniform behind him. He twists just in time for his sword to fend away a dagger, then he sees the face of his assailant and he can defend himself no more.

His sword is useless in his frozen hand and he can only watch as the other man draws back his blade.

"Father!" Willem cries, then comes a blinding pain in his chest, and the shock on the face of the man who attacks him is only a fading blur because the next thing is a wave of blackness and after that nothing.

RENDEZVOUS

Jack remembers the village well. It was a hospital the last time he was here. He remembers the surgeon who fixed the bone in his broken arm and wonders what happened to him.

He wonders what happened to the people who lived here. They were kind to him. But the village is deserted now and burned. He thinks they must have moved away. Somewhere better.

It has been a slow journey to get here. He dared ride only at night and even then would often seek shelter when he heard other riders on the road. He spent many hours quieting his tired horse in stands of trees or under bridges, waiting for French soldiers to pass by.

It is the third day of his journey and he worries that he has arrived too late. That no one will be here. That no one else is alive and free.

He ties the horse to a branch in the forest by a small stream, where Marengo can graze and drink. He walks slowly to the village, watching for any sign of danger. Trying to listen, like Lieutenant Frost, to sounds that are out of the ordinary.

He sees no one. He walks slowly through the streets, across the long grass of what had been the central village square. It is sad to see the lovely stone cottages lying in ruins, their roofs and doors blackened and burned, the glass of their windows smashed.

As far as he can see, it is deserted and he thinks he'll leave, but where will he go? Back to Antwerp? Try to make his way back to England?

Not for the first time in his life he feels totally and irrevocably alone.

It occurs to him to stay. To hide out in the ruined cottages, hunting and foraging for food in the surrounding forest. Perhaps if he waits long enough the others will come.

He circles the village one more time, looking for a building that is mostly intact. He is nearly at the church when a quick blur of movement catches his eye in the doorway of a ruined cottage.

He draws his dagger as he moves slowly in that direction.

Another small movement in the doorway of a different cottage catches his eye, and he turns that way, running, dagger raised, only to find the doorway, and the remains of the cottage behind it, completely empty.

Am I seeing ghosts? he wonders. *The spirits of the people who lived here?* He begins to feel frightened and turns back to his horse—to find his path blocked by a girl. A girl in rags, with hair cropped almost to her scalp. A girl he well knows.

"Come with me," Héloïse says.

He wants to hug her, so pleased is he to see her. But that is not proper, he knows that, and he suspects that she is not someone who likes to be touched. He gives her his widest smile instead and touches a hand to his heart.

"I am glad to see you," he says.

"And I you," is her reply.

Héloïse leads him into the church and through to a small kitchen at the back. There is a fireplace. She reaches up inside it and there is a click. Part of the wooden floor rises a few inches and Héloïse lifts it. Although it is heavy and appears solid, it rises easily.

The trapdoor reveals a flight of rocky stone steps.

Below is a cellar, surprisingly spacious. It is lit with candles. The faint glow reflects a thousand cracks in the rough-hewn rock walls.

In the center of the room, on a rough bed of sacking, lies Willem. The sacking beneath him is red with his blood.

Jack looks horrified for a moment, until he hears Frost's voice. "Is that you, Jack?"

He sees Frost in the far corner of the cellar.

"Yes, sir, it's me, sir," he says.

Now as his eyes adjust to the low light he takes in the rest of the room.

Captain Arbuckle stands at the base of the stairs.

There are others. A man, old and frail, sits in the far corner. A woman crushes herbs in a small wooden bowl. A young lady sits with Willem, wiping his face with a damp cloth. Jack remembers her from the hospital, although he does not know her name. Some British soldiers in ragged, dirty uniforms sit in a corner.

"What has happened?" Jack asks.

"An accident, nothing more," the woman says with a quick glance at the old man. His face, Jack now sees, is white, and his lips are tightly pressed together. His eyes never leave Willem.

"I am glad you are here," Frost says. "I feared you had been killed or captured at Krabbendijke."

"I almost was, sir," Jack says.

"What do you know of the others?" Frost asks.

Jack shakes his head. "All dead, sir," he says. "I saw their bodies on the meat cart. All except Lieutenant Hoyes and McConnell and Gilbert, sir. McConnell and Gilbert was captured, sir."

"Big Joe is with us," Frost says. "Where are McConnell and Gilbert being held?"

Jack looks at his feet.

"Jack?"

"McConnell is dead, sir," Jack says. "I think Gilbert is too. It was the devil himself. I saw him shoot McConnell, and I'm pretty sure he was going to shoot Gilbert. He would have shot me too if I had stayed. He wouldn't like no witnesses to what he done."

"What devil is this?" Willem's mother asks.

"Thibault," Jack says. "He killed Bony, so he did."

There is a shocked silence.

"Thibault?" Frost asks.

"Him that chased us in the sewers," Jack says. "He looks different now. He only has one eye and one hand, but it was definitely him."

"Thibault killed Napoléon?" Arbuckle says. "I heard it was a British prisoner. Cosette has a letter from Calais that confirms it."

"No, sir," Jack says. "I was there. He shot Lieutenant McConnell and Napoléon and put a pistol in McConnell's hand."

"Why would Thibault shoot Napoléon?" Frost asks.

"I been wondering about that, sir," Jack says. "He didn't seem angry with him or anything."

"Thibault will have assumed control of the army," Arbuckle says. "We must find a way to get this news to the French."

"What do you mean?" Jack asks.

"If we can spread this information it will cause unrest in the French Army," Arbuckle says. "They will not follow the man who killed their beloved Napoléon."

"If they believe it," Jack says.

"They will believe it," Arbuckle says. "They already think this man to be a devil."

"He is the devil," Jack says.

"Blücher marches to Calais," Frost says. "He will find the

French Army in disarray, but he will not attack, not while the French still have battlesaurs."

"Thibault knows about the rockets," Jack says. He feels that news is important, although he is not sure why.

"How?" Frost asks.

"I don't know, sir," Jack says. "That's what Lieutenant McConnell told me."

Frost is motionless, his face hard. Jack looks apologetic at having brought what is clearly bad news.

"They will use the rockets to lure Blücher into a trap," Arbuckle says. "He and his army march to their deaths."

PRIEST HOLE

Willem's eyes open and it is like curtains have been suddenly thrust back on an unclouded morning.

It is not bright, far from it, but the sudden intrusion of light, any light, into such a dark dream is both shocking and disconcerting.

There is no fuzziness, as there sometimes is when waking, just a sharp transition from one world to another. But this new world is strange. His bed is hard, perhaps wooden. The ceiling of the room is rock. He is underground, but that is disorienting because the last memory he has is of the forest. And it is not a cave, like those underneath the Sonian. The walls here are too smooth, cut and scraped by the hand of man.

There are people in this strange rock-walled room but he does not turn his head to look at them. Not yet. He is afraid to do that. He is afraid of what he will see. He is afraid that he has died. If so, this is not heaven.

A face moves above him and he blinks rapidly with relief. This is neither hell nor purgatory. It cannot be, for the face above him is the face of an angel. A pretty blond angel with a lazy eye that immediately snaps into direct focus with concern. For him.

"Cosette?" he asks, checking that this is not merely an interlude in his nightmare. That he has not simply exchanged one dream for another. The act of talking hurts his chest and makes him realize that even breathing is painful. He tries to sit up but a thousand tiny knives begin to plunge into his chest. He gasps with the agony and Cosette quickly places her hands on his shoulders to press him back down.

"Rest," she says.

Pieces of the puzzle start to connect in Willem's mind.

Cosette was a prisoner. Held in the abbey with his mother. If she is here, then he must also be a prisoner. That explains this room. It must be a dungeon beneath the abbey. He shuts his eyes in misery and defeat. He set out to rescue them, but has ended up sharing their cell. He has only made the problem worse.

He turns his head to look for his mother and finds her grinding some kind of paste in a wooden bowl with the end of a bayonet. A makeshift mortar and pestle.

"Maman!" he cries, despite the pain it causes in his chest.

She places the bowl down and comes to him, wiping his forehead with a cool, damp cloth. "Rest, Willem." She echoes Cosette's command.

There are other people in the dungeon, Willem sees. Frost is here, with Jack—kind, loyal, simple Jack. Two people Willem loves as if they were his family. The earl's man, Arbuckle, tough and capable, is here also; he sits on a wooden bench against the wall, cleaning a pistol.

On the floor at the far end of the room is an older man. He seems vaguely familiar to Willem, although he cannot say how he knows him. He is not someone from the village.

A pistol?

He flicks his eyes back to Arbuckle. This is not a dungeon, they cannot be captives of the French. Not if Arbuckle holds a weapon.

"Where are we?" Willem asks.

"Gaillemarde. Beneath the old church," his mother says. "Be quiet. There are French soldiers in the village."

Even as she speaks there is a creak from above, a footstep on a wooden floorboard.

"Why do they search so?" Cosette asks, her voice small, her eyes fearful.

Willem watches her. The thought of a return to captivity must be terrifying.

"They fear Willem," Arbuckle says. "They will not rest until they find him."

"I put all of you in danger," Willem says.

"We are in danger, it is true," Frost says. "But we go there willingly. And we are safe for now in our burrow."

"What about my father?" Willem asks. "François said that he lives. A lie? A ruse to lure us into a trap? Or was there truth behind the trickery?"

His mother smiles. "In that he did not lie," she says. She indicates the old man in the far corner. "He will be happy to see you so full of life."

And now Willem recognizes the old man. It is so many years since he has seen him, so many, many years, and the man has changed immeasurably. But there can be no doubt. It is his father.

"Papa?" he asks.

The man glances at him, then quickly looks away.

"Enough of your self-pity, Maarten," his mother says. "He is alive, and for the most part well. Come and greet your son."

Willem's father hesitates, then slowly gets to his feet. He walks unsteadily toward Willem and now Willem remembers. The darkest part of the dream. The flashing knife, the pain, the blackness.

"It was you," he says. "In the swamp."

"I am so sorry," his father says.

"Willem, do not blame your father," Frost says. "He did not see your face, only your French uniform. He saw you attack François. He did not know of François's treachery. Your father showed great bravery."

"I do not blame him," Willem says. "Where is François?"

"He escaped in the confusion after you were injured," Arbuckle says.

"He knows this place," Willem says. "Might not he tell the French of it?"

"For now, clearly, he has not," Frost says.

His father lays his hand on Willem's arm. "I have waited for this moment for so many years," he says.

For a few moments Willem cannot speak at all. "I truly believed I would never see it," he says finally. He wants to say more, there is so much to say after so many years apart, but he stops at a heavy bootstep right above them, on the wooden roof of their hiding hole. One soldier, more. There are crashes. Bangs that sound like musket stocks on the walls and floor. It seems inconceivable that they will not be found.

They wait, silently, motionless until the crashing and banging stops. The solid trapdoor has kept its secrets. The bootsteps slowly recede. Willem opens his mouth to continue, but the words he had are gone.

"They seem to be searching for the priest hole," Cosette says. "Perhaps François has told them about it."

Arbuckle shakes his head. "All churches have one. They know it is here somewhere."

Willem tries again to sit up, and this time succeeds, grimacing through the pain, although it makes his head swim.

"My wound," he asks. "Is it serious?"

His mother shakes her head. "The scrape of a knife along a rib, nothing more. You were lucky. Now lie back down."

She approaches with the wooden bowl, dipping her fingers into a gray-green paste.

"The danger is infection," she says. "I am doing what I can. Madame Gertruda's house was destroyed, but her garden remains and grows wild. I only hope that my memory, and the power of these herbs, will serve you well."

She applies the salve liberally to Willem's chest.

"What about Blücher?" Willem asks. "What of the attack on Calais?"

There is silence in the cellar. It is Frost who finally speaks.

"A disaster," Frost says. "Napoléon is dead, assassinated by Thibault."

"Surely that is good news," Willem says. "The tyrant is dead, his killer surely in chains in the deepest dungeon."

"Far from it," Arbuckle says. "Thibault now commands the French Army."

"Worse, he knows of our plans," Frost says. "He knows of the rockets and the meaning of their colors."

"How?" Willem asks.

"McConnell," Frost says. "But that is unimportant. What matters is that Blücher marches into a trap."

"Then we must warn him," Willem says.

"Indeed," Frost says.

"I have written a message for the old warhorse," Arbuckle says. "Jack will ride to Blücher to deliver it. If we can reach him before he begins his attack we may be able to avert a catastrophe."

"And if that does not work?" Willem asks. "If Jack does not reach Blücher in time, or if the message is not believed?"

"There is nothing else we can do," his father says.

"There might be," Willem says.

All eyes turn toward him.

"What are you proposing?" Frost asks.

"That we use Napoléon's weapons against him," Willem says.

There is total silence.

"That is foolish talk," Willem's mother says.

"Dangerous, but not foolish," his father says. "The French can ride the beasts; so too can British soldiers."

"It would even the odds if both sides had battlesaurs," Frost says.

Another long silence as they consider what has just been said.

"If we are to do this," Arbuckle says, "then we must do it now without delay."

Willem stands and has to put a hand to one wall to steady himself. His head swims.

"Not Willem," his mother says. "We go to La Hulpe, to seek refuge from the priest there. You must come with us."

"Mother," he says. "To ride the beasts we must mesmerize the beasts. I am the only one here who can do that."

He hears the words coming out of his mouth, and he knows they are right, but he can barely believe he is saying them.

"Not the only one," his father says. "I taught you, if you remember."

"Then we must both go," Willem says.

"You are wounded. You will come with us," his mother says, and in her voice is the same tone he heard so many times as a child, and that more than anything else is what decides him.

She is right, and Willem knows what he must face if he goes, and to be honest, he is not even sure if he *can* go. He can barely stand, let alone walk and crawl through black caves. Yet still he says, "I will go to the caves with the soldiers."

"No—" his mother starts, but he cuts her off, politely but firmly.

"Maman, if I go, then tonight you may be mourning me," he says. "But if I do not go, then many mothers will be mourning many sons in England and Prussia. And the devil himself will be the conqueror of all Europe, and who knows, soon, the world."

"We must all go," Cosette says.

"No, Cosette," Willem says.

"I heard your fine speech to your mother just now," Cosette says. "I fling it back in your face. What applies to you applies to me."

"I am needed in the caves," Willem says. "You are not. Go with my mother to La Hulpe."

"Do you imagine that the French are not expecting you?" Cosette says. "They anticipate just such an attack and the cavern will be full of guards to prevent it."

"And you, a mere girl, can somehow overpower these guards for us?" Arbuckle asks.

Cosette stares at him with such ferocity that Arbuckle—and Willem knows no braver man—quickly lowers his eyes. Cosette looks away, and when she turns back, her face and demeanor have changed; her voice too, its pitch and her accent are all subtly different. "No, a 'mere girl' cannot," she says. "But Lieutenant Horloge just might be able to."

THE WIZARD OF GAILLEMARDE

Workers in peasant smocks scurry around on the floor of the vast cavern beneath the abbey. Some wheel hay carts or trolleys piled high with the carcasses of goats, sheep, and small saurs. Others push barrows of watery steaming dung, the stench of which hangs thickly in the damp, cold underground air. The barrows buzz with saur-bugs, and moths create frenzied clusters around lanterns hung from the walls.

Deloque scratches at his beard, holding his musket loosely in the crook of his arm. He would rather be out in his garden, tending his vegetables, but he, along with almost every other available soldier, is on duty guarding the dark and smelly caves. Their commanders are expecting an attack.

He has been given one of the saur-guns today. A big musket for a big man. Some of the smaller and younger soldiers can barely lift such a gun. He likes it. It is big enough to kill a battlesaur. He almost wishes there would be an attack just so he can see what kind of a hole his gun will put in the chest of an enemy soldier.

A battlesaur growls nearby and all the eyes around Deloque flicker nervously in that direction. The saur, a greatjaw, is chained to the wall close—too close, Deloque thinks—to where the soldiers stand in rank. It is the only saur in the cavern. All the other sets of shackles are empty, the former occupants over in Calais, or Ireland. The greatjaw seems restless, shifting from one foot to the other and occasionally jerking its head against the heavy chains. *Perhaps it is lonely*, he thinks. Or perhaps it is frustrated at all the live meat in front of it, but out of its reach. It raises its head and growls again, a long moaning howl, so loud that he can feel it. It lowers its head and eyes the rows of soldiers. For a moment it seems to be looking directly at him. Deloque's palms start to sweat, despite the cold.

He thinks of the girl: Cosette. The prisoner, now released. He thinks of her often. He salivates at the thought of what he might do to her if he caught her. But she will be long gone now. To a new city. Perhaps to a new country. Somewhere she can hide. She will have to hide for the rest of her life after what she did to the lieutenant. After what she did to him! Stealing their uniforms and locking them in the prison cells.

Horloge is a weak, insipid little man. But now he, Deloque, has something to hold over him. Horloge's simpering cowardice in the prison cell. He will suffer for that. But not now. Later, when it is to Deloque's greatest advantage.

There is a murmur in the ranks; heads have turned from the greatjaw toward the darkness in the depths of the cavern. He follows the gaze of the others but can see nothing.

It takes his mind a few moments to work out what the other soldiers have already realized, what they are looking at. *Nothing.*

That is what is strange. The rear of the cave is muffled in darkness. All the lamps have been extinguished. He is mulling this over when it occurs to him that this could be the prelude to an attack.

"Hold fast," a voice calls out. It is the sergeant. A rougher, tougher man Deloque has never met, but there is an uneasy tone in his voice. The sergeant feels something, Deloque thinks, because he feels it too. A foreboding.

Two more lamps flicker out, the creeping blackness from the depths of the earth swallowing their light as it moves toward the soldiers.

"Make ready," the sergeant calls.

Make ready for what?

Deloque hoists his heavy gun, cradling it in his arms, raising the barrel to aim at the sky. Sky? There is no sky. Only a solid rock roof over their heads, trapping them underground with whatever now comes.

There is movement in the deepest shadows of the cave. Fading into view as if the blackness itself has swirled and formed and solidified into a living creature. It walks toward them, arms outstretched. Not it. *She!*

It is so incomprehensible that his mind cannot at first believe it. It is her. The prisoner. The escapee. Cosette. Or something that has taken her form.

She (it) walks forward slowly. She still wears the stolen uniform of the lieutenant but over it flows a long, black cape.

There are murmurs and movement around him, but the sergeant seems uncertain of his next actions.

Now she is fully in the light of the main cavern, her hair golden, shining like silk in the lamplights. Deloque almost breaks ranks; he wants to rush over to the girl, to wind his fingers through that beautiful hair, to feel the softness of the skin of her neck between his fingers as he snaps it.

But he fears that it would dissolve back into the blackness. And so would he.

He can do nothing but watch as she raises her arms slightly. The explosion at her feet is a bright flash and a brief puff of smoke with a sharp crack like musketshot. He blinks at the insult to his eyes and ears, and as the smoke clears, it is no longer the girl who stands before them. *It* has transformed into a young man, the cape flowing from his shoulders, a cowl shadowing his features. But Deloque does not need to see his face to know who this is. They all know. *The Wizard of Gaillemarde.*

"Present!" the sergeant calls, unable to keep a nervous quiver from his voice.

They all hear him but only a few raise their weapons. The rest stand, petrified at this manifestation of evil.

There are stories. The wizard is not human. He cannot be killed. They say he was shot in the chest with a pistol and, unharmed, spat the ball out of his mouth. They say he made an entire ship disappear into thin air. Some say that he can transform himself into a battlesaur.

Deloque does not know whom to believe. He is a simple man and has learned to trust what his eyes show him, and little else. He lowers the wide, wide muzzle of his huge saur-gun toward the wizard.

The robed figure raises his hands and begins to rub them together, faster and faster, until his fingers are no more than a blur. Steam begins to rise from the wizard's hands, drifting upward. Deloque's eyes are drawn to the roof of the cave where, miraculously, impossibly, storm clouds start to gather. Roiling, tumbling clouds inside the cave. It is not possible and yet it is real.

There are gasps from around him. Movement, too, as terrified cave workers run past the soldiers, heading for the surface.

From somewhere Deloque finds an inner strength. The wizard must be destroyed. He tries to steady his musket on the robed figure.

The clouds thicken and darken, and Deloque shivers and tightens his finger on the trigger. The wizard stops rubbing his hands and abruptly claps them together. Thunder roars and lightning flashes overhead just as the sergeant screams, "Fire!"

Deloque's musket jerks and the shot goes wild, high into the wall of the cave. But the air around him shivers with the sound of musketshots and is smeared with smoke from the gunpowder. The wizard is hit and staggers backward into the shadows. Deloque stares, his mouth open, as the thunder still echoes off the rock walls.

A cheer starts among the soldiers but it is cut short as the wizard steps forward again into the light. He spits one, two, three musketballs from his mouth and raises his hands again to the roof of the cave.

It begins to rain.

Deloque is the first to break ranks, throwing down his musket, pushing other soldiers out of the way as he runs, panic-stricken, toward the ramp that leads out of the cave. There are shouts, some screams around him, and the retreating ranks of the soldiers have become a rout. Deloque barely notices. He runs, pushing some out of the way, trampling over those who fall.

He is a man. A big, strong, brutal man.

But no man is a match for such magic.

TRICORNES

The simplest of tricks, given the right presentation, can perplex the brightest of minds. Yet even Willem is surprised at how well his illusion has worked.

The clouds were no more than steam, created by diverting the outlet pipe from the water boiler. The lightning, and its corresponding thunder, were achieved by cutting the thin lead pipe that carried the firedamp gas to the boiler. The firedamp, lighter than air, drifted up to the ceiling of the cavern, where it floated, waiting, until Arbuckle, on cue, ignited it at the pipe end.

It was as much good luck as good planning. Too much firedamp and the explosion would have annihilated everyone in the cavern. Too little, and it would not have ignited. But it did, with a huge flash that lit the clouds of steam and even to Willem looked just like lightning.

The rain was a bonus. The clouds of steam, condensing on the cold rock ceiling of the cavern and dripping down.

It was almost perfect. At that distance, in the darkness, it was always going to be a difficult shot, and he had hoped to unnerve the soldiers enough that they would not fire, or that their shots would go wild. It had worked. Almost. Just one soldier, somewhere in the ranks, had the steadiness of heart and aim, or the sheer good luck, to hit Willem dead in the chest.

For Willem the impact on the heavily padded metal plate

strapped to his torso was like being kicked in the stomach by a mule. His already injured chest had screamed fire, and it took all of his energy to regather himself, to step forward and spit out the three musketballs he had placed in his mouth earlier.

Cosette helps him remove the metal plate as Arbuckle and Big Joe seal the entrance to the cave, lowering a wooden gate that is suspended from the celing. It is a massive gate for massive creatures, constructed of hefty timber planks buttressed by poles as thick as the mast of a small ship. It is hinged at one end. A heavy chain runs from the bottom of the gate up though a large metal pulley system on the ceiling of the cavern and down to a chain-stay and winch on top of a jagged spur of rock, rising like a huge claw in the center of the floor.

The gate slams shut with a thud and a cloud of dust.

"Quickly," Arbuckle says. "That will hold them, but not for long. Where are the tricornes?"

"This way," Héloïse says.

Willem follows them around a sharp corner at the rear of the cavern, and under a low knuckle of rock into another large cave.

Here there are tricornes. Four of them. Each is almost twice the height of a man, with two great horns jutting from its head, in front of a large flare of bone. A third, shorter horn is at the end of the snout.

Despite the horns they seem placid, incurious; they do not look up at the entrance of the humans but continue calmly chewing hay. Their saddles are long with two pommels, for two riders. A rope ladder hangs from the center of each saddle.

Holsters for three pistols are attached to the rear part of the saddle on each side. Six pistols per animal.

"Each saur will need a rider and a gunner," Arbuckle says. "We have five soldiers, enough for only two of the beasts."

"I can ride," Cosette says.

"I will not allow it," Willem says.

"And who are you to say what I may or may not do?" Cosette asks.

"It is a job for soldiers," Willem says a little awkwardly. There are not enough soldiers.

"I do not know how to load or fire a gun," Cosette says. "But I can ride as well as any man."

Arbuckle chuckles and says to Willem, "I think there is no reasoning with your intended."

"She is not my—" Willem stops, because she *is* his intended. As he is hers. He has known this since Gaillemarde. That is why he cannot bear the thought of her riding into battle. Yet he knows he cannot stop her.

"I will ride also," he says. For many reasons he cannot let Cosette ride while he remains behind.

"Then we are short by just one rider," Arbuckle says.

Willem looks around the cave, his eyes passing over Frost and settling on Héloïse.

"I will not ride the great demons," Héloïse says. She stares at him, unashamed.

"Then I will," Frost says. "That will give us eight. Enough for all the tricornes."

"How can you ride?" Arbuckle asks.

"Put me in the saddle and I will show you how," Frost answers.

"He has no eyes, but makes use of his other senses in ways that would astound you," Willem says.

"Very well." Arbuckle gestures to the other soldiers. "We will guard the entrance while you prepare the saurs."

Cosette walks toward the nearest tricorne as Arbuckle and the other soldiers disappear back into the main cave. She stands in front of the first tricorne, well within range of its horns. Willem wants to cry out to her to be careful, but restrains himself. The tricorne looks up from its food and regards her briefly, then lowers its head again.

Cosette moves toward the hanging rope ladder.

"Wait," Willem says, but she ignores him and takes another step.

The great animal turns toward her, a low, rumbling growl warning her away.

"Wait," Willem says again.

Cosette remains perfectly still until the animal resumes feeding, then takes another step forward.

Willem holds his breath. He does not dare speak for fear of alarming the beast.

He examines the tricorne as Cosette moves closer and closer to the rope ladder.

Large metal blinders cover the beast's eyes. They are open, but can be closed by leather cords that lead up behind its neck. His father gave them detailed instructions on how to control the battlesaurs. To steer the great saurs you simply open one eye more than the other. It will turn in that direction. Leather flaps sit above the nostrils. Those too can be opened or shut. To stop, you shut both the blinders and the nostril flaps.

To get the beast to move requires something else. Something that seems magical, even to Willem. *Electricity.*

Cosette grasps the ladder and pulls herelf up the first step.

"They neither fear us, nor want to eat us," she says. "You do not need your sparkle tricks with these saurs."

Willem is not convinced, but Cosette skips lightly up the rope ladder without any reaction from the tricorne. She does not try to ride sidesaddle but adjusts her smock so that she can put a leg over the other side. She examines the reins for a moment.

"There is no battery," she says.

"The batteries are in the armory," Héloïse says. "I will get them."

Cosette climbs carefully down, patting the great beast gently on the side of its neck. It stirs, but makes no other movement nor sound.

Héloïse is quickly back with the battery, a small gray box. She carries four of them and places them at Willem's feet. "I will get the pistols," she says, and disappears once again.

"Let me try," Willem says.

Cosette nods.

Willem takes a battery and moves to the rope ladder, struggling to control his breathing. This is no meat-eater, he knows this, but its sheer size and power are terrifying. It could end his life with a misplaced footstep or a nudge of its head. He places a foot on the ladder, and before he can allow himself to think any further, he climbs.

The skin is rough and ridged. The beast feels cold to the touch. He reaches the top and slides a leg over the back of the animal, just behind the great bony shield. Here two wires protrude from the skin at the base of the skull, just like the ones he saw on that terrible night in the village.

The wires clip in to two connectors on the battery, and a small switch is marked ON and OFF. He ensures it is in the off position before connecting the wires.

Héloïse brings a supply of pre-loaded pistols from the armory, handing them up with one foot on the ladder. Willem slots them into the holsters by the rear saddles. He climbs down as Cosette climbs the ladder of the next tricorne.

Big Joe and Mogansondram arrive in the rear cavern just as Willem is slotting the last of the pistols into the last of the holsters on the last of the saurs.

"How are you faring?" Big Joe asks.

"I have just finished," Willem says.

"Good," Big Joe says. "There are sounds from outside the great door. We think they are preparing to attack."

"Then it is time for us to mount the beasts," Willem says.

"With your permission," Frost says.

"It would be my honor to have you on board," Willem says, as Frost, without any assistance, finds and begins to climb the ladder.

Willem turns his attention to the shackles chaining the tricorne to the rock wall. He releases a metal pin and slides out a heavy catch. The chains fall away. The beast is free.

It does not move at first, but merely stands where it was chained, as if unaware it has been released.

"You must hurry, Willem." Frost's voice comes from the rear saddle.

Willem pulls lightly on the cords so that the creature will turn to the right, then flicks the lever on the battery for the merest fraction of a second. There is no reaction from the tricorne. He presses the lever forward a little longer and the animal stirs and shakes its head, but does not move.

He presses it forward firmly and the beast shudders and begins to step forward, veering to the right. Willem releases the lever and the beast continues to trudge along. He turns to see the other tricornes slowly forming a line behind him.

They round the corner to the main cavern and his tricorne stops immediately at the sight of the greatjaw shackled to the wall. He has to nudge it again with the battery to get it moving.

He is halfway down the length of the main cavern when the great wooden door explodes.

The shattering crash of thunder that comes from the entrance is followed by a deadly whirlwind of smoke, dust, and shards of wood.

Willem ducks behind the bony ridges of the shield at the tricorne's neck, instinctively hauling the noseflaps and blinders shut to protect the tricorne from the worst of the blast that washes over and around them.

Light pours in through the gaping hole where the great wooden door used to be.

The battlesaur shackled to the wall close to the door is falling, hit by the explosion—dead, unconscious, or injured, Willem cannot tell. There is a loud, meaty thud as it hits the ground.

The French are inside the cavern now, marching down the main ramp.

In the confusion of the smoke and dust Willem sees Arbuckle stand up in full view of the oncoming troops, a huge saur-gun in his hands. He fires and a sheet of flame belches out of the end of the gun, a cloud of musketballs filling the air. French soldiers scream or grunt as they fall, but behind them are more, rank after rank.

Already Arbuckle has dropped the saur-gun and picked up another. Another roar, and more French soldiers fall, but now Arbuckle is running, ducking and dodging as metal balls dig rock chips from the wall and floor of the cave around him.

The unstoppable tide of French soldiers pours into the cave and Willem knows all is lost. They are too few. They have pistols against muskets. The great, audacious plan is over before it has really begun. He cowers behind the body shield of the tricorne as musketballs pound into it.

But now there is a sound of a different kind and through the swirling clouds of dust and smoke Willem sees the battlesaur, back on its feet, free of its shackles, raising its head to the roof of the cavern and filling it with its terrifying guttural roar. Its eyes sweep around the cavern, finding Willem, who shudders, but its gaze moves on and it rampages forward, toward the light, toward the ramp. The French retreat in confusion before the beast, leaving bloodied and wounded comrades littering the ramp and the cavern floor.

"Now!" Arbuckle cries. He scales the ladder up the side of Cosette's tricorne, then hauls it up, hooking it onto the saddle.

Willem needs no encouragement. He rams the lever on the battery forward. The animal shudders and begins to move. Willem flicks the lever again and the beast breaks into a trot.

The ramp is short and the sunlight in the courtyard of the abbey is sudden and shocking for eyes that have spent too long in the dark reaches of the caves. Blinking through the pain, his eyes filling with tears, Willem sees the French soldiers screaming, running, only a very few aiming their muskets at the beast that rages in the enclosed courtyard.

Then they are through the abbey gate and onto the wide path outside. Willem steers the great animal to the west and feels branches and leaves brush at his legs as they begin the long charge.

To Calais.

BY THE RIVER

She finds François kneeling by the riverbank, staring at the water. She knows this place, and knows it is his favorite part of the forest. She has seen him here many times, and knew it was where she would find him.

He does not seem to hear Héloïse approach and so she stands for a while behind him, also watching the water. The way it moves, ripples that merge and form whorls before spinning away into nothing. She listens to the sound of the river as she listens also to the sounds of the forest around them.

It has not taken her long to find him. There are places known only to those who know the forest. Places of peace, of sanctuary.

She slides the bayonet silently out of her smock and moves close behind François.

"Do not move," she says as she presses the edge of the blade against his neck. Her knees press into his back and her hand is on his forehead. He stiffens with surprise, but does not move.

"I was foolish," he says. "To think that she could ever love someone like me."

"Cosette," Héloïse whispers softly.

"She is not like us," François says.

"She is from a different world," Héloïse says.

"So it is," François says.

"I could kill you now," she says. "It would take no more than a twist of the blade."

"You will not," he says, though he does not know how he knows this.

"You are to blame," she says. "For everything. For everyone. I should kill you."

He waits and gradually the pressure on his neck eases.

"Today you live," she says.

With that she steps back and the bayonet suddenly juts from the ground next to him.

He grabs it, seizing her arm at the same instant, pulling her down, rolling on top of her, the bayonet now at her neck.

He presses down and she feels a trickle of blood on her skin.

"I do not do this lightly," François says. "I feel that if circumstances were different, it might be a ring, not a blade, that I press upon you."

"That is a choice you must make," she says, making no effort to fight.

"I serve Napoléon, and nothing, not even you, must divert me from my purpose," he says.

"Napoléon is dead," Héloïse says.

His eyes widen in shock, but then narrow.

"You speak the words of the devil," he says. "It is nothing but trickery to save your own life. Napoléon was sent by God to unite the world; God would not allow him to be killed."

"You know me, François," Héloïse says. "There is no deceit or trickery in me."

"Then you were lied to," François says. "How did you come by this news?"

"From Jack, the simple one," Héloïse says. "He is without guile."

François nods, acknowledging this truth.

"He witnessed the event with his own eyes," Héloïse says. "Napoléon is dead, at the hand of Thibault. It is Thibault who will unite the world under his banner."

"The devil!" François is aghast.

"It gives me no pleasure to speak these words," Héloïse says.

"But the things that I have done!" He raises his head and lets out a scream. A primal sound of fear and loathing, it echoes through the trees. "I did them for God!"

"You were deceived by the devil," Héloïse says.

"I will go to hell, and it has all been for nothing," François says.

"Not yet you will not," Héloïse says. "With confession and repentance can come absolution."

"I have sinned," François says. "I am responsible for many deaths. I killed my own cousin."

"That is the past," Héloïse says. "You must now look to the future. Stay with me. Here in the forest. Lead a good life with me. God will see this."

He sits with his head in his hands, quietly sobbing.

She makes a bowl out of a leaf and squats by the river, filling it with water for him.

When she straightens, he is gone and it is her turn to weep.

RIDING TO CALAIS

Jack has ridden up a long, winding slope, cresting it within sight of the walled city of Calais. The sun is bright and the sea sparkles beyond the walls. There are ships in the distance too, and he does not need to see their colors to know they are British.

Back in the priest hole, Frost had entrusted Jack with a mission: "Ride to Calais. Ride like the wind. Find Blücher. Stop him. At all costs he must not engage the French Army. Can you do this?"

"I can try, sir," Jack said. He hesitated. "But why would he listen to me, sir?"

Arbuckle pulled a sheet of paper from inside his tunic and wrote rapidly on it with a quill pen. He folded it and handed it to Jack.

"Give this letter to Blücher," he said. "Whoever you speak to, say this: *'Dringende Nachricht für Blücher.'* Repeat it back to me."

Jack tried his best, struggling with the unfamiliar sounds.

"Good enough," Arbuckle said. "It means 'Urgent message for Blücher.' Practice it on the way."

"You must stop Blücher at all costs," Frost said. "Do you understand?"

"Yes, sir," Jack said.

Arbuckle pulled a pistol from his holster. He took a pepper cartridge from his ammunition pouch and quickly loaded the pistol before handing it to Jack.

"Go, man," Arbuckle said. "Every second counts."

Now, after hours of hard travel, Jack has arrived. On the farmlands stretched out below him he sees the Prussian Army, neat rows of soldiers, cannon, and horses.

His own horse is almost spent, spittle coating the sides of his face, his labored breathing only easing when Jack lets him rest for a moment at the top of the hill.

"Good boy," he says affectionately, patting Marengo's neck. The horse shakes his mane and gives a soft whinny.

The army below him looks as if it has just got here; the soldiers are still setting up camp. Rows of tents at the rear are being erected. There are no signs of battle, no smoke, no sounds of gunfire. He thinks he might just deliver his message in time, and rehearses in his head the phrase that Arbuckle taught him.

Marengo is breathing a little easier and they are starting down the other side of the hill when Jack sees a streak of fire from within the walls of the city. A rocket sending up a flare on a parachute that drifts slowly to earth, a yellow star hanging above the city like in the stories from the Bible.

He digs his heels into the horse's sides and this magnificent stallion flies down the hill, mane streaming behind him.

From the base of the hill Jack rides through a small glade where leafy trees form a roof over the road, an oasis of peace that belies what is ahead.

Then it is farmland and Jack encounters the first of the Prussian soldiers, two light cavalrymen patrolling the rear.

"Dringende Nachricht für Blücher," Jack cries as soon as he is within earshot, before they have a chance to challenge him.

One of them starts to talk, a long string of incomprehensible sounds. Jack just keeps repeating: *"Dringende Nachricht für Blücher."*

He remembers the envelope and pulls it from his tunic, waving it at the men. *"Dringende Nachricht für Blücher!"*

They look at each other, then one of them nods and points down the road. Jack is gone before the arm is half-raised, spurring the horse forward. There are more soldiers here, the rear echelons of the army. The cooks, the engineers, the caravans of the merchants who trail behind the army.

To everyone he meets he repeats the phrase he has memorized.

The words as he says them start to get mixed up in his mind and he says them in the wrong order or misses words until he is so confused that he can only hold up the envelope and say, *"Dringende. Blücher."*

It is enough. Everyone nods and points him in a direction until he arrives at a tent, well guarded.

"Blücher," Jack says. *"Dringende!"*

A guard takes the letter from his outstretched hand and disappears inside. A moment later a man in the uniform of a field marshal emerges. He speaks at first in German, then switches to English when Jack shakes his head.

"Who are you?" Blücher asks.

"Sir, I'm Private Jack Sullivan, Royal Horse Artillery, G troop. I mean I used to be, before I went to work for Lieutenant Frost, sir." Jack stops, flustered.

"Is this information true?" Blücher thunders, waving the letter.

"You must not attack!" Jack cries. "The devil has battlesaurs!"

A peal of thunder comes from the front line and smoke and the smell of gunpowder are brought swiftly to them on the freshening breeze.

"Your message arrives too late," Blücher says.

IN THE NAME OF THE DEVIL

François wanders in the place that is most his home, the great forest of the Sonian.

He walks aimlessly, following routes instinctively, barely seeing the huge trees and the restless undergrowth, stumbling over rocks that normally his feet would know and avoid. Seeing shards of sky through eyes blurred with tears. He does not question the direction he is taking, allowing himself to be guided by unseen powers.

He prays as he walks. He prays in a shout that sucks the air from his body and leaves him panting and wheezing. His words echo from tree to tree, shimmering through the forest, but that is what he wants. He shouts to make sure God will hear.

"Forgive me, Lord," he screams in wretched pain and grief. "Forgive me for I have sinned. Forgive me, Lord, I believed I was doing Your work. Forgive me, Lord, the evil trickster had me fooled."

He does not see the forest because his head is full of images. The faces of his mother, his uncle, the people of the village. All dead at the order of the devil. His cousin, Jean. His eyes, shocked, frightened, and slowly growing cold as François sat over him with the bloodied knife.

So much death and destruction. François had not understood it, but he had accepted it as God's will.

But it was not God's will. It was the devil's.

That trickster. That fraud. That liar.

François comes to the top of a cliff and a waterfall. He blinks away tears. This is a place he knows well. It was here that he, Jean, and Willem found the firebird nest. It was here that it all began. It can be no coincidence that he has been guided to this place.

It is a place of peace. Around him the trees are full of birdsong. Far below, a horse, a British officer's horse still in its full regalia, lowers its neck to drink from the cool running water. There is no sign of the officer. The river sparkles in the sunlight, gurgling through boulders.

A winged saur swoops down the cliff, skimming the stream, its claws trailing in the water, then dipping in with a splash, emerging with a struggling fish. François looks down at the sharp rocks below and he thinks of Héloïse. He thinks of her forgiveness and her unconditional love, and finally, here in the open on the edge of the cliff, God speaks to him and he knows what he must do.

A breeze ruffles the leaves on the trees at the top of the cliff, a gentle hand at François's back, urging him toward the edge.

INTO BATTLE

The rain starts just after midnight. Softly at first, a fine mist, giving them enough warning to fold the leather covers down over the three pistols strapped to either side of the saddle. The rain intensifies, as does the wind, driving sheets of hard water at them sideways. Willem ducks behind the bony shield of the tricorne's head. In the saddle behind him, Frost is silent.

They have passed through many small towns on the road to Calais. Still nobody has seen them. The residents remain asleep, perhaps dreaming of thunder, as the huge hooves of the tricornes tear up cobblestones through the center of each town.

Occasionally Willem glances behind him, and each time he is awestruck at the huge horns of the beasts that follow. What will happen when they encounter the French greatjaws, he has no way of knowing.

It is only when they pass through the thriving city of Kortrijk that they are seen for the first time, by milkmen and delivery boys beginning their morning rounds. All watch with gaping mouths as the four massive horned creatures charge through the city streets.

The attacks continued throughout the night, growing more daring as the rain intensified. Jack makes sure to keep both of his pistols dry. When the time comes to use them he wants them to work.

Rain changes war. He knows this. It makes muskets harder and slower to load and fire. Cannon can get bogged down in muddy ground. As the meat-eaters have charged in from the sides, the Prussian soldiers have often had to defend themselves with only swords and bayonets, virtually useless against the great battlesaurs.

They roam now around the edges of the army, their very presence terrifying the soldiers in the formations. There has been no sleep tonight for the Prussians.

Jack, although just as terrified of the beasts, wishes that a battlesaur would attack where he is standing. One of his pistols is loaded with pepper. If he can get close enough to the saur and fire the pepper into its eyes, he thinks he can improve the odds for the Prussians on this wet and windy night.

Another scream comes from somewhere behind him and peering backward through the rain he sees a battlesaur stomping away from the lines with pieces of soldier falling from its mouth.

Everywhere the Prussians cower, useless, waiting for the next attack, wondering who will be next to be crushed and dismembered by that fearsome mouth and the teeth, those huge, terrifying teeth.

They cannot retreat and they cannot advance. All they can do is wait for morning and pray for dry weather.

Jack tends to Marengo for a while. The horse trembles when the battlesaurs are near but does not rear or shy away. He is a brave horse as well as a strong one. No wonder Napoléon chose him for his own.

Another scream comes from the far side of the army. A cannon fires, but there is no resultant cheering as there would be if the cannon had found its target.

Jack wonders about the others. How they got on in the caves.

He worries about Frost. How he will be without Jack to guide and protect him.

Still another scream, this time from the rear of the formations.

It will be a long night, Jack thinks.

The view from the top of the hill is shocking.

Willem brings his steed to a halt, surveying the scene that stretches out before them, describing it to Frost. Cosette stops her tricorne next to his.

In the distance, on the coast, is the city of Calais, surrounded by a high saur-wall topped with battlements, the clean hard lines broken at regular intervals by cannon ports. On the far side, by the seawall, a tall stone watchtower guards the harbor.

The overnight rain has stopped. The sun has not yet risen but the sky is alight with the red rush of morning. Below them, overturned ammunition caissons litter the flat farmlands before the city.

The Prussian Army is in disarray, their cannon broken and strewn around the paddocks. It is the French artillery that fires, each roar and gush of smoke matched by a great scar gouged into the ragged Prussian ranks.

And roaming free are the battlesaurs. Willem counts six of them.

They hunt at the edges of the battle, occasionally racing forward to pick off some hapless soldier as his comrades rush backward in terror.

A small group of Prussian soldiers break free suddenly from the main body of the army, running for a small forest and the meager shelter it offers. One of the greatjaws is on them before they are halfway to the tree line, stomping, slashing, and tearing with those terrible teeth. Their screams are piercing but mercifully brief.

"But why do the Prussians not retreat or surrender?" Willem asks.

"Thibault," Arbuckle says, his face grim. "He does not mean to defeat them. He intends to wipe them out. They have broken their alliance. They have proven themselves untrustworthy and Thibault will not want to leave such an army in his rear. He will not want to risk an attack on Paris while he is occupied over the English Channel. He will destroy them."

"It will be a massacre," Willem says.

"Then let us even the odds," Arbuckle says from the saddle behind Cosette.

She spurs her tricorne forward.

Willem says, "Cosette."

She looks back.

"I will look out for you down there," Willem says as he jolts his own saur into movement.

"And I you," Cosette says, and it is the closest thing to a declaration of love that has ever passed between them.

"The flare!" Big Joe cries, and they all look to the coast. A streak of light climbs from the stone watchtower, leaving a bubbling smoky wake. It bursts into a bright green star, drifting slowly back down over the city."

"What does it mean?" Cosette asks.

"The signal for the Royal Navy to depart," Willem says.

"We must hurry," Arbuckle says. "Or there will be battlesaurs in the streets of London tonight."

"Is there a signal that would tell the navy to remain here instead?" Cosette asks.

"A red rocket," Frost says. "We must find the red rockets."

"Where?" Cosette asks.

Willem points at the smoky trail that is dispersing slowly in the clear blue sky, tracing it back down to the top of the stone tower in the fort.

"There," he says. "The tower."

The hill shudders under the giant hooves of the four tricornes. Leaves whisper a rustling alarm and birds are shaken out of the trees. A dust cloud rises behind them as they pick up speed, thundering down the hill toward the flat fields beyond.

Only now does Willem think of Jack. Did he make it? Did he warn the Prussians but too late? Is he dead, or alive somewhere in the midst of the battle below?

There is the constant crackle of musketfire punctuated by the *boom, boom, boom* of the artillery.

Willem looks again at the wide flare of bone in front of him and wonders if it will stop a musketball. He hopes so.

The Prussian soldiers have spotted them now. There is confusion, perhaps because they see a woman warrior with blond hair waving behind her, still in the unbuttoned French uniform jacket of Lieutenant Horloge. But as the Prussians take note of the several red British uniforms, they let out a cheer that is quickly taken up by the entire army.

Just as the Prussians have spotted them, so have the French. Already one of the battlesaurs is heading toward them at a run, the lurching, two-footed stride of the greatjaw so different from the four-footed gallop of the tricornes. Willem's ride, without any encouragement from Willem, turns, aiming directly for the greatjaw. The ground is soft and the huge feet of the tricorne sink deeply but this does not seem to slow it down.

A gunshot sounds from over Willem's left shoulder. He jumps, and half turns to see Arbuckle in the rear part of Cosette's saddle already reaching for another pistol.

The greatjaw slides to a stop in the muddy field, standing its ground directly in front of the charging tricorne, its mouth open, those huge teeth glistening. Why does it not move out of the way?

Only at the very last second, the greatjaw steps nimbly to one side and the teeth slash down, but the tricorne has been expecting this and somehow shunts itself sideways into the chest of the greatjaw, unbalancing it. The greatjaw slips, falls, and writhes around in the mud, struggling to get back to its feet, but a second tricorne is there, one of its long horns driving up into the softer skin at the base of the greatjaw's neck as it tries to rise. It falls again and this time does not struggle.

Willem lets out a scream of excitement, which is matched by Cosette on the tricorne behind.

"To the cannon!" Arbuckle shouts.

Jack has watched the French cannon chewing into the ranks at the front, the Prussian artillery unable to respond. The six French battlesaurs have been roaming at will, rampaging through the Prussian infantry, which scatter before them, unable to hold their lines. The cavalry has tried again and again to charge at the saurs, but the horses always refuse, turning away at the last minute.

It has been a catastrophe.

But now Willem and the others are here, storming in on some new kind of saur that Jack has not seen before! The greatjaws are diverted, giving hope to the Prussian infantry, enabling their officers to generate some kind of order in the ranks.

In the field to his left Jack sees a tricorne hurtling toward a greatjaw, but the bigger beast steps out of the way, surprisingly nimble for a huge animal. It grabs down as the tricorne passes, its huge teeth clamping on to one of the rear legs of the three-horned saur. It lifts and the tricorne goes down, over on its side, creating a huge crater in the mud.

Jack runs to Marengo, springing up into the saddle. He whirls and gallops through the French ranks, which open to let him through.

The tricorne is trying to twist around to reach the greatjaw with its horns, but it cannot twist far enough. The greatjaw will not open its mouth to release the leg, and rakes at the stomach of the tricorne with its claws.

Jack clutches the reins with one hand and draws his pistol with the other. He thinks he has correctly remembered which pistol has the pepper and which has the ball. He hopes he is right. The rider of the greatjaw sees him approaching, raises a pistol, and fires, but misses wildly as the saur thrashes its head.

Of all the horses on the field, only Marengo will charge at a saur, Jack learns. The horse remains steady and true and Jack waits until he is sure of his shot, then pulls the trigger just as they come in range of the greatjaw. The crash of the pistol shot is followed by a brief mist of black powder and the greatjaw screams, thrashing its head from side to side, its rider barely holding on.

The greatjaw turns and runs, snorting, wild, crazed, throwing its rider before it has gone more than ten strides.

Willem steers his huge steed toward the French lines. To reach the enemy first they must pass over the remains of the Prussian artillery. Broken wheels, smoldering caissons, and the bodies of the artillerymen—a blackened, burning, hellish scene of devastation, mud, and carnage wrought by Thibault's battlesaurs.

Now in front of them the cannon of the French are lined along a cobblestone road in front of the saur-wall. The infantry and cavalry seem to have disappeared, but looking up Willem sees a long row of muskets lining the battlements. The cannon belch red and yellow flames and thick smoke and Willem feels the wind of one of the huge iron balls as it passes close to his leg. A little closer and he would have lost the leg, and his life soon after. Behind him he hears screams as the cannonballs wreak more damage on the Prussian lines.

Already the cannon crews are reloading. He sees the spongemen with their long ramrods frantically worming the barrels. The loaders with their heavy cannonballs or canister shot. The firers with their fuses and burning linstocks. He hears the officers shouting orders. But the French cannoneers are unused to being on this end of a battlesaur charge. They drop their ammunition, their ramrods and fuses, breaking ranks and running for the safety of the thick walls of the city.

The smoke from the last barrage is still hanging in the air as Willem and Frost reach the French front lines. Their tricorne brushes aside the first cannon as if it were a toy, smashing the wheels, dumping the weapon into the mud.

The air around him sounds as if it's alive with buzzing insects—musketballs! Glancing up, Willem sees puffs of smoke obscuring the French soldiers lining the battlements. A pistol sounds behind him, then another, as Frost returns fire.

"Ignore the cannon," Frost shouts. "Destroy the ammunition!"

Willem ducks down behind the bony shield of his tricorne and again hears Frost's pistol sound behind. He turns the beast, charging sideways along the artillery support line, just behind the row of cannon. They overturn caisson after caisson, strewing cannonballs, explosive canister shot, and gunpowder across the cobblestone road. A fire starts and quickly spreads to the gunpowder stores. The air fills with dense black smoke from the burning wagons, punctuated constantly by great flashes of heat and light as canisters and powder barrels detonate. The wind carries the smoke toward the city, and the sound of the muskets on the battlements ceases as the soldiers there are engulfed and blinded.

"We must get to the tower," Frost shouts, and Willem points his ride at one of the gated entrances to the city.

Where are the other tricornes? Willem wonders, even as he presses his mount onward.

A glance back tells him. Two are in battle with an equal number of greatjaws. The body of another tricorne lies in an empty field. He cannot see the riders and sight of the field is soon lost in the billowing smoke. He remembers his promise to keep Cosette safe. He prays she and Arbuckle are not the fallen riders, but there is nothing that he can do now but that: pray.

Before him, the large wooden gates are closing rapidly. Through them he can see two or three soldiers lending their shoulders to each gate. They slam shut just as Willem reaches them. They were built to keep out saurs, but the builders could not have imagined a saur like this. The wood splinters; the gates fall as if made of paper; the soldiers behind are tossed aside like toys under the creature's headlong rush.

The narrow streets of the city are choked with smoke and panicking soldiers who scatter before the huge horns and great thundering hooves.

One soldier bravely stands his ground, raising his musket toward Willem, but a pistol sounds behind Willem's ear and the man flies backward into a water trough.

"The tower!" Frost shouts.

A glance up, and even through the smoke Willem sees it. A tall circular watchtower in the distance to the south.

The battle of two armies has become the battle of the dinosaurs.

Men and horses scatter as the great beasts rampage across the battlefield, the tricornes charging, their horns lowered, the greatjaws dodging out of the way and snapping as they pass. Through it all rides Jack Sullivan on his fearless steed.

He races for a small hillock on the outskirts of the battle where two huge saurs are locked in combat.

The tricorne charges but the greatjaw steps nimbly out of the way. Its massive jaw latches on to the neck of the other beast. The rider disappears and the man in the rear saddle flings himself off as the greatjaw bears the tricorne to the ground and pins it there with a giant foot.

But Jack is moving without fear or thought. He spurs Marengo onward, drawing his pistol. There will be opportunity for only one shot and Jack knows how difficult it is to shoot from horseback. For that reason he waits until the very last minute. Riding right up toward the two great saurs locked in a dance of death. Only when he is right in front does he raise the pistol, utter a brief prayer, and fire. Not at the saur, but at its rider.

The man topples, clutching his neck, bright blood bubbling between his fingers. Still Marengo closes in on the greatjaw, right alongside now, and Jack raises himself up in his saddle and dives off, clutching at the base of the battlesaur's saddle and hauling himself up.

There are cords and wires, the controls of the saur, but he does not know which does what. A small box has a lever and on impulse he jams that forward.

The battlesaur rears in agony, thrashing blindly, tossing Jack off like a rag doll. It twists and bellows. The tricorne, released, wastes no time, sinking its horns deep into the belly of the vulnerable greatjaw, ripping it open, then charging in again, this time aiming for the neck.

Jack rolls away across the mud as the dying greatjaw slams into the ground next to him. A nudge on his shoulder and Marengo is there. He quickly mounts and surveys the field.

Of the mighty French battlesaurs, three are now dead or dying and two are riderless, disappearing into the surrounding forest. He searches for the other one, and to his horror, sees it disappearing into the walled city.

As the resurgent Prussian Army sets upon the small French garrison, Jack spurs Marengo forward, riding hard for the city gates.

Willem holds on tightly, keeping his balance, but barely, as the tricorne continues its charge, impaling soldiers on its horns, tossing them aside like garbage. An artillery troop is wheeling a cannon forward but before the firer can touch the fuse, the weight of the tricorne slams into it, sending the cannon and the French artillerymen flying.

They reach the harbor. It is packed with French ships, huge battleships, transport ships, their decks packed with soldiers.

"So many ships!" Willem gasps.

His words are swallowed by a thunderous, guttural roar that echoes off the walls of the buildings around them.

Willem looks around to see a greatjaw right behind them. The tricorne does not need jolting; it has heard the roar too. It jerks forward, throwing Willem back in the saddle. The streets are narrow, there is no room to turn and fight. The greatjaw's teeth slash through the air just behind them. The tricorne panics, running blindly from what comes after it.

Willem glances back again just in time to see Frost fire at the greatjaw. The sound of the pepper cartridge is unmistakable but Willem curses as the cloud of particles shoots high in the air, above the greatjaw's head.

He is almost thrown from the saddle as the tricorne veers around a corner. Behind him, Frost is hanging on by his fingertips.

The tricorne skids on the cobblestones and its hindquarters smash into a house. A wall collapses into a pile of bricks and dust. Still the greatjaw is right behind them, stumbling on the loose bricks that have spilled into the street. As it turns the corner the rider is revealed.

"Now!" Willem shouts.

The pistol kicks in Frost's hand. The rider shudders and slides backward off the saddle.

Willem gives a whoop, but his joy is short-lived. The greatjaw needs neither encouragement nor rider to chase a tricorne. Willem hauls on the reins, trying to regain control of his animal. He closes a blinder, steering the tricorne around another corner onto a small bridge across a river, heading for a church. Here the road curves again, toward the ocean. In the distance Willem can see the retreating masts of the Royal Navy.

He turns again, into a narrow street filled with market stalls. The wooden poles and awnings disappear, shredded to ribbons and matchsticks.

A quick glance confirms that the greatjaw is still right on their tail.

"We must find somewhere to turn around," Frost shouts, exactly what Willem has been thinking. If they can turn, the tricorne can fight, bringing its three great horns to the battle. But if they slow, the riderless greatjaw will be upon them.

VICTORIE

Thibault watches the battle from the crow's nest of the *Impérial*, where he has climbed since receiving reports of a group of tricornes approaching from the east. He slams his one fist into the wood of the mast in frustration and anger, seeing two of his precious saurs lying in the fields beyond the city. How could he have relied on that fool Baston to defend the abbey? He slams his fist again into the mast, drawing blood inside his black leather glove. Within the walls of the city he sees the greatjaw close on the tail of a tricorne.

"They are heading for the fort," he shouts to the officers below him. "Send the reserve artillery to the courtyard. I want those tricornes dead!" He thinks a moment longer. "Prepare Victorie," he shouts.

He finds the opening in the floor of the wooden platform and begins to descend. It is difficult with only one arm, but Thibault does not even notice. His mind is on Victorie, the one battlesaur he held in reserve. A good name for a battlesaur because today she will be the difference between defeat and victory.

He reaches the deck and runs for the gangplank, not minding that he is being watched by the lower orders of his troops. There is no time to waste.

Victorie is chained between two bollards on the dockside. Thibault leaps for the rope ladder that is unfurled from her side and begins to climb.

FINAL CHARGE

A crossroads is in front of him but Willem ignores it, heading for what appears to be a town square. Perhaps here there will be room to turn and fight. A blur of movement catches his eye and he looks sideways to see Cosette on her beast, in full charge, Arbuckle still with her.

A crash comes from behind him and he glances around; the greatjaw has completely disappeared. He reaches the square and turns, heading back the way he came. Cosette's animal blocks the crossroads. The greatjaw is embedded in the side of a house, covered in bricks and dust, impaled on the two longest horns of Cosette's tricorne. The greatjaw struggles in the cavity that has been created in the side of the building, clawing at bricks with its massive hind legs, turning its head and trying to reach the tricorne with those massive teeth. Cosette's tricorne backs away and a rush of blood pours from the two gaping holes in the greatjaw's side. It continues to struggle feebly but makes no effort to get up.

Cosette spurs her tricorne forward, taking the lead with Willem following, toward a small bridge over the river. On the other side of the bridge, the wall of the fort is high and strong, but the gates seem no more sturdy than those of the city wall. Willem finds himself yelling with excitement, as is Frost behind him.

Cosette's saur slams its head into the gap between the two gates, which burst open in a spray of splintered wood.

"Cosette!" Willem screams, but he knows she has seen what he has seen. A row of French cannon lined up facing the gates. She is barely through and into the fort when the cannon roar and Cosette, Arbuckle, and her saur are enveloped in a cloud of smoke. There is a thud as the tricorne hits the ground and slides toward the cannon, smashing into them, sending them flying backward into their own ammunition caissons.

Willem bursts through the gates to see to his horror another cannon battery to the right.

Another thunder of gunpowder, long fingers of flame stretching out toward him, and Willem's saur shudders under the impact of cannonballs.

The great steed is dead on its feet and falling sideways. Willem rolls away as the beast crashes into the stone floor of the fort. A wave of the most intense pain spreads like lightning from the wound in his chest. The world spins, then turns to black.

"Willem!"

He wakes to find Arbuckle dragging him and an unconcious Frost behind the wall of the fort for safety. A group of cavalry soldiers charge toward them and for a moment Willem is sure he will die, but the uniforms are Prussian; no longer allied with the French, the red plume of the emperor has been stripped from their shakos.

The soldiers dismount, drawing their sabers, and follow Arbuckle into the courtyard of the fort.

It takes every effort that Willem can muster to drag himself back to the doorway and peer around. He sees the bodies of the French artillerymen strewn among their cannon. He sees Cosette lying by her tricorne, her leg trapped under the huge bony flare at the top of its skull. He sees Arbuckle and the Prussian cavalry officers disappearing into the door of the tower.

Then he sees the battlesaur.

It has arrived through a far gate, on the coastal side of the fort. But it is the rider, not the mount, that most terrifies Willem. Thibault.

Pain or no pain Willem drags himself to his feet, leaving Frost propped against a wall. He has no pistol, only his sword. He takes a single faltering step toward Cosette. The world swims but he does not fall, and he takes another step, then another.

The greatjaw steps over the remains of a shattered caisson, a few meters from Cosette. She screams and scrabbles about for a pistol in the saddle behind her.

Willem is still trying to get his legs to work properly, staggering across the courtyard, his head swimming with the pain.

Cosette reaches the pistol, cocks it, and fires it up at Thibault. There is a thud and a metal object flies out of the devil's hands. She has missed, Willem realizes, and hit the battery.

Not that Thibault needs the battery. The saur has its eyes fixed on Cosette, still trapped on the ground in front of it.

It lunges down, its huge jaws widening.

And it stops.

Its eyes are fastened on the flickering light that has appeared in Willem's hands. A sparkle stick. Even as he struck the flint he was suddenly aware of the gunpowder, loose and in kegs, in the crushed caissons around them. A single spark and they will all go up in a sheet of flame. A lit linstock lies perilously close to a dark pool of spilled powder.

Willem holds the stick in his left hand and draws his sword with his right. The pain in his chest is almost overwhelming but he knows he must not lose focus. Without the battery, Thibault cannot jolt the saur out of the mesmerization. Willem moves closer and tries to lift the sword, his eyes fixed on the soft skin under the battlesaur's neck. He can barely raise the sword off the ground.

Something is torn in his chest and no amount of strength nor will-power will make his arm go higher.

"Willem!" Cosette calls.

The neck of the beast is right above her, Willem realizes. He drops the sword to the ground, kicking it across to her with his foot, and uses the sparkle stick to bring the snout of the beast down even lower. She waits, ready to thrust upward as soon as the neck is within reach.

But then the animal jerks and breaks free of the mesmerization. Willem looks up to see Thibault with the battery back in his hand.

The head of the beast snaps toward Willem but he is thrust suddenly to the side; someone is there, a tall strong boy, whose shape Willem knows well. The boy holds a canister shot. He grabs the sparkle stick out of Willem's hands and touches it to the fuse of the canister even as the mouth of the beast crunches down.

François's head and torso disappear inside the great mouth.

Willem throws himself to the ground next to the trapped Cosette, shielding her as best he can, and a moment later there is the roar of an explosion and a spray of blood and bone fills the air. A giant tooth clatters off the cobblestones near Willem's face.

When he can look he sees the saur still standing. Its head no longer exists, there are just bloody tatters of flesh at the end of its neck. There is no sign of Thibault.

There is no sign of François either.

The saur slowly topples, blood pouring through its shattered neck.

Willem lies back as Prussian soldiers flood into the courtyard. The tall shape of the tower is spinning in circles above him, and a moment later so is a streak of light and an explosion, and a red star burns hot in the cool blue sky.

* * *

The red glow of the flare illuminates the smoke of the battle as Jack and Marengo gallop into the courtyard of the fort, skidding to a halt on the paving stones.

Willem and Cosette, bathed in blood, lie in a butcher's yard of dinosaur flesh. Thibault lies nearby, his grotesque face lifeless, his head all but removed from his body.

"Mr. Willem!" Jack cries, jumping down and crouching beside him.

To his amazement, Willem's eyes open. "Cosette?" he croaks in a harsh whisper.

It only takes a moment for Jack to ascertain that Cosette also lives, and although unconscious, seems unharmed. The blood is that of the dinosaur.

"She's alive, Mr. Willem! So is Lieutenant Frost."

Only now does Willem relax. His eyes close and he rests.

A voice comes from behind Jack, shouting in a language he does not understand, though he thinks it is French. He spins around to see Field Marshal Blücher.

"It is a bad business," the Prussian commander says. "Are they dead?"

"No, sir!" Jack cries.

"Then I will call for the medical cart immediately," the field marshal says, and speaks rapidly in German to his aides.

"Blücher, late as always!"

Jack looks up to see Captain Arbuckle running out of the tower, sword in hand, the blade dripping red.

"I would not be here at all if not for you and those horned dinosaurs of yours," Blücher says.

"Nor would any of us, if not for Willem," Arbuckle says, kneeling beside Willem and checking his pulse, before moving to

Cosette. He stands. "Get your best gunners onto the cannon of the fort, and do it quickly. The French ships are trapped between us and the Royal Navy, which even now returns to Calais. Napoléon is dead; Thibault is dead; the French coalition will be in disarray. This battle is already won."

Again Blücher rattles off orders in German and aides run to see them carried out.

Jack stays with Willem and Cosette, even when the hospital wagon arrives. He wipes blood from their faces and presses damp cloths to their lips.

He hears a cheer, and even without seeing it, he knows that the French ships have struck their colors.

In the sky above, a yellow rocket soars and fizzles, followed by a red one, then a green one. The drifting colors combine and make rainbow patterns on the gradually clearing smoke.

EPILOGUE
March 3, 1816

THE MAGICIANS

The hospital is a quiet place where white-frocked nurses hurry down long corridors with jugs of water or clean bedding in their hands. Set among green English gardens, it is as different as it is possible to imagine from the blood-soaked field hospital set up in Gaillemarde after the battle of Waterloo.

The orderly assigned to take Willem and Cosette to see their friend is a large, cheerful fellow of many smiles but few words. He stops at a room and ushers them inside, but does not enter himself.

A heavy curtain has been drawn across the doorway and they must push through it to enter.

"Willem! Cosette!" The voice is Jack's as he rises from a chair in the corner of the room, beaming. He grabs Willem's hand and shakes it, and then, unsure of the proper greeting for Cosette, takes her hand and shakes it too, as if she were a man.

She does not mind and laughs, a delightful sound that has become one of the everyday joys in Willem's life.

"Mr. and Mrs. Geerts," Frost says. He is lying in the hospital bed, his eyes heavily bandaged.

Willem smiles with a shy glance at Cosette. "How was the operation?" he asks.

"Exceedingly painful," Frost replies. "And yet I still live and breathe."

"And your eyes?" Cosette asks.

"That remains to be seen," Frost says. "My surgeon was the king's own, and there is none better. But the procedure is still experimental. In a week I hope to finally gaze on this wife of yours, Willem, and if she is as pretty as you say, I may have to steal her for myself."

"It's all right, ma'am," Jack whispers to Cosette. "He's only joking."

"I hear your opening night was the toast of London," Frost says. "A husband-and-wife magic show, with electricity! Such a thing has never been seen before. And Jack tells me you made a dinosaur disappear right from the stage. Such an illusion! Or was it in fact real magic after all? I would not be surprised, with you two."

"A true magician will never say," Cosette says.

"Let us just say that we had a little help from my father, and an old friend," Willem says.

Frost loses his smile. "How is Sofie?"

"She mourns her son," Willem says. "As many mothers have mourned many sons over the many months of this war. But she has great spirit, and she is enjoying London."

"What of Héloïse?" Frost asks. "I heard you had sent people to look for her."

Willem smiles.

"They did not find her," he says. "But I did not need them to. I know where she is."

"And where is that?" Frost asks.

"She is home," he says.

AUTHOR'S NOTE

Unlike *Battlesaurus: Rampage at Waterloo*, this book is pure fiction. *Rampage at Waterloo* was as historically accurate as I could make it, right up to the actual Battle of Waterloo. However, this alternative history diverged significantly from real history at that point.

Even so, I have again tried to accurately portray the times and locations: the forts in Ireland and France, the streets of London, and the peculiar and terrifying world that was the Bedlam Lunatic Asylum.

I again owe a great debt to some excellent books:

Bedlam: London and Its Mad, by Catharine Arnold
Ten Days in a Mad-House, by Nellie Bly
The Art of Warfare in the Age of Napoleon,
    by Gunther E. Rothenberg

Many of the characters in this story are real historical figures. I have tried to depict them as accurately as possible in this alternative version of our history. My apologies for any inaccuracies.

Some of the fictional characters are named after real people. These are the grand-prize winners of my school competitions. Congratulations to:

- Ethan Arbuckle
- Hunter Frost
- Joe Hoyes
- Sam Roberts
- Jack Sullivan
- Dylan Townshend
- Harry Wacker
- Dylan Wenzel-Halls
- Ben Wood
- Lewis Wood

And a special thanks to:
Sofie Thielemans, Somerset College, Gold Coast, Australia